"Did I hear you right? He was with a boatload of *Vikings*?"

Grant nodded. "They looked like pictures I've seen."

Mariah eyed him suspiciously. "Where would he find Vikings?"

Grant looked at her with angry impatience. "How the hell do I know? I can only tell you what I saw—a bunch of men in armor carrying shields with swastikas on them."

"Swastikas?" echoed Brigid in disbelief. "Are you sure?"

Growling deep in his throat, Grant limped over to a desk. He snatched up a pen and a notebook and hastily scrawled a design on the paper. He handed it to Brigid. "That's what I saw. Is that not a swastika?"

Brigid stared at the drawing for so long and so silently, Grant almost repeated the question. When she finally spoke, her voice was a hushed, hoarse whisper. "Yes and no. It is a swastika but not the type we associate with Nazi Germany. It's something a lot worse."

Other titles in this series:

James Axler
Outlanders

EQUINOX
ZERO

A GOLD EAGLE BOOK FROM
WORLDWIDE.

TORONTO • NEW YORK • LONDON
AMSTERDAM • PARIS • SYDNEY • HAMBURG
STOCKHOLM • ATHENS • TOKYO • MILAN
MADRID • WARSAW • BUDAPEST • AUCKLAND

First edition February 2003

ISBN 0-373-63837-X

EQUINOX ZERO

EQUINOX
ZERO

The Road to Outlands—
From Secret Government Files to the Future

Almost two hundred years after the global holocaust, Kane, a former Magistrate of Cobaltville, often thought the world had been lucky to survive at all after a nuclear device detonated in the Russian embassy in Washington, D.C. The aftermath—forever known as skydark—reshaped continents and turned civilization into ashes.

Nearly depopulated, America became the Deathlands—poisoned by radiation, home to chaos and mutated life forms. Feudal rule reappeared in the form of baronies, while remote outposts clung to a brutish existence.

What eventually helped shape this wasteland were the redoubts, the secret preholocaust military installations with stores of weapons, and the home of gateways, the locational matter-transfer facilities. Some of the redoubts hid clues that had once fed wild theories of government cover-ups and alien visitations.

Rearmed from redoubt stockpiles, the barons consolidated their power and reclaimed technology for the villes. Their power, supported by some invisible authority, extended beyond their fortified walls to what was now called the Outlands. It was here that the rootstock of humanity survived, living with hellzones and chemical storms, hounded by Magistrates.

In the villes, rigid laws were enforced—to atone for the sins of the past and prepare the way for a better future. That was the barons' public credo and their right-to-rule.

Kane, along with friend and fellow Magistrate Grant, had upheld that claim until a fateful Outlands expedition. A displaced piece of technology…a question to a keeper of the archives…a vague clue about alien masters—and their world shifted radically. Suddenly, Brigid Baptiste, the archivist, faced summary execution, and Grant a quick termination. For Kane there was forgiveness if he pledged his unquestioning allegiance to Baron Cobalt and his unknown masters and abandoned his friends.

But that allegiance would make him support a mysterious and alien power and deny loyalty and friends. Then what else was there?

Kane had been brought up solely to serve the ville. Brigid's only link with her family was her mother's red-gold hair, green eyes and supple form. Grant's clues to his lineage were his ebony skin and powerful physique. But Domi, she of the white hair, was an Outlander pressed into sexual servitude in Cobaltville. She at least knew her roots and was a reminder to the exiles that the outcasts belonged in the human family.

Parents, friends, community—the very rootedness of humanity was denied. With no continuity, there was no forward momentum to the future. And that was the crux— when Kane began to wonder if there *was* a future.

For Kane, it wouldn't do. So the only way was out— way, way out.

After their escape, they found shelter at the forgotten Cerberus redoubt headed by Lakesh, a scientist, Cobaltville's head archivist, and secret opponent of the barons.

With their past turned into a lie, their future threatened, only one thing was left to give meaning to the outcasts. The hunger for freedom, the will to resist the hostile influences. And perhaps, by opposing, end them.

Chapter 1

The metal monster roared, squealed, clanked and swerved as if in a panic. The pebble-strewed sand of the California coastline spumed from behind the full-track treads in double rooster tails.

Sitting in the caged gunner's saddle on one side of the revolving coaxial post, Chaffee glanced out of the topside turret bubble toward their back trail. He reflected dourly that if there were a convoy rolling behind the Sandcat, the drivers of the wags would be digging bucketfuls of grit out of their teeth for the next couple of days. But since he had allowed Bertram to get behind the wheel, he was in no position to complain about his piloting.

The vehicle that carried Chaffee was known by assorted names—Fast Attack Vehicle, Armored Personnel Carrier or simply a wag—but was most often referred to as a Sandcat. Built to serve as an FAV rather than a means of long-distance ground transportation, the vehicle's flat, retractable tracks supported a low-slung, blunt-lined chassis. The armored topside gun turret held a pair of USMG-73 heavy machine guns.

The Cat's armor was composed of a ceramic-armaglass bond, which shielded against both intense and ambient radiation. The turret in which Chaffee was seated appeared to be a transparent half dome, but at the touch of a button microcircuitry would engage, feeding an electric impulse to the chemically treated armaglass bubble. It would instantly become opaque when exposed to energy-based weapons, such as particle-beam emitters—not that there was much chance of encountering such weapons. Like most everything else used by the Magistrate Divisions, the Sandcat was based on predark tech and had been built to participate in a ground war that was never fought.

Chaffee unconsciously shifted his weight in the gunner's saddle to compensate for the incessant swaying of the vehicle. He was slightly built for a Mag, with an overlarge head, narrow shoulders and long, spindly legs. His helmet concealed his grizzled, prematurely gray hair. He kept it cropped to little more than stubble in an attempt to hide the gray, but everyone in the division knew he was getting old—too old to be leading dark-territory probes like this one.

The controlled roar of the 750-horsepower engine sounded uncomfortably loud, even through the polystyrene lining of Chaffee's helmet, but he managed to focus past it. The rhythm and noises of his mechanical environment had long since become part of the substance of his life as a patrol commander in the Snakefish Magistrate Division. It wasn't much different than growing accustomed to the rolling of the Cific Ocean, off to the Sandcat's right, which fostered sea legs.

He looked out the turret blister to the Cat's left. A solid forest wall loomed, the spaces between the tree trunks dim and shadowy. The woods looked like the haunted forests he had heard stories about as a child, full of mystery, gloom and demons. Chaffee was glad the Sandcat, even with its armor and armament, wasn't rolling through that black wood—not that the view on the vehicle's right was much more comforting.

The black waters of the Cific glimmered with the ghostly reflections of the full moon, gleaming like a polished medal high in the cloudless sky. The pebbled beach ahead of the Cat gleamed wetly under the moonlight, which allowed the pilot to dispense with the headlights.

The glistening pebbles skirted the edge of the sea and led to a crowded labyrinth of black rotting timbers half a klick ahead. The spectral moonlight made the ancient marina look even more haunted than the woods. The place had probably been in poor condition even before the skydark of two centuries earlier. Chaffee knew that most of the open boathouses cradled partly submerged and barnacle-covered wrecks from those days.

Chaffee looked down at his squad, their faces cast into eerie shadow by the dimly glowing red bulbs on the bulkheads. The Sandcat's interior comfortably held four people. At the front of the compartment, right beneath the canopy, were the pilot's and copilot's chairs. In the rear, a double row of three jump seats faced each other. Four Magistrates in full armor stared at one another, anxious for the three-hour journey from the barony to end one way or the other, either with action or ennui.

Chaffee was anxious, too, but for a variety of reasons. His years as a hard-contact Mag had taught him to hate forestalling preemptive action. He had always silently cursed the long hours of preparing for a mission, the seemingly endless briefings and strategy sessions that burned the details of the operation into his memory. The other five members of his team were recently badged recruits, and though they may have been superbly conditioned by a constant regimen of merciless training, they lacked the regimen of even more merciless experience. That was the main reason he had chosen them for the mission.

"Coming up on the cove, sir!" Bertram announced from the pilot's seat. He spoke very loudly, far more than he needed to be heard over the engine noise.

Chaffee repressed a smirk at the young man's nervous exuberance. It was a silly idea, he reflected, for the division administrator to authorize such an important mission with such a cherry crew. Still it pleased the forty-five-year-old Magistrate in a very personal way to know that he could still charm, persuade and hoodwink his superiors. But after the siege of Cobaltville and the battle of Area 51, there were few Mags with his seniority remaining in Snakefish.

"Ease off on the throttle," Chaffee called down. "No sense in giving them advance notice of our arrival."

Bertram obediently lessened the pressure of his foot on the accelerator and downshifted. The engine roar became a muted growl. Bertram, like Daley, Abel, Saxton and Quinones, wore the black polycarbonate body armor. The lightweight exoskeletons fit snugly over undersheathings made of Kevlar weave. Small, disk-shaped badges of office were emblazoned on the arching left pectoral, depicting stylized balanced scales of justice superimposed over nine-spoked wheels. The badges symbolized the Magistrate's oath to keep the wheels of justice turning in the nine villes.

Like the armor, their helmets were made of black polycarbonate and fitted over the upper half and back of his head, leaving exposed only a portion of the mouth and chin. The red-tinted visors were composed of electrochemical polymers and connected to a passive night sight that intensified ambient light to permit one-color night vision.

"Sir, do you really think we'll catch Breeze and his smuggler crew this time?" Bertram said.

"I'm sure of it," Chaffee responded. "Double-check each other—make damn sure you've got all your seals closed and helmets secured."

"Yes, sir." Bertram and the other Mags hammered one another on the shoulders to make sure all the pieces of the armor were fully sealed and tested the locking guards of their helmets.

Chaffee resettled the small headset under his own helmet's liner as a sudden hissing of static filled his left ear.

"Breeze One-Niner to Cat Walk One," a cultured male voice spoke softly.

Chaffee kept his face immobile as the voice said,

"We see your approach. We're all prepped for the surprise party."

Chaffee didn't respond. The owner of the cultured voice hadn't expected him to say anything, as per their plan. He kept the radio frequency open and Chaffee had to focus through the static, just as he had learned to do with the distraction of the engine rumble.

Climbing down from the turret, Chaffee tapped Bertram on the shoulder and ordered, "Stop us here. Kill the engine."

Bertram obediently downshifted. His hands were firm and quick on the braking lever, and he brought the Cat to a complete halt with scarcely a squeal of metal on metal. Chaffee could tell by the set of his lips he didn't care for the place they'd stopped in—reeds grew high and there were dense stands of sycamore trees nearby, the trunks snarled with undergrowth. The place was perfect for an ambush.

Chaffee reached over and unlatched the gull-wing door, swinging it up and out. Bertram stiffened as Chaffee slid over the copilot's seat and out of the vehicle. "Sir—"

"I'm going to take a quick recce," Chaffee stated gruffly. "The rest of you stay put until I come back or you hear otherwise."

Because of the visor, Chaffee couldn't tell if suspicion glinted in the younger man's eyes and at the moment, he really didn't care. Chaffee raised his right arm, bending it at the elbow. A tiny electric motor whined as he flexed his wrist tendons. Sensitive ac-

tuators activated flexible cables in the forearm holster
and snapped the Sin Eater smoothly into his gloved
hand. The gesture was performed simply for effect,
to show his team he meant business.

"I'll be back," he said flatly and set off toward the
distant marina.

The cultured voice spoke into his ear again.
"We're all set here. Find some cover."

Chaffee's eyes darted to and fro across the beach,
then settled on a large boulder, half the size of the
Sandcat, jutting from the shoreline. He strode swiftly
toward it, intending to put it between him and the
vehicle. He cast an over-the-shoulder glance toward
the Cat just as the RPG-4 rocket streaked out of the
woods and exploded to the left and rear of the wag
in a flare of orange flame and a bone-knocking con-
cussion. The shock wave slammed Chaffee off his
feet and rolled over him like an extended thunderclap.
Shrapnel clanged off the armored hull in a series of
very nonmusical chimes.

Chaffee swore under his breath, then scrambled to
his feet. At that range the rocket should have hit dead
on target unless the man handling the launcher was
unforgivably green—even greener than the Mags inside the Sandcat.

He sprinted to the boulder and circled its base,
looking back toward the Sandcat. Through the open
hatch, he glimpsed Bertram frantically stretching
across the seat, clawing to grab the door handle to
pull it down and seal it. But before he was able to
secure a hold, another rocket sizzled from the thicket

of reeds, inscribing a smoking trajectory barely four feet above the ground.

The sleek, two-foot-long RPG-4 rocket lanced into the Sandcat through the open hatch. The warhead detonated with an earsplitting explosion. The wag kicked over sideways, driven by the detonation from within that gutted the cab and incinerated Bertram. The Cat swerved into a crazed fishtail, strewing the ground with engine parts. Chaffee felt a blast of withering heat right through his armor. Flames spewed from every port, weld and seam.

A rain of debris filled the air, jagged pieces of metal banging and clattering all around him, mixed in with chunks of men's bodies. Chaffee ducked back behind the boulder and waited until the echoes of the explosion faded and the clank and clatter of falling wreckage became a series of sporadic thumps and thuds.

He didn't have to guess what happened to the Mags, particularly Bertram. When the warhead exploded, splintered shards of metal were propelled at thousands of feet per second. At such close range, the jagged daggers of steel, impacting at over eight hundred pounds per square inch, penetrated the polycarbonate armor like hot needles through paraffin. Bone crumbled into sugar-cube-sized chunks and spinal columns splintered like rotten latticework. There was absolutely no chance that any of the crew survived.

Carefully Chaffee inched away from the boulder, sweeping his gaze from the woods to the reed-choked thicket.

"Satisfactory?" the smooth voice inquired into his ear.

Chaffee started to nod, then remembered there was no reason for him to observe radio silence any longer. He made sure the throat mike adhered securely to the side of his neck before retorting, "Very much so."

He eyed the burning heap of wreckage. Despite its metal hide, the Sandcat reminded Chaffee of a giant burst-open animal. Spark-shot columns of acrid smoke poured from the splits in the hull, and the odor of scorched oil and seared human flesh cut into his nostrils.

"There's no way individual identifications can be made now," Chaffee stated. "As far as Baron Snake-fish is concerned, I died along with my team."

The voice in his ear purred gloatingly. "Just the way you wanted it. Now get over here—our partners will arrive any second now."

Chaffee started walking in the direction of the marina, then he paused. "Who fired the first rocket?"

"Ah." The voice sounded genuinely apologetic. "That was little Moxie. His first outside job with me. I hope you understand he was overzealous."

"I do. Are you comm-linked with him?"

"Of course."

"Send him out, would you?" Chaffee's tone suggested mild amusement.

There was a moment's hesitation, then the voice said, "He's on his way. Don't be too hard on him."

"Don't worry," Chaffee replied. "I understand the eagerness to make a kill."

A figure appeared, stepping out of a dark place between the sycamore trunks. He was a small man wearing an olive-green, baggy bodysuit. He had dark, swart features and his black hair was arranged in short, beaded dreadlocks. He angled the long hollow tube of the rocket launcher over his left shoulder. He gestured to Chaffee and an abashed, jittery smile played over his lips.

"Sorry about that, sec man," he said in a lilting soprano. "Never used one of these things before."

Chaffee forced a smile to his lips. "Sec" man was an obsolete term dating back to preunification days when self-styled barons formed their own private armies to safeguard their territories. It was still applied to Magistrates in hinterlands beyond the villes, so Chaffee figured Moxie was an outlander by birth.

Lifting his right arm, the barrel of his unholstered Sin Eater pointing at the sky, he called Moxie, "What about one of these? Ever used one of these?"

Moxie came to a halt near the burning Sandcat, the flames sending dancing orange reflections across the blunt planes of his face. Petulantly he said, "I know how to use a blaster."

"Good," Chaffee responded. "Then you know what has killed you."

He dropped the barrel of the Sin Eater and two shots roared, sending out almost physical waves of sound. Moxie kicked backward, as though performing an acrobatic trick. A crimson, wet blossom appeared on the front of his bodysuit.

The two rounds smashed into Moxie's heart, turning it into pulverized meat. He slapped down onto the ground with a rattle of beads. Blood from hemorrhaging lungs bubbled from his nose and mouth.

After a moment, the cultured voice whispered dryly, "Y'know, I figured you'd do that."

"Figured you did," Chaffee bit out. "The stupid son of a bitch missed his target and came close to flash-blasting me. We don't need a stupe like that in our crew."

"Oh, it's 'we' now, is it?" A mocking laugh filled Chaffee's ear.

"It had damn well better be," Chaffee snapped, a flinty edge in his voice. "I took a big risk stealing the launchers from the armory because you told me you had people who knew how to use them."

"Fine. In that case, it's time you meet another member of 'our' crew."

Chaffee didn't react to the sarcastic emphasis on "our." Nor did he hear the footsteps behind him, but he felt a presence. If nothing else, his thirty-plus years as a hard-contact Magistrate had bequeathed to him something of a sixth sense. He whirled on a heel, leading with his Sin Eater, finger hovering over the trigger stud. Then he half stumbled, feeling his jaw drop open in astonishment. Unconsciously he let his Sin Eater dangle at the end of his arm. A woman sidled out of the reed thicket, the long column of a rocket launcher cradled in her arms.

Chaffee estimated her height at close to six and a half feet. She was full breasted and large limbed. She was all woman, in spite of the rocket launcher and her garments—which were so unusual, Chaffee had difficulty identifying them as such.

Long golden hair flowed out from under a winged helmet, falling in two thick braids halfway to her waist. They framed a square-jawed face with broad cheekbones, and a straight nose above a wide, thin-lipped mouth. Her eyes were big and so pale a blue they appeared gray.

She wore a deep blue, low-necked tunic that left her magnificent arms bare except for gleaming silver wristbands. On one ample hip she wore a straight double-edged sword at least four feet in length, and on the other hip a battle-ax dangled from a thong. Leather boots rose almost to her knees. Her legs, like her arms, were bare. Her limbs gleamed like polished opals in the moonlight. A full, flowing crimson cloak billowed behind her.

Chaffee gaped at her, all the moisture in his mouth drying to a dustlike film. He realized the wings of her helmet were made of thin alloy, fashioned to resemble those of a hawk, and a mesh of chain mail glinted dully at the bodice of her tunic. Her lips were set in a grim, taunting smile, almost as if she dared him to point his pistol in her direction.

Although Chaffee stopped short of rubbing his eyes in disbelief, he husked out incredulously, "Who the hell are you?"

The giantess didn't answer, but the voice in his ear responded crisply, "You may call her Sif."

Squaring his shoulders and doing his best to sound

in control of himself again, Chaffee demanded, "*What* is she? Your strong-arm?"

"Hardly. She calls herself a Valkyrie, but over the past couple of months she's been acting in the capacity of an ambassador."

"Ambassador?" Chaffee repeated impatiently.

Equally impatient the voice snapped, "Join me and all will be explained."

Chaffee eyed Sif suspiciously, and the giantess jerked the hollow bore of the rocket launcher suggestively toward the marina. Hoping she didn't interpret his momentary hesitation as fear, Chaffee started marching across the gravelly beach. Sif fell into step beside him, striding along with a swaggering gait. Chaffee noted how his breath plumed out before his eyes and he realized the air temperature was close to freezing. Sif, in her abbreviated tunic, seemed perfectly at ease.

They passed through the chain-link restraining fence and climbed onto the wooden pier. Their footfalls echoed hollowly on the planks and timbers as they walked toward the boathouse at the far end. A light glowed from within it, and a figure stepped onto the pier.

Chaffee looked at the man emerging from the boathouse with dislike, but he covered it with a smile. He was a very handsome man with longish, carefully styled black hair and a neatly trimmed, waxed mustache. His face was deeply bronzed, which Chaffee knew derived from a sunlamp, not from exposure to the elements. He wore a long coat, the hem of which nearly dropped to his ankles. A fur collar that was almost ridiculous in its luxuriant fullness puffed up around his jawline.

Breeze Castigleone didn't look like the boss of the Snakefish barony's Tartarus Pits. Named after Tartarus, the abyss below Hell where Zeus had confined his enemies, the Pits were the planned ghettos of the baronies. The Pits were melting pots, swarming with slaggers and cheap labor.

The barons had decreed that the villes could support no more than five thousand residents, and the number of Pit dwellers could not exceed one thousand. Part of every Mag's duty was to make Pit sweeps, seeking out outlanders, infants and even pregnant women and either ejecting them from the barony or killing them. Despite the ruthless treatment of the Pit dwellers, one constant, in any version of any ville, was a Pit boss. By no means an official title or position, Pit bosses nevertheless served a purpose of varying degrees of importance, depending on the ville.

Part crime lords, part information conduits and part procurer of luxuries, most villes tolerated Pit bosses as long as they knew and kept their place. If they maintained a certain order among the seething masses in Tartarus, Magistrates were inclined to look the other way if they engaged in limited blackmarketeering or the elimination of troublesome elements.

Not only did Breeze Castigleone not look anything like a Tartarus resident, but he also didn't resemble his predecessor in the slightest. Boss Hamhock Hiney had been pretty much standard issue, much like the self-styled barons who had tried to rule the country before the unification program—fat, brutish, bullying braggarts whose sexual appetites tended toward the depraved. Castigleone appeared almost fey and feminine in contrast to the late Hamhock.

But Chaffee knew Castigleone hadn't risen to prominence in the Tartarus Pits of Snakefish on his looks alone. He possessed a cunning and absolutely ruthless brain, which in tandem with his talent for manipulation and unlawful acquisition of goods, made him something of a genius.

Chaffee looked out at the Cific past the end of the pier. Mist floated above the water, wreathing the waves with vapors. The fog felt like the touch of a clammy hand on his skin.

"Where are the partners you spoke of?" he asked.

Castigleone chuckled patronizingly and removed a small object from his coat pocket. It emitted a faint buzz, and he passed it before his face. Chaffee knew what it was and ignored the affectation. At some point in his life, Castigleone had come across a tiny, battery-operated fan with plastic vanes. When he adopted it as a personal signature, his nickname naturally followed. Chaffee found it silly, but "Breeze" was certainly preferable to "Hamhock."

"They're on their way," Breeze replied, gesturing toward the ocean.

Sif stepped forward, gazing eagerly out at the fog.

She spoke a few words Chaffee didn't understand, ear-filling conglomerations of consonants.

"What the hell did she say?" he demanded.

Castigleone shrugged. "I have no idea. I'm just the go-between, not a linguist. I'm just a hired man with a hired man's interest in your situation."

Chaffee ground his teeth together, tamping down a sudden surge of the righteous rage of a Magistrate when scorned by a slagger. It was a struggle to remind himself than when he led his crew into an ambush, he had ceased to be a Mag.

A sound floated to them, vague and watery. Out of the vapor a shadow appeared. Chaffee stiffened, squinting as the shadow shape resolved into a looming, elongated outline. It was a ship, he realized, but a ship that might have been gliding in eerie silence out of the mists of history.

Double ended, perhaps sixty feet long, the vessel reminded Chaffee of some aspects of a giant, wide-bodied canoe. Stern and bow reared up to support platforms amidships. On the outside, along the rail were fastened gleaming disks of steel, objects that Chaffee recognized as shields. Each one was inscribed with the same symbol—a black cross canted clockwise, with the arms curving backward. The tall mast had a sail draped around it, unfilled because there was no wind to speak of. The sail seemed to be made of animal skins from which the fur had been scraped. The black sideways-cross insignia was either painted or sewn onto it.

The prow that faced them arched upward rather like

the trunk of an elephant. Positioned uppermost on the trunk was a snarling dragon's head, its long snout gaping open to reveal rows of inward-pointing fangs. On either side of the head-flared fins, scalloped at the ends so they resembled bat wings.

Chaffee stood rooted to the spot, too numbed by astonishment to move or even speak as the dragon ship hove closer to the end of the pier. For a reason he couldn't understand, the sight of the vessel evoked visions of limitless ice fields, of sunlight twinkling on hoarfrost and of a soul-numbing cold. He shivered involuntarily. At the edges of his hearing he heard a distant, rhythmic throb that he absently recognized as the growl of an engine.

On the deck stood dark, silent figures, giant men wearing helmets of burnished steel that were adorned with curving horns or outspread wings. The moon-light glittered on their scale-mail corsets as though they were dusted with diamond chips.

The engine sound changed, lowering in pitch, and the dragon ship bumped gently against the end of the pier. Sif strode out eagerly as the figure of a man leaped gracefully from the vessel and into her arms. She caught him up in a brief, fierce embrace. Chaffee stared so long at the figure without blinking that his eyes began to sting and water.

The man seemed very tall in the dim illumina-tion. From neck to thigh his lean body was cased in black link mail, and under that a fur-trimmed tunic. Light winked dully from an amulet hanging around his neck.

His head was completely concealed by a helmet wrought of black, gleaming metal, presenting a blank visage of slitted eyeholes and a small grilled slot for breathing. At the crest and sides of the helmet sprang out thin, sweeping curves of steel that were mates to the bat-winged fins on the ship's dragon figurehead.

The dragon-helmeted man disengaged from Sif, and Chaffee noted he wasn't as tall as he had first thought, but he still topped six feet. He appeared underweight at first glance, but the effect was caused by a total absence of excess flesh. He strode purposefully toward him and Castigleone.

The Pit boss spoke to the helmeted man in a whisper, gesturing toward Chaffee. The man's eyes glittered behind the slits of the helmet, then he strode toward him. As he did, he lifted the helmet from his head. The man's face was aquiline, with hollow cheeks that stressed his broad, pale forehead. Sleek black hair fell to his shoulders in a tangle of witch-locks. A streak of white that was several inches wide slashed straight back from his hairline over the crown of his head to his nape. Across his forehead crooked a wealed scar, bisecting his right eyebrow.

The slight slant of his gray eyes lent his pale face a vaguely sly cast. His mouth turned up at the corners, so that he seemed to be constantly smiling over some amusing incident only he was aware of.

At first he struck Chaffee as an aesthete, an effete intellectual. There seemed to be a smug serenity about his bearing and smile, but there was none in his eyes. They blazed in his gaunt face with haunted memories of suffering, of fasting, of a soul-deep pain. He had unusual hands, too—the palms very broad with exceptionally long and powerful-looking fingers. His right hand was encased in a glove of black leather, but the left hand went bare.

The man handed his helmet to Sif and absently toyed with the amulet hanging from his neck. With a start, Chaffee realized it was a tiny wooden phallus with stylized crystal testicles affixed to it.

In a voice that bore traces of a metallic accent, he asked, "My friend Breeze tells me you wish to become an expatriate? That you seek asylum?"

Chaffee's gaze flicked from the strange amulet to the dragon ship and back to the man's high-planed face again. "You can offer me asylum?"

The dark-haired man gestured negligently to the vessel. "That is the mobile embassy of the nation I represent. Once you set foot upon it, you will be under the protection of Ultima Thule…and therefore saved from the coming Ragnarok."

It took Chaffee a few seconds to work out the subtleties of the man's accented pronunciation. Trying to mimic it, he echoed, "Ulteema Thoo-lee? Is that where you're from?"

A smile tugged at the corners of the man's thin-lipped mouth. "*Nyet*. I hail from a land much, much different."

"If I go with you, I'll be saved from…what did you call it?"

The man's smile faltered and turned into a frown. Gesturing to Castigleone, he said, "I presumed our mutual friend had explained our doctrine to you. Ragnarok, the conflict of ice and fire—the last day. But the discussion is not about my origin but about your choices."

Chaffee took a deep breath. "Yes. I wish your protection."

He took a step toward the ship, but the man stopped fondling his amulet and restrained him by a hand on the shoulder. "However, tovarich, I have a few questions."

Chaffee scowled. "So do I. First of all—who are you?"

"I have been known by several names. However, the easiest for you to pronounce is Grigori Zakat. It's not my real name, but it will suffice."

He paused and added coldly, "Now I have a question for you. I am curious about a man I once knew who wore the same armor as you."

Surprised, Chaffee inquired, "You mean a Magistrate?"

Grigori Zakat nodded. "He was a former member of that fraternity, I believe, only recently disaffected when I first met him."

"Do you know his name?"

Zakat chuckled, but there was no humor in it. It was a sinister, sibilant hiss of a laugh that set Chaffee's nape hairs to tingling. "I do indeed. I shall never forget it. Perhaps you can give me a hint of where I might find the man named Kane."

Chapter 2

Two months later

"Kane," Domi whispered. "Where can I find you?"

Kane's strained voice issued from the trans-comm unit Domi held to her ear. "About three-quarters of a klick northeast of you, right at the river, halfway up a tree."

Domi couldn't help but smile. "What the hell are you doing up there?"

"What do you think?" His whispering tone was harsh and tense. "I'm building a house."

"Why are we whispering?" Domi asked, imitating his low tones.

The transmitter accurately conveyed Kane's sigh, but he didn't raise his voice. "I'm above a place where animals come to drink. I might be able to see Monstrodamus's tracks if he's been here recently."

"Has he been?"

"I don't know."

"Okay," Domi replied. "I'm near a bog, but I don't see anything that looks like dinosaur tracks or dinosaur shit."

"We know he's here on the island," came the terse reply. "That's enough." Kane fell silent for such a long tick of time, Domi was on the verge of calling his name. When he spoke again, there was a perceptible note of anxiety, if not fear, underscoring his voice. "I'll call you back."

Domi heard the click of the circuit closing. She folded the cover over the palm-sized radiophone and stowed it back in her war bag, blinking back sweat from her eyes. She guessed the humidity was about ninety percent, and even the chirping of birds sounded lethargic in the moisture-drenched air.

She accepted the discomfort as part of the mission, but she found Thunder Isle, as the natives of New Edo called it, almost as inhospitable as rad-hot hellzones. As she had crept through the jungle, waterfowl whirred up in clouds from pools of stagnant water, unseen animals snorted at her from tall breaks of cane and swarms of insects hummed all about her.

Domi had needed all of her wilderness craft to make any kind of progress. She had seen narrow animal paths beaten through the undergrowth, but she didn't follow them. Curiosity was not much of a motivating force with her. She learned early that too often curiosity killed not only the cat, but also everything around it. People who grew up outside the sheltered walls of villes accepted that as gospel.

She slunk through the vines and underbrush like a creature born to jungle life. In many ways, she had been. A thicket ahead of her was suddenly violently agitated, as if shaken by a stiff breeze. Dropping to one knee, Domi knew she couldn't be seen. An albino by birth, her complexion was normally pale as creamed milk. Since being on the island, she'd taken care to cover her exposed skin with a mixture of berry and grass juices that kept most insects away. She'd scrubbed in mud to allow her skin to blend in easier with the shiftings of light and shadow.

Domi's close-cropped bone-white hair was wilder than normal because she'd braided broken twigs with green leaves into it to disguise most of the color. She was every inch of five feet tall and weighed one hundred pounds. On either side of her thin-bridged nose, her ruby eyes glinted like drops of blood.

She wore a camou-striped tank top, so soaked with perspiration it adhered to her body like a second layer of epidermis, and a pair of high-cut shorts. A zippered canvas bag and holstered blaster were attached to a web belt cinched around her narrow waist. She wore no shoes, since her feet were thickly callused on the soles. Her small breasts thrust tautly against the damp fabric because of her youth and, at the moment, the tension in her body.

One of the genetic quirks of the nukecaust aftermath was a rise in the albino population, particularly down south in bayou country. Albinos weren't exactly rare anywhere else, but they were hardly commonplace.

The former Pit boss of Cobaltville, Guana Teague, had found Domi particularly unique and smuggled her into the Pits with a forged ID chip. In exchange, she gave him six months of sexual service. When seven months had passed without his releasing her from their agreement, she terminated the contract by cutting his throat.

The shrubbery rustled again and Domi held her breath, trying very hard to look like one of the ferns sprouting all around. She gripped the M-14 rifle she'd chosen from the Cerberus redoubt's extensive armory. The blaster was serviceable, with a matte black finish and fired heavy, 7.62 mm rounds. She kept the weapon below the line of underbrush but above the marshy ground so the bore wouldn't be fouled.

A lean creature, very low to the jungle floor, crept into view. It wasn't large, only two feet long or so. With its rich chocolate-colored fur and short legs, the animal reminded her of a ferret or weasel. The head was shaped differently than such animals she had seen in the Idaho Outlands where she grew up. The snout was pushed back bulldog fashion, and the canine teeth protruded down from its upper jaw like a pair of discolored daggers.

The ferret's head rotated on its neck in a jerky fashion, its nostrils dilating as it sniffed the air. It froze, its black button eyes fixed on her. Domi expected it to dash off in a panic once it caught her unfamiliar scent. To her astonishment, it lowered its head and leaped, extending its jaws wide.

She had no time to draw either her handblaster or the knife sheathed to her calf. Leaning back, she lifted the blaster and buttstroked the ferret out of the air. It landed in the nearby brush, twisted, squeaked in fury and lunged at her again.

In the short span of time between knocking the

animal out of the air and its next leap, Domi whipped the serrated, nine-inch-long knife from the sheath at her leg. The only memento of her seven months as Guana Teague's sex slave, it was the same knife with which she had cut the man's triple-chinned throat. The long blade in her hand flickered just a shade more swiftly than the reflexes of the ferret. It sliced the air in a flat arc, then cleanly sheared through fur, muscle and bone. The fanged head jumped from the lean body amid spouting blood.

The animal's decapitated body dropped to the ground, and it thrashed around in a series of twisty convulsions. The head landed between her feet, its jaws still champing. Domi backed away from it, grimacing at the speckles of the creature's blood shining wetly on her legs. She had seen and killed any number of mutie animals in her young life, so encountering a vicious throwback to an earlier form of existence didn't disturb her overmuch.

Standing, Domi swished her knife through the air to clean it of blood, realized that was a mistake, plunged the blade into the ground and resheathed it. She cursed silently at herself, knowing there could be other creatures nearby, far larger than a ferret, that would be attracted by the scent of blood.

For a moment, Domi considered giving up the hunt for the creature Kane had christened Monstrodamus and returning to the Cube. She wasn't enjoying her return to ferality as much as she had hoped she would. She wondered briefly why she was not experiencing the ecstasy of the hunt as she had so many times before. The delicious sense of peril, the feeling her most precious possession—her life—was at stake, didn't excite her as it had in the past.

The prospect of stalking and killing a raptorial dinosaur had sounded uniquely entertaining when Kane first proposed it. Now it seemed like a recklessly foolish way to spend the day, since there were far more dangerous animals on Thunder Isle than vicious prehistoric ferrets. As she recalled what Kane had told her about the huge cave bear that had pursued him during his second visit to the island, she repressed a shudder.

The ferret and just about every bit of flora and fauna on the little island were prehistoric in nature, brought there through science gone awry, not violated Mother Nature run amok. Even knowing that still didn't make the place feel any less ominous.

There was something ominous about all of the Western Isles, and this one, named Thunder Isle by its nearest neighbors, was extremely disturbing. The Western Isles referred to a region in the Cific Ocean of old and new land masses. The tectonic shifts triggered by the nukecaust dropped most of California south of the San Andreas Fault into the sea.

During the intervening two centuries, undersea quakes raised new volcanic islands. Because the soil was scraped up from the seabed, most the islands became fertile very quickly, except for the Blight Belt— islands that were originally part of California and were still irradiated.

The volcanic isle upon which New Edo was built

was not irradiated. New Edo had been settled by the House of Mashashige, fleeing political unrest in Japan. It turned out to be a richly forested isle, the tip of a larger landmass that had been submerged during the nukecaust. Evidently it had slowly risen from the waters over the past two centuries, and supported a wide variety of animal and vegetable life. The exiles from Nippon claimed it as their own and named it New Edo, after the imperial city of feudal Japan.

Of course there were many problems to overcome during the first few years of colonization. Demons and monsters haunted the craggy coves and inland forests. They had a malevolent intelligence and would creep into the camp at night to urinate in the well water or defecate in the gardens. More than one samurai was slain during that time, their heads taken. These depredations were the acts of creatures who had made their way from Ikazuchi Kojima, Thunder Isle to the people of New Edo.

According to Lord Takaun, daimyo of the House of Mashashige, a cyclical phenomenon occurred on the neighboring isle. He described lightning that seemed to strike up, accompanied by sounds like thunder, even if the weather was clear.

Takaun had no explanation for it, but he knew that on the heels of the phenomenon often came incursions of what the more impressionable New Edoans claimed were demons. Months before, Brigid Baptiste, Kane and Grant were shown the corpse of one such demon—which was tentatively identified as a Dryosaurus, a man-sized dinosaur.

Brigid was able to identify other artifacts found on the shores of Thunder Isle—a helmet from the era of the conquistadores, and a stone spearhead that resembled a Folsom point, so named for Folsom, New Mexico, the archaeological site where the first one was found. It was evidence of a prehistoric culture, many thousands of years old. When she, Grant and Kane went to Thunder Isle, all of them glimpsed another dinosaur, far larger and more vicious than the Dryosaur. In fact, it killed a group of Magistrates they had been tracking.

Domi stumbled slightly in a depression on the ground. Looking down, she saw deep parallel tracks that had squashed and flattened the vegetation on the jungle floor. The outside edges of the prints showed a pattern resembling splayed, three-toed feet. They were many times the length and breadth of her small feet.

Her breath caught in her throat and she looked around, her heart beating hard and fast. The hunt for a carnivorous dinosaur—a full-grown Allosaurus according to Brigid, and a stunted Tyrannosaur according to Kane—was no longer an entertaining abstraction. The instant she saw the tracks, the albino girl felt a cold wash of fear and an awareness that death was very close.

Moving carefully and stealthily, she slid into the jungle. All around were growing plants, most of them ferns. The size ranged from tiny seedlings to mon-

strous growths the size of oak trees. Tangles of
creeper vines carpeted the jungle floor. The atmosphere was like that within a greenhouse—impreg-
nated with the overwhelming odor of vegetation and
nearly impenetrable with water vapor.

Leaves crunched somewhere ahead of her. Still
holding her breath, she sank down on her belly, waiting for another sound. It wasn't long in coming.
About fifty feet away, a great form came crashing out
of the underbrush. The animal resembled a half-
starved, mangy cougar, except for its size. It was almost as bulky as a bear. Domi estimated it was at
least twelve feet long from its blunt, bewhiskered
snout to the tip of its stubby tail. Its shoulders and
forelegs were so massively muscled as to give it a
top-heavy appearance, although its hindquarters were
more powerful than those of mountain lions she had
seen.

The animal's oversized head was definitely feline
in configuration, with huge jaws equipped with fangs
that curved out fully a foot from the gums. During
the briefing before the op at Thunder Isle, Domi had
been shown pix of the type of animals she might encounter, and she remembered seeing a depiction of a
creature similar to this one. It was called a saber-
toothed tiger, but the artistic rendering she saw didn't
do justice to the living, breathing reality of the monster. For one thing, the creature exuded a revolting
odor.

It swung its head to and fro, making soft grunting
sounds as it sniffed the air. Hunger burned in its wide,

unblinking eyes. Then the creature turned in her direction, laying its ears flat against its head. A low growl rumbled in the big cat's throat. A pink tongue emerged briefly to lick its black chops, and its fearsome teeth gleamed wetly.

Domi felt her heart hammering in her chest, but kept her breathing under control. Carefully, slowly, she brought the M-14 blaster to her shoulder. It could be set for semiautomatic or automatic fire, and its magazine contained twenty rounds. She set the selector switch for single shot.

Still lying prone, the Outland girl sighted on the saber-tooth through the open sights, then kept both eyes open as she moved up to the sniper scope. Experience told her that she had to aim slightly under her target to properly hit it. The great cat sank into a crouch.

Breathing in, Domi put the crosshairs over the center of the animal's chest. The giant beast suddenly surged over the ground in a juggernaut-like charge. Its lips peeled back from the huge fangs, its greenish eyes glistening. She exhaled half a breath as Grant had taught her, held it, then squeezed the trigger.

The bore of the M-14 lipped flame with an ear-splitting crack. The heavy rifle stock slammed back into her shoulder. The joint twinged in protest. Well over a year before, a bullet had shattered the bone. DeFore had replaced the shoulder joint with an artificial ball and socket. After long weeks of painful therapy, Domi had returned to full strength. However, impacts against the joint still caused occasional pain.

The slam of the blaster butt against her shoulder was nothing compared to the bone-shattering impact of the 7.62 mm round into the saber-toothed tiger's body. Blood fountained from between its gaping jaws and it pitched around furiously, making great gurgling yowlings. Domi watched as its huge body spasmed wildly, its claws tearing up great clots of earth and shredding the undergrowth. It flipped and flopped and struggled crazily, as if its brain refused to admit that its body was dying. She was horrified by how long it took the frightful monster to die. Finally its wild wallowings ceased.

The tiger was still twitching and vomiting crimson when an eardrum-compressing, trumpetlike cry pierced the murk, followed by a deep-throated bawling that sounded almost petulant.

Vegetation swished and crashed and the ground shook, as if from a series of heavy blows. Domi dropped her head lower, putting her chin into the muck as a dark shape loomed out of the foliage, propelled by a pair of massively muscled rear legs. The sunlight shafting down into the clearing revealed its monstrous form.

The clawed forelegs were small in proportion to the rest of its body, but the curving, steel-hard talons tipping each of the three fingers were at least six inches long. Bulging with ropes of muscle, they were drawn up to its chest almost in an attitude of prayer. Grinning jaws bared two rows of glistening yellow fangs beside which those of the saber-tooth were like fingernail parings. The mouthful of teeth lent the creature's face the aspect of a grinning skull. It was a nightmare come to life, radiating menace and death.

The saurian snout bore a pair of flared nostrils that dilated and twitched in tandem with the motion of the forked, snakelike tongue darting out between the fangs. The head, twice the size of that of a horse, turned this way and that upon an extended scaled neck.

Two huge legs, almost as big around as some of the fern trees she'd seen, supported the massive, barrel-shaped body. They were enormously overdeveloped, the thighs and calves slabs of scale-coated muscle. A long tail trailed out from behind, disappearing into the undergrowth. Domi guessed it used its thick tail to balance itself.

The nauseating reek of rotten meat and the sour stench of reptiles clogged Domi's sensitive nostrils. So great was the monster's weight that its huge, three-toed feet sank deep into the damp ground with each hopping step.

Huge cold eyes like those of a serpent a hundred times magnified stared unwinkingly from beneath a pair of scaled, knobby protuberances. Thick swellings at the sides of its head told of the great muscles that worked its maw. In the damp air Monstrodamus's pebblelike pattern of dark-brown scales glistened like a coating of molten metal.

Domi saw a ridged pattern of wealed scars on his neck, where the flesh wasn't covered by the scales. They were the healed wounds inflicted by Kane's combat knife during his first meeting with the huge reptile, some three months before.

Monstrodamus swiveled his head on his neck like a gun turret, then he bent and sniffed at the saber-tooth's body. Leaning over, his huge jaws opened and closed, crunching noisily on the heavy bones of the animal. He ripped out a hunk of flesh and stood upright, fresh blood splattering the ground. His eyes surveyed the landscape, looking for a challenge to his meal, then he bent again toward the cat carcass.

Muscles turned to stone by fear, Domi didn't move, watching the giant saurian feed. Brigid had told her that it was generally believed dinosaurs were attracted mainly by movement and smell, so Domi figured if she remained motionless, the odor of the saber-toothed tiger's blood would overwhelm her own scent and she would remain undetected.

Her fear receded enough so more details of Monstrodamus became apparent. The creature wasn't as large as it initially seemed when it first appeared, perhaps twenty-five feet long and fifteen feet tall. Also, though its body was thicker than any animal's Domi had ever seen, it wasn't fat. In fact, it looked gaunt and half-starved, which fit in with Brigid's hypothesis that there was simply not enough food on Thunder Isle to support a population of creatures of Monstradamus's size.

Moving as deliberately as she could, Domi carefully reseated the stock of the M-14 against her shoulder again and placed the scope's crosshairs over the dinosaur's left eye. A fresh round had been automatically cycled into the rifle's chamber, so she took careful aim and curled her finger around the trigger. Her heart pumped hard and her body quivered with the adrenaline flowing through it.

Her finger began to tighten—then the trans-comm unit in her bag shrilled loudly.

Chapter 3

"Okay." Domi's voice floated from the trans-comm unit in Kane's left hand. "I'm near a bog but I don't see anything that looks like dinosaur tracks or dinosaur shit."

"We know he's here on the island," Kane replied tersely, hoping the tension in his voice wasn't conveyed to Domi over the little radiophone. "That's enough."

Kane pressed his chest into the tree trunk and tried to suppress his trembling. He bit his lips and clutched a branch so tightly with his right hand it was a wonder he didn't sink his fingers through the wood. "I'll call you back," he whispered and thumbed down the cover of the trans-comm.

Kane surveyed the narrow river below him, focusing on the way the sunlight danced over the muddy brown water. He didn't want to think about moving for fear of either falling out of the tree or dropping his USAS-12 Remington shotgun into the river.

An inch over six feet tall, Kane was long-limbed and rangy, a lean, sinewy wolf of a man who carried most of his muscle mass in his upper body above a slim waist. His skin was lightly bronzed from exposure to the elements, except for a long, hairline scar that stretched whitely across his left cheek. His dark hair hung in damp strands from the oppressive humidity, blackening even the sun-touched highlights at his temples and nape. His pale eyes, blue with just enough gray in them to resemble the high sky at sunset, were narrowed to slits behind the dark lenses of sunglasses.

He wore an olive-drab T-shirt tucked into camouflage pants and high-laced jump boots. A Colt Combat Elite autoblaster was snugged in a canvas holster at his right hip, and the zippered war bag slung over his left shoulder held two spare clips for the handblaster, an extra rotary drum magazine for the shotgun, a canteen, a pair of grens and a length of nylon tipped with a small grapnel.

Remaining absolutely motionless demanded every ounce of concentration. He had to ignore all the twinges of pain in his extremities and the residue from the terrible shock that had temporarily paralyzed him less than two weeks before. Now he almost wished he were still incapable of movement as he felt the weight of the great snake sliding over the backs of his thighs. He had always prided himself on being free of phobias, but with a surge of shame he realized he had developed a fear of reptiles over the past couple of years. It wasn't an irrational fear, but derived from unpleasant experience.

First there was his encounter with Lord Strongbow and his mutagenically altered Imperial Dragoons, with their scale-ringed, snakish eyes. Then there was his terrifying battle with a gigantic constrictor atop a ziggurat in South America, one of the natives had been decked out in a feathered headdress and christened Kukulkan, in homage to the ancient Mayan god. That incident was followed only a short time later by walking a gauntlet of diamondbacks in California. His fear of things reptilian had reached its culmination a few months before during his nightmarish bareback ride on Monstrodamus through the jungle of Thunder Isle.

The serpent crawling over him as it slithered down the tree was in no way as large as Kukulkan or as fierce as Monstrodamus, but it was at least ten feet long. Its mottled hide was a greenish-gray with odd markings that reminded Kane of an overlapping series of aces of spades. He had no idea what kind of snake it was, but it didn't possess the distinctive wedge-shaped head of the pit viper. But that didn't necessarily mean it wasn't vicious or a constrictor.

He could only hope the serpent slid over his body simply because he was in its way as it went down to the river, and thus ignore him. But since most of the creatures he had seen on his two prior visits to the little island seemed obsessed with eating one another, he doubted the snake would simply pass up even an unpalatable meal.

All in all, Thunder Isle was not only one of the most inhospitable places Kane had ever visited—and he had quite a number of unpleasant memories—but it was also the most unlikely of locations to head-quarter a major subdivision of the Totality Concept.

The Totality Concept was the umbrella designation

for predark American military supersecret researches into many different but interconnected subdivisions. The many spin-off experiments were applied to an eclectic combination of disciplines, most of them theoretical—artificial intelligence, hyperdimensional physics, genetics and new energy sources.

As in all scientific endeavors, one research spawned another and then another, regardless of the success or usefulness of the forerunners. There were successes, of course. There had to be, since the Totality Concept wasn't limited by a budget nor was it answerable to any government agency. In fact, very few military and government executives even knew of its existence. There were rumors, of course—there were always rumors, but the people in power worked very hard to squash, deny or ridicule them.

The primary subdivision of the Totality Concept was Overproject Whisper, which in turn spawned Project Cerberus and Operation Chronos.

Cerberus dealt with the transfer of organic and inorganic matter from one location to another, and Chronos focused on transtemporal interphasing—time travel, or in the vernacular of the Totality Concept scientists, time "trawling."

The seat of Operation Chronos, code-named Redoubt Yankee, was built on one of the Santa Barbara, or Channel, Islands, disguised as a satellite campus of the University of California. As it was one of the finest and most secret research establishments in the world, its engineering and computer centers were second to none. Its accomplishments in the field of physics were never matched, much less exceeded. The personnel of the installation cracked the so-called cosmic code within the walls of the main building, known as the Cube.

According to Brigid, the cosmic code was vernacular for the unified field theory, which referred to the mathematical reconstruction of the first few seconds of the big bang when the universe was a primal monobloc without dimensions of space.

But even if that were true, it was cold comfort to Kane at the moment, with the pressure of the snake's body sliding over his legs. To his immense relief, the serpent paid him no more attention than if he were part of the tree itself. It continued to slither down the trunk, and when he no longer felt the dry touch of its hide, he blew out his pent-up breath in a long sigh. He began to flip up the cover of the trans-comm in order to call Domi back as he watched the snake reach the ground. It began a leisurely, undulating crawl toward the river.

Kane was at the river because he had been following three-toed footprints in the spongy ground. Although they were larger than one of his hands with the fingers spread wide, he knew they weren't tracks made by his quarry. He also knew, however, that wild carnivores often hunted near streams and rivers, attacking unsuspecting prey when they were bent over to drink. He had hoped to at least find a clue that Monstrodamus had been in the vicinity recently.

As he started to scoot backward down the tree, Kane heard a faint swish in the air. He caught only a brief, almost subliminal streak of flashing movement, and with a resonant, meaty thud a spear nearly five feet in length drove into the body of the serpent, right behind its head, pinning it to the ground.

The spear was a crude thing, with a wooden shaft wrapped with leather thongs.

The creature's trunk knotted, looped, unlooped and whiplashed in maddened efforts to free itself. It whipped its tail back and forth, and its jaws opened and closed with a castanetlike clacking, forked tongue flailing, as if it were trying to dislodge a bone stuck in its throat. Paroxysms shivered through the snake as its mottled length thumped violently against the ground. The entire body coiled and uncoiled.

Spine stiffening in tension and surprise, Kane swept his eyes over the underbrush in the direction from which the spear had flashed. A heavyset figure stepped out of the foliage, with a pair of arms that might have been fashioned out of the thick tree limbs sprouting around Kane.

The man was about five feet five with very rounded shoulders and a forehead that bulged out like the edge of a cliff. His eyes were set deeply under a bulging supraorbital ridge. His beard was gray. He was almost naked, wearing only a few bits of hide held up with intertwined vines.

Kane knew he shouldn't have been surprised to see a form of primitive man on the island, since Brigid had identified a stone spear point found there and he had seen a couple of pelt-wearing brutes in the Cube's stasis chamber. But to actually watch one of the progenitors of humanity shambling out of the underbrush was a sight that sent a chill up and down the buttons of his spine.

He received another surprise a second later when he realized the subman wasn't alone. A group of people wearing little more than their own shaggy hides crept out of the undergrowth. Kane studied their harsh, strong features. Their hair ranged in color from dark to fair to brindled red. All of the men affected grizzled beards. The women wore their unruly mops of hair bound up with rawhide thongs. Necklaces of painted bone and animal teeth banded their throats. In fact, all of them, men and women alike, had the bearing and feral expressions of animals.

At a quick count, Kane estimated there were perhaps a dozen adults, with a few children mixed in. He groaned inwardly at the concept of primitive people cruelly snatched from their own time and clime and dropped in an alien environment. What made it worse was that they were abducted at the whim of a machine, a malfunctioning computer program. Even the people who had written the programs were two centuries dead.

Kane couldn't help but feel a surge of pity for the hapless subhumans who clustered in the brush and waited for the snake to die so they could eat. Wherever or *when*ever they came from, he doubted Thunder Isle was much of an improvement.

A mission a few months ago had brought him, Grant and Brigid to the Operation Chronos installation, a place they assumed had been uninhabited and forgotten since the nuclear holocaust of two centuries before. Only much later did they find out the installation was inhabited by an old enemy, the brilliant but deranged dwarf, Sindri. He himself told them while he investigated the installation, he found that the temporal dilator's chronon wave guide conformals ran wild on random cycles. They either reconstituted trawled subjects from the holding matrix or snatched new ones from all epochs in history. Thus, everything from people, to animals and plants were randomly trawled from past epochs.

Sindri managed to get control of the dilator and use it a bit more judiciously. One of the uses to which he put it was trawling Domi out a microsecond before her death in Area 51. Whether the little man was responsible for bringing Monstrodamus out of the Chronos holding matrix was still unknown. His tamperings with the technology caused it to be dangerously unstable. With a contribution from Brigid, the dilator overloaded and reached critical mass, resulting in a violent meltdown of its energy core.

When the radiation in the installation ebbed to a nonlethal level, Kane, Grant and Brigid returned. No trace of Sindri was ever found, but none of them believed he had perished, since he had escaped what appeared to be certain death twice before. It was a more likely scenario that he used the facility's mattrans unit to gate to his space station haven, *Parallax Red.*

In the weeks following the incident, Brigid and Lakesh made several visits to the Operation Chronos redoubt, salvaging what could be salvaged. However, the predatory dinosaur had become a definite menace to not only the people of New Edo, but also to the Cerberus personnel who made frequent visits to the Chronos station. Only a few days before, the monster had pursued and nearly devoured Philboyd, who had been foolhardy enough to stroll outside the facility's perimeter.

Kane had no great admiration for the supercilious astrophysicist, but when Lakesh asked him to end the threat of Monstrodamus in order to make Thunder Isle a viable alternative to the Cerberus redoubt in Montana, he eagerly accepted. Over the past month or so, living in Cerberus had grown more and more claustrophobic with the infusion of new arrivals—one in particular.

Ordinarily Grant would have acted as Kane's partner in the monster hunt, not the diminutive Domi. However, the big former Magistrate was still recovering from the same neurological trauma that had incapacitated Kane a short time before. Kane noted sourly that Grant had felt well enough to gate to the Cube in the company of Shizuka, the commander of New Edo's military arm, the Tigers of Heaven. Even now Grant, Brigid and a couple of other Cerberus personnel waited for him and Domi to return—or at least receive a report about the progress of the hunt.

Kane saw how the heavy trunk of the snake drooped limply to the jungle floor. Although postmortem spasms still rippled along its body, the grizzled man Kane thought might be the chief of the tribe stepped tentatively toward the serpent. In one blunt-fingered hand he grasped a stone-bladed ax by its gnarled wooden haft.

Straddling the snake's body from the rear, he brought the ax down swiftly, chopping off the reptile's head with a single blow. The people whooped in a gleeful chorus and rushed out of the underbrush. They fell onto the snake with stone knives and even bare hands, slashing, slicing and tearing. Within seconds all of them were blood-spattered as they stuffed dripping gobbets of raw reptile flesh into their mouths.

The stench of fresh blood and burst bowels wafted up to Kane in the tree, but he didn't look away even though he felt a little sick to his stomach. Moving very slowly, he put the trans-comm back in the war bag. Despite being concealed by leafy branches, he didn't want to do anything that might draw the attention of the subhumans. As far as he knew, they very well could consider his flesh a lot more appetizing than snake. He wished they would take their kill and move on, since other predators could get a whiff of the blood and viscera, move in to investigate and keep him treed even longer.

Almost as soon as the thought registered, he sensed rather than felt a sudden displacement of air, then he heard a flapping, as if a wet strip of carpet were being shaken out above him. He looked up just as the bird-thing landed on the limb only a couple of feet above him. Although the creature wasn't fearsomely large, the bough sagged beneath its weight, bringing it even closer to Kane.

Gripping the limb with hook-clawed feet, the thing was at least four feet tall with a wingspread of not less than ten feet. It was covered not with feathers but a pimpled, naked hide that reminded Kane of the skin of a shaved dog. The leathery, membranous wings resembled those of a bat, but it didn't look like a bat in any other particular. Sprouting from the first joint of the wings were four curving talons.

The creature's long beak darted toward Kane's upturned face. He glimpsed how it was spiked full of sharp, conical teeth as he evaded it with a sideways twist. His sudden motion half dislodged him from the branch on which he lay, and he clutched at the monster's feet. He got two fistfuls of the wings, noting that the flesh felt like damp doeskin.

The bird-thing struggled, pecking at the back of his skull, whipping its head and neck about and trying to flap its wings all at the same time. The point of its beak stabbed down on the back of Kane's right hand, bringing with it blood and a fierce pain.

Kane lost his grip and dropped down the tree, angling his body to land on a limb. Leaves slapped his face in a rush, swiping his sunglasses away. A momentary glimpse of a thick branch below filled his vision. Twisting, he managed to loop an arm over it, feeling the tough bark scrape against his flesh. The branch shook and bowed as it took his weight. He held on tightly, kicking with his feet as though he were running in place as he tried to find some purchase, desperately afraid the branch would crack at any second.

Making a whistling, squawking cry, the bird-thing dropped to a lower branch. A spot of his blood shone on the tip of its beak. Apparently the monster had gotten a taste of him and wanted more.

Barely able to throttle the panic filling him, Kane glanced down, spotted another limb five feet below and dropped. Better prepared this time, he easily caught hold of the limb, swung himself under and over it, coming to a three-point rest on the thick limb just as the winged thing landed on it. The limb bent, sagged, and then the splintering crack of wood filled Kane's ears for an instant. Right at his feet, the crack opened like a gaping mouth pulled back in a death rictus, showing more and more of the white wood inside.

The winged monster slipped on the bough and nearly spilled down the smaller branches feeding out from the main one. It caught itself, throwing its head forward desperately to shorten its center of balance. It fluttered its wings frantically.

Kane clawed for the strap of his USAS-12 shotgun, trying to bring it around, but the barrel caught in twigs and smaller branches. Before he could free it or draw his handblaster, the split in the limb widened, dropping it to fashion a reversed L.

Kane fell and the creature came down on him hard, falling on him and enfolding him in its wings like an overeager lover. He secured a hold on its head, one hand around its neck, the other clasping its beak, keeping it closed. As he and the winged monster plunged down, the rough bark of the limbs scratched his arms and drew blood, and he banged his head against the tree trunk.

A pained grunt escaped between his teeth as he slammed hard against the ground, but the impact was considerably softened by the marshy soil. The air wasn't even driven from his lungs. He struggled against the winged carnivore's weight, trying to push it off him, expecting to feel the frenzied rake of hind claws that would disembowel him at any moment. To his surprise, all it did was flutter its wings feebly. He had wrung the creature's neck as they fell together, its hollow bones breaking easily.

He flung the body away from him and was immediately encircled by a knot of subhumans. They glared at him from beneath their beetling brows. The men didn't appear to be afraid of him at all. Instead they seemed angry that his sudden appearance had interrupted their feast.

The man Kane had christened Chief bared blood-filmed teeth at him in either a snarl or a ferocious grin. He gestured with his ax, and two men pulled Kane to his feet. As outnumbered as he was, he decided not to struggle even though his shotgun and pistol would have evened the odds within seconds.

Chief eyed Kane suspiciously and made a gobbling sound. If there were words within the gobble, they were completely unintelligible. The man had to have commented on Kane's clothes because the others gathered around him. The men and women showed great interest in the fabric, fingering the cloth of his shirt and pants, putting their hands into the pockets. All of them stank with a strong, vile smell as human as it was animal. A woman showed a great interest in the zipper of his fly. It seemed to intrigue her more than anything else.

Chief tried to tug the shotgun from his shoulder, but Kane grasped the strap tightly and shook his head. "Nope. Can't let you have it. Sorry."

With a snarling grunt, the man yanked more insistently on the strap. Kane didn't relinquish his grip. "It's dangerous," he said, trying to sound very earnest and reasonable. "You could hurt someone."

Chief glared at him, shook his ax under his nose and uttered several slobbery grunts. Kane figured he was being warned to cooperate. He smiled sweetly into Chief's face. Chief didn't smile back. Instead he uttered more gobbling grunts and clucked a couple of times.

Two subhumans grabbed Kane's arms and tried to force them up behind his back. Before they could complete the hammerlock, Kane said, still as inoffensively and unthreateningly as he could manage, "I'm about to break some of your bones. I hope you don't take it personally."

Kane lifted his leg and stomped down as hard as he could with his boot heel, mashing it into the instep of the man on his left. Since the subhuman wore no shoes, Kane heard and felt the delicate metacarpal bones break beneath his heel.

The sudden, overwhelming pain caused the man to

involuntarily release Kane's upper arm, freeing him to deal with the second captor. Kane fell back, wrenching free of the man on his right and shooting his left elbow into his throat with a meaty thud. The man staggered, holding his throat in both hands, his tongue protruding from his mouth. His feet skidded on the slippery bank of the river, and he toppled into the water with a great splash. The woman who had been interested in Kane's fly shouted something. She sounded very angry.

Growling deep in his throat, Chief lunged forward, swinging his ax. Kane easily avoided the blow by pivoting his upper body to the left. He swung out with his right fist. He felt a good solid impact run up his arm. His knuckles connected squarely against Chief's jaw, snapping his head over with a small spray of spittle and blood flying from his mouth. Chief didn't fall, but he dropped his ax and stumbled for several feet, arms windmilling as he tried to keep upright.

The subhuman thrashing in the water suddenly screamed, a hoarse shriek of mingled terror and pain. Involuntarily every head turned toward him.

A serpentine body lashed out from the foaming surface of the river, coils of scaly, sinewy flesh looping and humping. Jaws at least two feet across grabbed the subhuman by his right shoulder. It dimly resembled an eel.

The subhuman screamed again as he was slung around like a rag doll, his feet kicking the water to a froth. He beat on the creature with his free hand. His companions on the bank screamed, as well, and hurled their weapons at the water monster. The spears and stone ax heads rebounded from the muscular coils. The creature gave them no notice.

Kane moved on impulse. He unholstered his pistol and shouldered the primitives aside. He slid down the bank into the river. Still holding its captured prize, the creature turned toward him, the black eye on the side of its wedge-shaped head glinted as it focused on him, trying to decide whether he was a new meal or a threat.

Wading forward, Kane didn't wait for the creature to make up its mind about him. He slammed the bore of the handblaster into its eye and squeezed the trigger. The sharp report of the shot was muted, but the shock of impact registered strongly up his arm. Shudders ran through the serpentine creature, and the grip of its jaws on the subhuman weakened. A moment later, it released its hold and sank beneath the surface, coils still quivering.

Breathing raggedly, the wounded subhuman allowed Kane to drag him out of the river and back onto the bank. Blood streamed from the subhuman's gnawed flesh, but the wound didn't look particularly serious. Kane smiled at the tribe. "See, I'm somebody you should thank, not eat."

The tribe glared at him, and Kane wondered if they were unhappy that the monster eel had submerged and was thus beyond their bellies. The men and women shifted closer, growling angrily. Kane had no idea what the growls meant, but he stayed balanced on the balls of his feet, raising his hands for protection, waiting for the next assault although every instinct told him to attack.

Magistrate martial-arts training borrowed shamelessly from every source—from tae kwon do to savate to kung fu. The style was down and dirty, focusing primarily on the aspects of offense rather than defense. Magistrate doctrine taught never to be defensive when any opportunity presented itself to go on the attack. Most Mags had no idea when or even how to back off, but over the past couple of years Kane had learned the wisdom of a discreet withdrawal.

He didn't want to fight the primitives, and he certainly didn't want to be forced into a position where he had to use his blasters on them. They were abductees, prisoners on Thunder Isle, and though they might be better off dead in the long run, Kane had no intention of making that decision for them. By the same token, if the situation turned really ugly, he wasn't about to fend off a mob of subhumans with only his bare hands, compassion be damned.

Sliding his finger into the trigger guard of the shotgun, Kane considering firing a round over their heads, in the hopes of driving them off. Before he made up his mind, he heard a loud, earsplitting crack that he recognized as the report of Domi's blaster. As the thunderous echoes rolled across the sky, the primitive clan clapped their hands over their ears, eyes wide in astonishment, their mouths forming Os of wonder and fear.

Kane took instant advantage of their surprise and lunged into the foliage on the other side of the tree.

From behind him he heard a savage cry of anger erupt from many throats simultaneously. Heart pumping hard, he felt his familiar angry repugnance at being forced into the role of prey. His many years as a Magistrate had accustomed him to being the hunter, not the hunted.

He plunged through the closed-canopy foliage, and though sun shone bright in the sky, little of it penetrated to the treacherous morass of foul water, giant ferns and creepers that formed the jungle floor. It was like a world of endless green twilight. The heat was suffocating, and sweat saturated his shirt. His breathing was labored.

Slogging through a patch of mud, the stench of marsh gas filled Kane's nostrils and awoke nausea in his stomach. Still, the sulfurous stink wasn't much more nauseating that the effluvium exuded by the subhumans.

His wet boots squished loudly with every footfall. Kane wished he could be stealthy, but he knew he couldn't without sacrificing speed. He wanted to put as much distance between himself and the tribe of primitives as quickly as he could, and then make contact with Domi. He sucked in great gulps of the humid air as he struggled across roiling, muddy creeks, sinking almost to his knees in some places.

Reaching higher ground, he stopped to catch his breath and listen. He heard the bawling of the pursuing subhumans, but they sounded far away. The chief, though angry, probably wasn't too enthusiastic about a prolonged chase, not when they had fresh meat to eat.

Kane unzipped the war bag and withdrew the transcomm. He thumbed up the cover and pressed the key to open the channel to Domi. He heard the circuit engage—then the flat snapping of a rifle shot followed a second later by a roar that combined the worst aspects of a siren, steam valve and the howl of a dying dog.

The sweat beaded at his hairline instantly turned ice-cold. He had no doubt that the roar had erupted from the throat of Monstrodamus.

Chapter 4

At the first trilling of the trans-comm, Monstrodamus jerked erect with a startled snort. The noise sounded like an old man clearing his nasal passages, but a thousand times magnified.

Almost in the same instant, Domi's finger reflexively squeezed the trigger of the M-14. The shot sounded obscenely loud and the round missed the dinosaur entirely, smacking into a tree fern amid a mushy explosion of splinters. Monstrodamus paid no attention. Its maw gleaming crimson with the saber-toothed cat's blood, it voiced a prolonged bellow that to Domi carried in it notes of outrage.

Before she could track the creature with the blaster, Monstrodamus bent over so its upper body was parallel to the ground and charged her with long, hopping steps. Domi sprang to her feet and cartwheeled out of the creature's path, ducking under a canopy of overlapping ferns. The carnivorous dinosaur heeled around, trampling her blaster underfoot and making a panting sound that reminded her of an idling engine. She guessed it was trying to fix her new position.

Monstrodamus pounded across the ground toward her again, lowering its head and opening its jaws wide. Fetid breath that stank of rotting meat washed over her, and she swallowed bile. An instant before the monster's jaws would have closed around her, Domi jumped to one side. The momentum of the dinosaur's charge carried it crashing and roaring into the undergrowth.

Domi ran to the nearest copse of tree ferns. She selected one with no branches for some distance, and its trunk was so glossy and smooth she shinnied up it with difficulty but without abrading her skin. Her toes braced against the bark and shoved her body upward. She went through the branches as if she were falling up the tree instead of down.

She reached a limb and ran lightly along a frond just as Monstrodamus head-butted the trunk. Before she could be jarred from her perch, Domi leaped and landed on an adjacent fern. From there, she swung to another tree fern with the effortless agility of a monkey. She remembered how Grant had commented once or twice on how nimble she could be, and her reply that she would be happy to show him the variations to which she could put her acrobatic prowess to use.

But the memories brought her pain and she closed her mind to them, concentrating on leaping from tree fern to tree fern. She couldn't afford the distraction of old emotional wounds. The greatest danger was that she might misjudge the strength of a handhold and go crashing down at Monstrodamus's feet. She could hear the swishing of vegetation and crashing crackle of foliage as the enormous creature blundered along after her.

Although she regretted it, Domi dropped her war bag, which contained a canteen, an MRE pack, a spare clip for her handblaster and her trans-comm unit. Its weight was throwing off her balance as she climbed, leaped and climbed again. But after ten minutes she tired of climbing and leaping, her arm and leg muscles complaining at the stress put upon them. She slid down a trunk to the ground and went racing through the jungle toward the river, hoping she might reach it before Monstrodamus caught her scent again.

Her hope was in vain. The huge saurian bounded out of the thickets and blocked her path, its tail lashing the undergrowth, sending up showers of leaves. Ignoring the Detonics .45 holstered at her hip, Domi reached down and drew the knife from the scabbard tied to her right calf. She started walking toward the huge creature, both hands in front of her and arms spread out to the sides. She fixed her gaze on Monstrodamus's head.

There was no choice about heading directly toward the gigantic reptile. If she tried to hold back, to keep herself prepared to dodge to one side or the other, her reflexes wouldn't be as fluid as she needed them to be. Despite being drugged at the time, Domi recalled vividly squaring off against a monstrous constrictor in Amazonia, the god-snake the Indians believed to be Kukulkan. The memory comforted her, fueled her with a defiant self-confidence.

In a low, crooning voice, she addressed Monstrodamus. "I'm not afraid of you. I've fought bigger scaly bastards than you."

Her boast wasn't true, but she figured the dinosaur didn't know that. Domi kept her face composed, as blank as a porcelain mask. Only a couple of months after the nightmarish encounter with Kukulkan, she had walked a gauntlet of rattlesnakes in California. Not only had she survived, but she had also killed most of them with the very knife she held in her hand. She waved the blade back and forth in a regular, hypnotic rhythm, the diffuse sunlight winking from the polished steel.

Monstrodamus blinked repeatedly down at her, as if confused by the small, white wraith that approached steadily and fearlessly, with a single shiny tooth in one hand. Snorting, it snapped the air and bent its upper body toward her. Domi kept walking forward. Then the dinosaur charged. The ground shook to its thundering tread, and great clods of earth were torn up and sent flying by the clawed feet, its counterbalancing tail held straight out.

Domi stood her ground. A fraction of a second before the huge feet would have crushed her into the jungle floor, she bounded forward, slashing widely, and felt her knife blade cut into the scales that coated the monster's snout. The jaws of Monstrodamus snapped shut, and a sideways toss of its head hurled her into a thicket, rolling and tumbling head over heels.

Gasping, dazed and her rib cage flaring with pain, Domi somehow staggered to her feet. More quickly than she expected, Monstrodamus untangled itself from the undergrowth and, roaring in fury and pain, pivoted. Scarlet gleamed from the knife-inflicted gash on its snout. Rather than being cowed by Domi's show of defiance and attack, the dinosaur seemed more infuriated than ever. If any cogent thought had ever crossed the predator's mind, the concept of retreat was apparently not one of them.

Domi fought down a surge of panic. She had proved her courage hundreds of times in her young life, in bloody battles on sea and land, against human and nonhuman. But Monstrodamus no longer seemed like an animal. It was a demonic force unleashed from some unknown, nameless hell that pursued her for its own reasons.

Domi turned and ran as she had run few times in her life. Ferns and thorns whipped at her naked limbs. The needled tips of coniferous shrubs scored red lines across her arms and legs. Drooping lianas snagged at her neck and head, but she fought free.

Behind her thundered the reptilian leviathan. Great divots of the soggy earth, ripped up by the taloned, churning feet, pattered down all around like a solid rain. She finally realized her hubris was going to be her doom. She knew she could not outrun Monstrodamus nor could she hide—the monster would smell her out. Every time she glanced over her shoulder she saw its grinning, fang-filled head looming above her like the face of an ageless god dedicated only to bringing about her agonizing death.

Domi clamped her jaws shut tight on a cry of fear

working its way up her throat. Then she stumbled and fell, directly into a deep trench gouged in the ground. She dropped with a splat in the dark, foul-smelling sludge at the bottom. With a pang of disgust, she realized she had fallen into an open-air latrine, filled with dinosaur feces. Monstrodamus ran over the trench and the walls collapsed under its vast weight.

Domi managed to wriggle forward as the mounds of muck fell onto her. She held a quantity of air in her lungs and she kept it there, not moving a muscle. She heard the thudding footfalls of Monstrodamus recede. When she realized the monster had not seen her fall and the soft earth covering her blocked her scent, she almost sobbed in relief. Then her sob turned to a gagging gasp of suffocation.

Domi squirmed about, threshing in the mire, trying to get her head clear. Her lungs ached fiercely as she clawed aside the thick, semiliquid mixture of mud and fecal matter. For a moment she thought she was buried alive, and she fought wildly in a convulsive flailing of arms and legs. Then she felt a hand close in her hair and pull upward. Although the pain in her scalp was fierce, she felt herself rising and when her head broke the surface, she gasped in a mouthful of the warm, humid air.

"Hell of a time to go swimming in fertilizer," Kane commented quietly.

KANE ANTICIPATED a reaction from Domi, expected her to spit profanities at him for both pulling her hair and speaking to her sarcastically. He was surprised and a little dismayed when she cried out in wordless relief and threw her arms around him. As she clutched him tightly, almost desperately, Kane sat with her on the ground while she tried to regain control of herself.

She buried her face against his shoulder and shuddered violently. He felt her heart beating hard and fast like the wings of a captured bird. Although he restrained the impulse to push the reeking Domi away from him, for a moment he wished he shared Grant's impaired sense of smell. Grant's nose had been broken three times in the past, and always poorly reset. Unless an odor was extraordinarily pleasant or virulently repulsive, he was incapable of detecting subtle smells unless they were right under his nostrils. A running joke during in his Mag days had been that Grant could eat a hearty dinner with a dead skunk lying on the table next to his plate.

It took Kane a few seconds to realize her little high-pitched pants were actually words. "Almost... buried...in *shit*...thought I...*dead!*" Under stress, her abbreviated mode of Outland speech became more pronounced.

Kane clumsily patted her muck-coated back and started to stroke her thickly clotted hair, then reconsidered. It was almost impossible to tell its true color was bone-white. He had never seen her so frightened. "You're fine," he said soothingly. "I got you out."

Dragging in a long, shuddery breath, Domi pushed herself away from him and hugged herself. Tears had cut runnels in the dirt caked on her cheeks. Although her voice still quavered with fear, Kane heard the edge of accusatory anger in it when she snapped, "Good thing, since it was your fault I was in there!"

Kane glanced at the trench and, for lack of anything else to say, commented, "Some big animal must've dug that out."

Domi's eyes sparked redly at his bland remark. "I had the drop on the son of a bitch—straight shot through the eye into the brain. Would've dropped his scaly ass dead. Then you commed me!"

Kane shrugged. Inanely he said, "Sorry. I'd told you I'd call you back, but I got delayed. Thought you might be worried you hadn't heard from me."

"I was too busy to worry about anybody but me."

"When I heard your first shot," Kane went on doggedly, "I needed to find out what was happening."

Domi looked at the raw scrapes on his arms and the still bleeding wound on the back of his right hand. "What happened to you anyhow?"

Tersely, swiftly, Kane told her. "I just followed all the racket Monstrodamus made while he chased you," he concluded.

Domi nodded. She had stopped trembling. Regarding him gravely, she declared, "This dinosaur-hunt idea of yours was triple-stupe."

Kane didn't dispute her, nor did he agree. "We've got a better idea of what's here on the island now. I found a group of people...sort of."

"Who cares?" Domi stood up and brushed irritably at the flakes of drying mud and feces on her legs. "Let Shizuka and her samurai take care of the things here. They're the ones who live next door."

Rising to his feet, Kane let the remark pass without responding to it. He knew there was no love lost between Domi and Shizuka.

"Wish we'd never heard of this nuke-shitting place," she continued sullenly, waving away flies that started to buzz around her.

Kane opened to his mouth to voice a rebuke and once more decided not to respond—or to remind her that if they had never heard of Thunder Isle, she would be no more than a memory and a black smudge mark on a concrete slab in Nevada.

Pointing with the barrel of the shotgun, he said, "There's a stream over there if you want to clean up a little."

"Why bother?" she snapped, but she started marching in the direction Kane indicated.

The stream was narrow and shallow, but the water was fairly clear and fresh smelling. Standing on the bank, Domi and Kane surveyed it, trying to see any movement beneath the surface. Domi picked up a stone and threw it to see what it stirred up, but nothing threatening arose.

"Good enough," Domi announced flatly, unbuckling her web belt and handing it and the holstered pistol to Kane. "The way I feel, I'd climb in there with a scalie."

She stripped off her top and shorts and waded without shame or conceit into the stream, carrying her clothes with her. Kane wasn't surprised by her lack of modesty. He had seen her naked before—everyone in Cerberus redoubt had, particularly during her first few weeks there. The girl wasn't accustomed to wearing clothes unless circumstances demanded them, and then only the skimpiest concessions to weather, not modesty. Born a feral child of the Outlands, she was always at ease being nude in the company of others, and if those others didn't share that comfort zone, she couldn't care less.

The stream was shallow, reaching only the tops of Domi's thighs, but it was deep enough to submerge her entire body when she knelt. The water grew cloudy around her as the coating of sludge dissolved and was swept away by the current. Standing, she swished her shorts and tank top around until most of the muck adhering to them floated away.

Eyes concealed behind the dark lenses of his sunglasses, Kane watched her, cradling the shotgun in his arms. Despite the new scratches and old scars marring the pearly perfection of her skin, particularly the one shaped like a starburst on her right shoulder, Domi was maverick beautiful. Her body was a liquid, symmetrical flow of curving lines, with small porcelain breasts rising to sharp nipples, and a flat, hard-muscled stomach extending to the flared shape of her hips. With droplets of water sparkling on her arms and legs, her skin looked opaque, its luminosity heightened by an absence of color. Even her patch of pubic hair was white.

As she splashed water over her breasts, she glanced up and caught Kane's gaze. She stuck out her tongue at him. "You feel like fucking?"

He was barely able to keep the surprise he felt from

showing on his face. Instead, he forced a lopsided grin. "You mean with you or anybody in general?"

"What do you think?" she challenged.

"Neither one is really practical at the moment."

Domi laughed a little scornfully. "It never is practical with you, unless you're drugged or hypnotized or something."

Kane's hands tightened around his shotgun. "What the hell do you mean by that?"

Shaking her head in exasperation, Domi waded out of the stream and wrung out her shirt and shorts. "I mean if you keep on pretending you're too professional for Brigid, she'll find somebody who doesn't think he is. You've got competition for her now, you know."

After two years of being in her company, Kane was accustomed to Domi's forthright and freewheeling manner of expressing herself, but the fact she raised such a personal topic in such circumstances surprised him into speechlessness for a long moment.

He snorted derisively. "You mean Philboyd? He's a geek."

She smiled slightly at his slang. As she pulled on her tank top, she said with studied nonchalance, "So is Lakesh. That hasn't stopped him."

Kane frowned. "How do you know?"

In the process of stepping into her shorts, Domi favored him with an up-from-under stare that was profoundly pitying.

He was only dimly aware of his jaw sagging open before he blurted, "Lakesh and you?"

Domi nodded, hitching up her shorts. "Me and Lakesh…for quite a while now."

She stared at him steadily, waiting for a reaction or daring him to express one. Instead, he shoved her belt into her arms. "Put it on," he said gruffly. "I think we'd better get back to the installation. We're underarmed now."

Domi continued to stare at him, then buckled the belt. "Whatever you say." Her voice was unusually even and toneless. "But I want to backtrack a little."

"Why?"

She gestured to the underbrush in the direction from which they came. "I lost my knife back there."

"You can get another one in Cerberus." He spoke more peremptorily than he intended.

Domi walked around him as if she hadn't heard. Kane thought about grabbing her and carrying her out of the jungle, but decided to let her indulge her whim. He knew the knife meant a great deal to her, since it symbolized the end of her period of slavery. Besides, she would fight like a leopard. Domi glanced over her shoulder at him. "You don't have to come with me. You could go back."

"Right," Kane drawled, catching up to her with two swift strides. "Let's just be careful."

Domi nodded in agreement. Cautiously they moved parallel to the tracks of Monstrodamus that led into the thickets. The soft ground was deeply sunken where the dinosaur had trod in pursuit of Domi. They followed the tracks into the denser growth and saw little scarlet spottings of blood on shredded leaves and twigs.

"Put my mark on the bastard, at least," Domi commented.

Metal gleamed dully a few yards ahead, and Domi increased the speed and length of her stride. She bent over and uttered a small cry of triumph. She brandished her knife and stated, "Now we go back."

Kane nodded. "Good."

The two people moved into the tree ferns, heading in the general direction of the Operation Chronos complex. They walked carefully, alertly, along a game trail, scanning their surroundings for any hint of movement, for any sign that Monstrodamus or some other beast was hidden in the jungle along their path. The trail led them near a boggy area. Ahead of them they heard heavy, snuffling grunts.

Domi and Kane halted, looked at each other, then crept forward on all fours, barely breathing. They reached a stand of cane and pushed the stalks aside to peer out. Both people froze, their lungs seeming to seize.

They saw Monstrodamus barely thirty feet away, standing spraddle-legged over a shallow depression gouged in the soft earth, wet earth. Its lips were drawn back over its teeth and from them dangled the blood-dripping carcass of the saber-toothed tiger. The dinosaur panted heavily around the body.

"Bastard backtracked on us," Domi whispered.

Kane noticed how the predator's cold eyes, sunk beneath knobs of scaled bone, were fixed on some distant point. Between its powerful legs lay a cluster of white, oval objects about the general shape and size of footballs. Kane also saw jagged shards scattered within the depression.

Domi, her face a pallid oval in the greenish gloom, said lowly, "Eggs...some of 'em have hatched."

Cold sweat formed on Kane's face as Monstrodamus dropped the animal's body near the nest. Lifting its head high, the flesh at the dinosaur's throat swelled and from its open jaws blared a long, trumpeting bawl.

"What's he doing?" Domi demanded.

"Mess call," retorted Kane flatly.

A moment later, Domi husked out, "Monstrodamus is a *girl*. A mama!"

In a faint whisper, Kane asked, "If that's the case, where's the papa?"

Suddenly the foliage erupted with high-pitched hisses and squawlings. Two miniature versions of Monstrodamus, the largest only about four feet tall, burst out of the ferns and raced toward the nest. Their heads were fierce-looking, since most of their bulk seemed to be concentrated in their mouths. The infants' reddish-brown skin looked leathery and dry. Monstrodamus greeted the pair of creatures with a rumbling growl that reminded Kane of a cat's purr. Looking at their three-toed feet, he realized one of the infants had made the tracks near the river.

"There's the kids," murmured Domi. "Baby Monstrodamuses."

"Monstrodami," Kane suggested absently.

The infant dinosaurs instantly fell onto the corpse of the saber-tooth and began ripping shreds of flesh from it, uttering little chirps of happiness in between loud and fast chewing noises.

Domi swallowed hard and replied quietly, but emphatically, "We are *definitely* underarmed."

The two people backed away, the sound of their retreat covered by the noises made by the creatures. They stood and began a quick march out of the area. Within a minute they rocked to a halt when they heard a crashing in the underbrush ahead of them. Before they could even begin to formulate a plan of action, another baby Monstrodamus burst through a thicket of ferns. It saw them, shrieked and leaped.

Chapter 5

Grant fumbled with the cigar and the lighter, transferring both from the nearly numb fingers of his left hand to his right before he finally achieved the proper balance to light up. As he thumbed the lighter to life and touched the flame to the end of the cigar, it occurred to him that with one arm essentially useless, he was occupying his gun hand. He had barely given his surroundings a cursory glance.

Some old habits died far easier than others, he thought a little sourly as he snapped shut the lid on the lighter. He hadn't bothered making a threat assessment, and the flare of the lighter, the crimson glow of the cigar tip, could easily turn him into a target in one second and a corpse in the next.

But the sun was at midpoint in the sky, and the area in which he stood barely provided enough cover for a cockroach, much less a blasterman—or a hungry inhabitant of Thunder Isle. Grant's long, heavy-jawed face was twisted in a scowl. Droplets of perspiration sparkled against his coffee-brown skin. Standing four inches over six feet tall, Grant was an exceptionally broad-chested and -shouldered man. Gray sprinkled his short-cropped, tight-curled hair, but it didn't show in the heavy black mustache that swept fiercely out from either side of his grim, tight-lipped mouth.

He wore jeans and a black T-shirt. A pair of microbinoculars hung around his neck from a leather strap. His left arm was crooked in a canvas sling, positioned across his midriff. Strapped to his right forearm was his Sin Eater snugged in its molded plastic power holster. He blew a wreath of smoke toward the distant tree line, glad to be out in the fresh air, yet noting the irony of polluting it with his cigar. But then, the air wasn't all that fresh around the Operation Chronos installation. In his opinion, a thousand tobacco smokers couldn't make the heavy, humid air of Thunder Isle any worse.

Hardly anyone used tobacco in any form nowadays. There were mild drugs available that were much safer, less offensive to others and just as sedative. But both Kane and Grant had learned to appreciate good cigars during their many Pit patrols back in Cobaltville, and having the freedom to enjoy them when they wanted to was one of the few advantages of being an exile, even though no one in Cerberus smoked but he and Kane. But as time went on, Grant perceived fewer and fewer advantages to living in Cerberus.

Certainly having his left arm and almost the entire side of his body rendered numb to all sensation wasn't one of them. Nor was standing in a dead zone, a flat, sandy plain at least a half mile in diameter. At its leading edge, the vegetation and shrubbery dropped away as if the foliage dared not cross an invisible boundary. The open place marked a zone of demarcation across the ground. On the far side of the circle grew thick, lush grasses and ferns. On Grant's side of the invisible boundary, the grass was thin and brown, little more than stubble.

Only a few feet inside the circle, the fronds and leaves were stained and spotted with livid streaks of yellow. Sprinkled across the barren and sere landscape were the browned skeletons of birds, their featherless wings outstretched as if they had dropped dead in midflight. Here and there were smaller collections of bones, those of rats and other animals.

Grant absently kicked at the ground, toeing up a clod of dirt. It lifted out easily, with no resistance. The blades of grass were lank and pale, the roots brown and dead. The dead zone was the result of radiation poisoning. Months before, when he, Brigid and Kane made landfall on the isle, they found evidence of radiation poisoning that extended from the Chronos facility in a parabolic shape. Later they learned the affected area was regularly subjected to short bursts of high-power pulses of microwave radiation from the temporal dilator, probably in the 10^{14} kilometer band.

Even though the dilator no longer functioned and hadn't in months, the barren zone had yet to show any appreciable signs of recovery. Grant puffed on the cigar, releasing a plume of smoke that made his eyes sting. He fanned the hazy cloud away from his face and kept his gaze fastened on the tree line, at the far edge of the circle of defoliation. It wasn't that he expected Kane or Domi to return without a heads-up call, but there was always a possibility.

Although he would never voice it, Grant felt terrible not being able to assist Kane and Domi in the hunt. Still, he was levelheaded enough to realize that there were very few situations that either one of them wasn't equipped to handle.

Grant and Kane, although they had served for many years as highly decorated Magistrates in Cobaltville, had been anomalies in the ranks of the baron's enforcers. Teamwork, acting as cogs in wheels was encouraged, but true friendship between Mags was frowned upon. Devotion to duty, to serving the baron, was paramount, not esprit de corps. Kane and Grant had broken this cardinal rule. Grant had sacrificed everything that had given his life purpose in order to save his partner, and more important, his friend.

If Grant had not made that choice, resistance against baronial rule would have been futile, regardless of all Lakesh's plans, hopes and schemes. Shortly after the nukecaust, Lakesh had volunteered to be placed in suspended animation. He was revived nearly two centuries later to contribute to the Program of Unification, a plan designed solely to bring what was left of the world under a single, controlling authority.

After his resurrection, Lakesh recognized the errors in his judgment and he began secretly plotting against the ruthless barons. It took him nearly thirty years to find a group of people with enough courage, strength and cunning to stand against the cushioned tyranny of the villes.

The people Lakesh had initially recruited to staff Cerberus were primarily academics, tech-heads, specialists in a variety of fields. All of them had led structured, sheltered lives in their respective villes. Until the arrival of Grant, Brigid, Domi and Kane, the Cerberus resistance movement consisted of little more than intelligence gathering.

Kane and Grant acted on that intel, performing as the enforcement arm of Cerberus. In that capacity, they not only scored a number of victories against the barons, but also contended with other threats.

But over the past few months, Grant realized he was weary of contending with threats, with menaces, with madmen and with violence. He had witnessed many violent deaths, and even been responsible for dozens of them during his Mag days and after. But his last five years as a Magistrate were fairly routine. He could count on the fingers of one hand how often he had fired his service weapon in the performance of his duty. His transfer to an administrative position was pending, and if he hadn't opted to join Kane in exile, he would now be sitting at a desk reading requisition reports. The prospect of hanging up his blaster and putting his armor in storage hadn't bothered him at all.

The trans-comm unit clipped to his belt suddenly gave out a shrill warbling. He jumped in surprise, cursed and nearly dropped his cigar. Brows knitting at the bridge of his nose, he decided to ignore the insistent warbling. He was ninety-nine percent certain of the caller's identity, and it wasn't Domi or Kane.

The comm continued to trill and with a profanity-seasoned sigh, Grant jammed the cigar between his teeth and fumbled with his good hand to unclip the comm and bring it to his ear. His "What?" was a ferocious snarl.

"What the hell are you doing?" Reba DeFore's voice demanded angrily.

"Just what you told me to do," he lied. "Sitting down and taking my medication."

In a tone of exceptionally weary exasperation, DeFore's voice responded, "I can see you from the Cube, you know."

Grant turned to face the Chronos installation and waved the trans-comm over his head. A black, almost featureless shape lifted out of the ground a quarter of a mile away. It was like a miniature mountain of black stone squatting in the center of the circle of dead vegetation.

The huge structure lay partly in ruins. It resembled a fortress, but of a streamlined architectural type. Made of a very dark stone, it rose in a complex of pillars and overhanging buttresses. Cubical in configuration, the building loomed above smaller structures like a squared-off mountain peak towering over foothills. Months before, when the dilator had reached critical mass, the resulting explosion had blown out chunks of the facade. Grant assumed DeFore stood at one of the openings, observing him with binoculars.

Some of the smaller buildings around the Cube had eroded so much they had fallen completely into ruin. Roofless arches reared from the ground, and a few storage buildings were scattered around the outer perimeter of the walls.

A broad blacktop avenue ran in toward the Cube. The asphalt had a peculiar ripple pattern to it, and weeds sprouted from splits in the surface. All three of them had seen the rippling effect before, out in the hellzones. It was a characteristic result of earthquakes triggered by nuclear-bomb shock waves.

Lampposts lined the road, most of them rusted through and leaning over at forty-five-degree angles. The avenue widened inside the walls, opening into a broad courtyard filled with great blocks of basalt and concrete that had fallen from the buildings. Secondary lanes stretched out in all directions, a spokelike pattern of streets, bike paths and pedestrian walkways.

All along the streets husks of buildings stood like the skeletons of sentinels, their soft flesh eaten away by the hungry teeth of time. One of the structures had collapsed entirely, folded in on itself like a house of dominoes, with the fallen rear wall knocking down all the interior sections one by one.

"I just wanted to stretch my legs," he said. "Besides, I really hate that damn place."

Most of the Totality Concept–related installations he had ever visited always seemed haunted by the ghosts of a hopeless, despairing past age, and Redoubt Yankee was no exception. The walls of the Cube seemed to exude the terror, the utter despondency of souls trapped there when the first mushroom cloud erupted from Washington on that chill January noon.

"I don't care much for it, either," came DeFore's

voice. "But there's a lot of material and equipment here that's been useful to us…and a lot more that has yet to be inventoried."

Grant couldn't argue with her statement, even if he had been so inclined. Most of the Operation Chronos machinery was damaged beyond any reasonable expectation of repair, but the data pertaining to the so-called Parallax Points program was retrieved and put to good use, including the protective garments Kane had named shadow suits.

"But that still doesn't change anything," DeFore continued, an acidic edge to her voice. "I still don't know the extent of the neurological trauma you suffered, if it's actually damage or not."

"Kane recovered," Grant replied a little sullenly, "with no problem."

"There are a lot of reasons for that," she responded bluntly. "One of them is the fact he's several years younger. You're reaching a dangerous age."

Grant struggled to tamp down a surge of anger. "And you're overstepping, Reba."

There was no response from the trans-comm, and his anger was suddenly replaced by a feeling of guilt. Not for the first time he reflected how he—all of them in the redoubt—treated DeFore as little more than a doctoring machine. He and Kane were the worst offenders, dealing with her only when they had a wound for her to suture or patch.

When DeFore spoke again, her voice was cold. "Then I'll let others who feel the same way about this place as you do give you a prognosis. Brigid, Philboyd and Shizuka are on their way to you.''

''What about Nora?'' Grant asked.

''She volunteered to stay in here with me and catalog the medical stores. I'm glad there's somebody in this crew who remembers what the whole point of gating here was.'' She added a little bitterly and unnecessarily, ''And it wasn't hunting dinosaurs.''

Narrowing his eyes, Grant saw a group of figures emerge from around the corner of a fallen wall. Sunlight winked from metal. ''That might not have been your point, but if we're going to make this place a branch of Cerberus, we can't have our personnel being eaten.''

He thought his point was valid, but the effort to make it was wasted since DeFore had already cut the circuit. He smiled a little, knowing how the medic always took every opportunity to get the last word. Closing the cover of the trans-comm unit, he returned it to his belt and waited for the group of people to reach him.

Brigid Baptiste was in the lead, due in the main to her brisk, almost mannish stride. As she walked, she absently combed a hand through her thick hair. It tumbled in waves from beneath the long-visored olive-green cap on her head, spilling artlessly over her khaki-clad shoulders like a red-gold mane. Her delicate features had an almost feline cast to them. Her complexion, fair and lightly dusted with freckles across her nose and cheeks, held a rosy hue.

Her eyes weren't just green; they were a deep, clear

emerald, glittering like jade. Tall and willowy, her slender, athletic figure reflected an unusual strength without detracting from her undeniable femininity, despite the unflattering shirt, whipcord trousers and high-topped jump boots she wore. An Iver Johnson TP9 blaster was holstered at her hip.

As a former archivist in the Cobaltville Historical Division, Brigid's knowledge on a wide variety of subjects was profound, due in the main to her greatest asset—an eidetic, or "photographic," memory. She could instantly and totally recall in detail everything she had read, seen or experienced, which was both a blessing and a curse.

Walking on her left and little behind was Shizuka. A little over five feet tall, she wore her luxuriant blue-black hair piled high. The tumble of glossy black hair framed a smoothly sculpted face of extraordinary beauty. Her complexion was a very pale gold with peach and milk for an accent. Beneath a snub nose, her petaled lips were full. The dark, almond-shaped eyes glinted with the fierce, proud gleam of a young eagle. She wore a billowy, pale-green *kamishimo,* the formal attire of a daimyo's retainer, with both a *katana* and shorter *tanto* sword thrust through the bright-red silk sash.

Brewster Philboyd was the tallest of the three, a little over six feet, long and lanky of build, seeming to be all kneecaps, elbows and knuckles when he walked. In his left hand he carried a small black plastic case. Blond-white hair was swept back from a receding hairline. He wore black-rimmed eyeglasses.

The right lenses showed a spiderweb pattern of cracks. His cheeks appeared to be pitted with the sort of scars associated with chronic teenage acne.

Philboyd was one of several scientists who had recently arrived in the Cerberus redoubt from a forgotten Moonbase. Like Lakesh, he was a freezie, postnuke slang for someone who had been placed in stasis following the war.

A contingent of Tigers of Heaven brought up the rear. Despite the heat and humidity, the four soldiers were attired in suits of segmented armor made from wafers of metal held together by small, delicate chains. Overlaid with a dark-brown lacquer, the interlocked and overlapping plates were trimmed in scarlet and gold. Between flaring shoulder epaulets, war helmets fanned out with sweeping curves of metal. Some resembled wings, others horns. The face guards, wrought of a semitransparent material, presented the inhuman visages of snarling tigers.

Quivers of arrows dangled from their shoulders, and longbows made of lacquered wood were strapped to their backs. Each samurai carried two longswords in black scabbards swinging back from each hip. None of them carried firearms, but their skill with *katanas* and the bows was such they didn't really need them. Grant had been told that ammunition was hard to come by, nor did New Edo have the natural resources to manufacture it themselves.

Grant had offered to supply the Tigers with guns and ammunition from the Cerberus armory, but he had been politely refused. The samurai code practiced by the Tigers considered blasters unmanly weapons, despite the fact they did have a few old World War II–vintage carbines in storage.

Shizuka spoke first. "Your healer is very put out with you."

Grant forced a smile. "Then our relationship is about normal."

Shizuka didn't return the smile. "She told me we would be wasting our time if we asked you to come back inside."

"And she'd be right," Grant replied agreeably.

"Any word from Kane or Domi?" Brigid asked.

Grant shook his head. "Not yet. I thought I heard a gunshot on my way out here, but it was so far away I couldn't be sure."

"Do you want us to track them?" Shizuka asked, gesturing to the Tigers.

Grant shook his head again, this time far more vehemently. "Abso-damn-lutely not. I don't want anybody else going through that shit until we found out if that tyrannosaur has been neutralized."

"Our boat is on the beach," Shizuka reminded him gently. "The only way to reach it and return to New Edo is through that shit."

"I know," Grant agreed. "Let's give Domi and Kane a little more time."

With a sour smile, Philboyd said, "If the damn thing hadn't chased me the other day, I wouldn't have believed it was real."

Brigid regarded him with an eyebrow arched at a supercilious angle. "You were briefed about Thunder

Isle, Operation Chronos and Monstrodamus. We told you everything before you agreed to leave the Moon.''

He nodded, his sour smile turning to one of shame. Philboyd, as well as the other members of his astrophysicist team on the Moon, had heard whispers of the Totality Concept during the twentieth century, but by his own admission they knew very little about it beyond the name. Brigid had explained that most Totality Concept–related redoubts were buried in subterranean military complexes mainly in the United States. There were, as they had reason to know, Concept-connected redoubts in other countries.

''I'm not complaining,'' he said a little defensively. ''But hearing about time-trawled dinosaurs is a hell of a lot different than having one snap at your ass.''

Brigid smiled wanly. ''Point taken.''

Nodding to the case in Philboyd's hand, Grant asked, ''What've you got there?''

Philboyd's face lit up as he unlatched it. ''Remember these things? Brigid said none of you could identify them.''

Resting on a layer of foam rubber Grant saw several small, flat curves of brass-tinted metal, barely an inch long. There were also a number of tiny rectangular wafers from which steel pintels protruded.

''What are they?'' he asked.

''He said they're comms,'' Brigid answered.

''Comm*tacts*,'' corrected Philboyd smoothly. ''They were state-of-the-art multiple-channel communication devices at the end of the twentieth century, used only by high-priority security forces."

Grant looked at them carefully, aware of a niggling sensation of familiarity, but he couldn't place it. "How do they work?"

"The sensor circuitry incorporates an analog-to-digital voice encoder," Philboyd replied, poking at one of the tabs with a forefinger. "This is subcutaneously embedded in the mastoid bone...the pintels connect to input ports in the comms. Once they make contact, when you receive a transmission, it's picked up by your auditory canals and the dermal sensors transmit the electronic signals directly through your skull bone. Even if you went deaf, as long as you wore the Commtact you'd still have a form of hearing."

"They can replace our trans-comms," Brigid declared. "Reba says the surgery to implant the sensors is very minor, just a matter of making a small incision and sliding them under the skin."

"What's the range on those things?" Grant asked, eyeing them dubiously.

"That's the main drawback," said Philboyd. "Due to their size, the range of the Commtacts is very limited. For line of sight transmissions, clear voice signals will only travel five miles."

Grant's eyebrows rose. "Only five miles? That's about three more miles than the range of the trans-comms."

The range of the radiophones was generally limited

to a mile, but in open country, in clear weather, contact could be established at two miles.

"Also," put in Brigid, "if we go with the Commtacts, it's one less piece of equipment we'll have to pack out into the field. That should make you happy."

Grant suddenly felt the pressure of Shizuka's eyes upon him, and his throat constricted. He didn't glance in her direction, but he knew not only what she was thinking, but also what she was expecting—that he would finally reveal to his friends his intention to leave Cerberus and live with her on New Edo. Because of the injuries he and Kane had suffered, he had yet to mention his decision to anyone and it was past time for him to do so. It was, after all, his idea.

Ever since he had met Shizuka and first visited New Edo, the concept of remaining on the little island monarchy had been very appealing. However, Shizuka had never extended an invitation to him. Grant hadn't felt it was his place to raise the issue with her until the past few weeks, after the op to the Moon and the arrival of the Manitius Base personnel.

Despite the new influx of people to Cerberus, Grant was fairly certain Kane would accuse him of desertion, despite the fact he had taken no vows or sworn oaths of service to battle the barons. Kane was his partner, true enough, and it was a matter of Mag policy never to desert a partner regardless of the circumstances, but they weren't Mags any longer. Kane had more of a personal, vested interest in seeing the barons overthrown than he did. It was Kane's vendetta, his vengeance trail, not Grant's. His primary contribution was to cover Kane's back. But now there were other people who could be trained to perform that function just as well.

Clearing his throat, Grant turned toward Brigid. He opened his mouth to speak—but shut it almost immediately when the thundering echo of a shotgun blast reverberated out of the jungle.

Chapter 6

Kane was astonished by how high Monstrodamus leaped—at least six feet straight up, then over their heads, tail held out stiffly. It landed behind Domi and its head darted toward her, jaws snapping open. With lightning swiftness the albino weaved away from the razored teeth, clawing for her holstered pistol.

As soon as she was out of the spread area, Kane squeezed the trigger of the shotgun. The sound of 12-gauge buckshot exploding from the bore of the Remington was deafening. The dinosaur took the shot in its lower belly. As though it had been slapped off its three-toed feet by a giant invisible hand, the creature catapulted backward into a clump of bushes. Its tail thrashed and whipped the shrubbery violently. It voiced a high-pitched quavering squall.

Its cry was answered by a ferocious bellow. Kane and Domi didn't hesitate. They whirled and ran, legs, arms and hearts pumping. Behind them they heard heavy, squashing footfalls as of great weights pulling free of mud.

Domi and Kane sprinted across an open patch of ground. His left boot sank into a section of swampy ooze and he stumbled, nearly falling. The mire sucked at his foot, refusing to release it. As he struggled to free himself, from behind them came a prolonged, screechy roar.

Her ruby eyes glittering with fright, Domi yanked on Kane's leg. "She found baby!"

They glanced back just as Monstrodamus crashed through the foliage, running at full speed with its head low, jaws wide in an unmistakable posture of attack.

With Domi's help, Kane pulled his leg free and the two people resumed their frantic dash again. The monster bellowed behind them, a roar so loud and full of fury it hurt their ears and chilled their blood. They plunged on, trying to not waste time or risk a misstep by looking over their shoulders. Both people wheezed, more from fear than exertion. They felt like foxes being chased by the hounds, and it was a feeling Kane despised.

The two people sprinted among the fern trees, tearing their way through clumps of shrubbery. With Monstrodamus gaining ground with every second, they realized the chance of eluding the dinosaur, now driven to a murderous frenzy by the death of one of its hatchlings, was so slim as to be not worth considering.

"Make a stand?" Domi panted, her hair plastered to her head by sweat.

Kane gulped in air and nodded. "Make a stand."

When they reached a copse of evergreens, the two people stopped, turning to face their gigantic pursuer. They scarcely had time for that single, swift movement before Monstrodamus bounded between them. The two people sprang away on opposite sides of the hissing, snarling saurian. They tried to disorient it by ducking behind tree trunks. The carnosaur stumbled to a clumsy halt, huge, splayed feet trampling the spongy ground. It snapped viciously at the treetrunk behind which Kane had jumped, and its teeth sheared away a bushel of bark.

Kane bounded toward another tree, and Monstrodamus followed him. Even though Domi shouted and waved her arms, she failed to distract the dinosaur from going after Kane. He wondered briefly if the gargantuan reptile remembered him from their first encounter months before.

He slid around another tree and the thickly muscled, scale-sheathed tail of Monstrodamus battered deep into Kane's midsection, slamming him off his feet and driving him against an evergreen trunk. All the breath left his lungs in an agonized bleat between his teeth. Sour bile climbed up his throat in an acidic column.

Kane was only dimly aware of collapsing to the jungle floor in a heap, but he knew Monstrodamus's open jaws hovered above him. Although his vision was blurred, he glimpsed the salvia-slick fangs. It was like seeing something out of the darkness of a midnight nightmare, moving in slow-motion but with crystal clarity. He retained vividly unpleasant memories of how those huge jaws ripped the head from the shoulders of a hapless Magistrate and months later how they bit Sindri's lobotomized henchman completely in two.

Through the pain haze swimming across his eyes,

he caught a foggy impression of Domi bounding forward, her long knife raised. She slashed at the creature's right flank, scoring a shallow, scarlet-leaking gash along the pebbled pattern of scales and then flitted away like a wraith. Voicing a sibilant snarl of anger, Monstrodamus spun toward her.

Gasping, Kane forced himself to his knees. He braced the shotgun against his left forearm and squeezed the trigger. He had chosen the Remington from the Cerberus armory because it was fairly lightweight, could be manipulated with one hand and the recoil was manageable because of the gun's gas system operation.

The roar of the USAS-12 was only a little more loud than the scream of pain erupting from the throat of Monstrodamus as the buckshot pounded into its upper chest. Its neck arched backward, head shaking furiously, flinging a spray of blood in all directions. At that instant, Domi bounded from behind a tree and, balancing on the balls of her feet, ran up Monstrodamus's tail to her back. She locked both arms around the dinosaur's neck, just behind the thick knots of jaw muscles.

The monster reared as Domi stabbed with her knife, the blade sinking to half its length through the tough scales. In a volcanic convulsion Monstrodamus's tail whiplashed against the trunk of a tree with sledgehammer force, flinders of bark flying from it and showering Kane with wood chips.

Monstrodamus bent over suddenly, nearly flipping Domi over the carnosaur's head. White legs kicking empty air, Domi hung on to the knife handle, goring, ripping, working the blade through the saurian's bulk.

Monstrodamus reared again, and slammed Domi into a tree. The impact sent shivers of pain from the crown of her head to the backs of her knees. She slashed at Monstrodamus's right eye, the point scoring a bloody cut in the scales beneath it. Kane stepped forward, drawing his handblaster even though he knew shooting at the creature's body would have little effect.

He could waste an entire clip trying to hit a vital organ. Only a head shot would kill the thing, and with Domi still clinging tenaciously to the carnosaur's whipsawing neck, she would be at as much risk of being shot as Monstrodamus.

He framed the gaping jaws in the blaster's sights, planning to put a round through its palate and thus through its brain. The creature's tail suddenly looped outward, catching him at ankle level and bowling him backward, the pistol flying from his hand.

"Will you shoot this fuckin' thing?" Domi shrieked. She still clung tenaciously to the creature's neck, hanging on like a bulldog to the hilt of the knife, which she could not withdraw.

Regaining his feet, Kane shouted back, "Let go of her and get clear!"

Domi instantly obeyed, releasing her hold and pulling her knife from Monstrodamus's neck. She fell to one knee, then dropped flat. Kane fired the Remington again. She rolled frantically toward him, beneath the barrage of buckshot, barely avoiding a pair of vicious, disemboweling swipes of the saurian's taloned feet.

Bracing his legs wide, Kane continued to fire the Remington at the predatory dinosaur. Round after round after round penetrated the scales and flesh and muscle, but Monstrodamus continued advancing. He kept pumping the trigger, bright brass flying up and out from the smoking ejector port. The 12-gauge shot pounded into Monstrodamus's body, tearing away fistfuls of flesh and muscle amid sprays of dark blood. The monster's sibilant snarling took on a high-pitched, keening note. Then the firing pin clicked dry on an empty chamber.

In the short tick of silence following the last explosive report, Domi said tonelessly, "Oh, fuck."

She worked the trigger of her Detonics Combat Master, holding it in a two handed grip, sending out booming shock waves of ear-shattering sound. The first .45-caliber round hit the creature on its massive left thigh, gouging a bloody furrow through the scales. The autopistol bucked and thundered in her hands, and the impact of another steel-jacketed block-buster sent Monstrodamus staggering sideways.

The dinosaur continued to turn in the direction Domi's bullet slammed it, spinning and swinging its tail laterally. The tip struck Domi in the side, knocking her headlong to the earth, the handblaster skittering end over end from her hand.

Monstrodamus lifted a big, hook-clawed foot, preparing to stamp on the fallen girl. Yelling at the top of his voice, Kane bounded forward and buttstroked the creature directly in the mouth with the USAS-12. He heard the crunch of teeth splintering under the force of the blow.

With all its other wounds, the clubbing blow to its fangs should have been no more painful than a flea-bite. To Kane's surprise, Monstrodamus stumbled backward, balancing itself on its tail, lowering its head and covering its mouth with its clawed fore-paws. It made a spitting noise as if it were trying to blow lint off its lips. He glimpsed little splinters of bone falling from her maw.

Without hesitation, Kane dropped the shotgun, heaved Domi up from the ground and began running. He half carried, half dragged the dazed girl, her toes barely touching the earth as he bore her along. As he expected, Monstrodamus recovered quickly from the strike to the teeth. Within seconds he heard the snap of twigs and crash of shrubbery as it rushed after them like a ship pushed in front of a hurricane.

They had gone less than a hundred feet before Kane was forced to stop at the edge of a big patch of open marshland. The slough area was well lit by the afternoon sun. The mud shone golden in places. Flying insects like dragonflies darted low over the morass, preying on gnats.

Still holding Domi, Kane slogged and struggled across the mudflat, sinking to his knees almost immediately. He plowed onward. Eyes glassy, Domi asked in confusion, "What are you doing?"

Hoarsely, his throat raw, lungs laboring, Kane declared, "I've had enough of this shit. It ends now."

He released Domi, who nearly fell face first into the morass. Facing Monstrodamus as she crept cautiously out to the edge of the marsh, Kane opened his war bag. He looked the creature over with a critical eye, noting the number of blood-streaming wounds all over her body. None of them appeared to be mortal, but it was hard to tell.

Tentatively Monstrodamus touched the soft, yielding surface of the mudflat with one three-clawed foot and withdrew it. Kane was reminded of someone testing the temperature of a stream. Carefully the big saurian began to back away.

Kane snapped to Domi, ''Make a fuss—yell, jump, sing, do anything to bring her out here.''

Domi shot him an incredulous look but did as he as directed—whooping wordlessly, waving her arms over her head, digging up handfuls of mud and hurling them at the carnosaur. Monstrodamus snorted, growled, pawed at the ground and snapped at the mud clots when they flew by its head.

From his war bag Kane removed an apple-sized and -shaped grenade. Withdrawing the coil of nylon rope, he attached a three-pronged grappling hook to the triggering ring of the grenade. The grenade was an M-68 fragmentation type, equipped with an impact fuse. The detonation mechanism was armed electrically three seconds after making a hard contact.

He stepped closer to the edge of the marshland, holding the grenade in one hand and the rope's slack in the other. He stared at Monstrodamus defiantly, a direct challenge.

"Come on," he called tauntingly. "You already had a couple of chances to bite my head off—I'm giving you one more. After that, you're done."

Monstrodamus growled again, and the growl built to a roaring crescendo of frustration. It paced back and forth along the marsh's edge as if suspicious. Domi kept up a yelling, mud-throwing racket, and Kane joined in, cradling the gren protectively in the palm of his hand.

Kane moved much closer. He and the dinosaur faced off. Monstrodamus shifted its weight from foot to foot. The monster somehow suspected he was luring it in. Slowly, with a deliberate provocativeness, Kane turned his back on the saurian and began to walk toward the far edge of the mudflat. Domi came after him, jeering and still throwing mud at Monstrodamus.

They kept walking, senses alert for any change in sound from the dinosaur's position. "She's not falling for it," Domi sidemouthed.

Kane gloomily agreed. Suddenly the trans-comm in his war bag began warbling, the high-pitched electronic trill seeming to vibrate in the air. Monstrodamus roared in fury, an eardrum-compressing bellow. Kane and Domi spun just as Monstrodamus lowered its head, extended its neck forward and opened its jaws wide.

"The comm is pissing her off," Domi observed breathlessly.

"I know just how she feels," he retorted.

Monstrodamus came blundering out into the marsh

like an out-of-control locomotive. The creature sank flank deep into the mud very quickly but kept making a floundering and flailing progress, snarling all the while.

Kane waited, fingers closing over the gren, watching the creature wallow and stumble in the sucking mud. Objectively three seconds was a very fast fuse, but subjectively was another matter. Three seconds was an eternity in which he would be completely vulnerable to its vicious fangs.

"Keep going," he snapped at Domi.

"No," she snapped back.

Kane didn't argue. He stood his ground, a dark and mud-streaked figure. He whirled the rope with its grenade-weighted end over his head, carefully gauging the distance.

When Monstrodamus was less than fifteen feet away, he gave the lariat a final, humming spin and launched it at the dinosaur's head. The rope wrapped itself around her neck, and the grenade slammed solidly against the side of her skull. Kane whirled, grabbing Domi around the waist and pushing her down into the mud.

Facedown in the mire, Kane felt and heard the heavy bass note of the explosion. Flame, smoke and shrapnel bloomed in a hellfire flower atop Monstrodamus's body. He caught only glimpses of pieces of the dinosaur's head hurtling in all directions. The razor-edged fragments spread in a killing radius of thirty feet, tearing through the brush and gouging long trenches in the surface of the marsh. If either Domi or Kane had been standing, they would have been ripped to pieces. Hunks of flesh and bone splatted down all around. Blood sprinkled the marsh in a crimson rain.

Kane hazarded a glance over his mud-caked shoulder and saw the body of Monstrodamus slowly sagging into a strange, half-crouching posture. Although the general configurations of its head could be discerned atop its neck, it was only a flensed, charred and thoroughly maimed travesty of the fearsome sight it had been only a moment before.

Choosing every movement with care, almost as if he were afraid that if he rose too quickly Monstrodamus would be restored to full, vengeful life, Kane climbed to his feet. He was only dimly aware of extending a hand to Domi and how she used it and his arm to heave herself up from the morass. As they stared at the settling corpse of the dinosaur, Kane was also only dimly aware of the irritatingly persistent warble of his trans-comm.

"Well," Domi said at length, her voice hushed with awe, "you by God got her."

"Yeah," Kane said laconically.

He reached into the war bag and pulled out the comm unit, flipping up the cover and keying in the channel. "Yeah," he repeated just as laconically.

"Kane?" Grant's deep voice exploded out of the little device so loudly and forcefully that Kane recoiled, wincing, holding it away from his ear.

"Yeah."

"What the fuck is going on?" Grant's voice was

a lionlike roar of anger, relief and consternation. "Sounds like a goddamn war zone!"

Realizing that Grant had to be within a mile's radius, Kane replied a bit more briskly, "In a way it was. But it's all over now. We took care of Monstrodamus and me and Domi are all right."

He broke off to glance questioningly at Domi. "You are, aren't you?"

"Sure," she chirped cheerily, raising her mud- and blood-spattered shoulders in a shrug. "Just wet my pants, that's all."

Kane grinned and said into the comm, "You hear that?"

"Unfortunately." Grant's voice softened to a rumble. "Me, Brigid and Shizuka are trying to find you."

"Don't bother," Kane told him. "We'll find our way to you. No sense in any more of us wandering around in here and getting in trouble."

"That's for damn sure," Grant agreed emphatically.

"We'll hook up with you shortly." Folding the comm, Kane glanced into the sky at the flock of carrion feeders already beginning to circle the mudflat on outspread wings.

"Time for us to go." For the first time, he noticed that he and Domi were covered with a film of wet brown muck. "We could both do with a scrubbing now."

Domi shrugged. "Don't mind being dirty as long as I don't stink."

As they struggled to lift their feet clear of the mire,

Domi commented, "There's still those baby monsters out there, you know."

Kane nodded. "And we haven't found out if there's a papa monster anywhere around, either. But both of those questions can keep for another day."

In the process of working a leg free of the mud, Domi stumbled. Kane grabbed her to keep her falling face first into the morass. One hand cupped her left breast, and he felt the desire-hard nipple pressing against the palm. Her heart beat fast.

Kane righted her but when he tried to remove his hand, she clapped her own over it, keeping it in position. She coyly glanced up over her shoulder at him. A hint of a challenge glinted in her eyes. Kane met and held her gaze. Despite himself, he felt his body responding to her, to the musky scent and heat radiating from her body. He hardened and rose and he had difficulty breathing.

For a long moment they stood there in silent surmise. Then in a silky-soft whisper, Domi said, "I made up that part about wetting my pants."

Kane laughed and the chains of tension fell away from him. He slid his hand up Domi's chest to her shoulder and pushed her ahead of him. She flashed him a grin, her teeth startlingly bright in her muddy face. She said, "We'll talk more about this after we've scrubbed."

Kane returned her grin, but he tried to dismiss Domi's comment as just another one of teasing innuendos, ultimately meaningless. With a slight quiver of surprise, he suddenly realized that not only could he not dismiss it, but also he didn't particularly want to.

Chapter 7

No one, not even Grant, Brigid, Shizuka and particularly Philboyd was happy to hear Kane and Domi's report. The strong possibility that Monstrodamus had a mate on Thunder Isle was more discouraging than being told about either the subhumans or the dinosaur infants.

"Don't think we have to worry about the babies," Domi said confidently as she marched along with the others back to the installation perimeter. "They'll probably starve to death and other animals will eat the unhatched eggs."

"Yeah," Grant said dourly as they skirted a great heap of broken stone and debris, "but what about their daddy?"

"What about him?" Shizuka inquired. "Reptiles aren't generally renowned for their devotion to their offspring, are they?"

Domi snorted in derision. "How would you know?"

Nobody was surprised by Domi's display of rudeness. Everyone knew how Domi had attacked Shizuka with a knife during their first meeting months before—and how the female samurai had easily disarmed her. Only Kane wondered whether Domi's resentiment of the woman stemmed from the memories of that humiliation, or whether it was due to lingering jealousy over Shizuka's relationship with Grant. Even sharing the dangers of the mission to rescue the abducted Quavell a short time before had done nothing to ease the tension between the two women.

Shizuka scowled in Domi's direction, and Brigid interposed hastily, "Actually twentieth-century paleontologists found fossil evidence to suggest that dinosaurs were more attentive to their children than was generally accepted. Most scientists developed their ideas about dinosaur behavior by observing alligators and monitor lizards."

Kane ran his fingers through his snarled, mud-caked hair. "Whatever kind of dinosaur the Monstrodamus family is—?"

"Definitely from the tyrannosaur group," Philboyd interrupted. "Judging by her tracks and general appearance, I'd say Monstrodamus is Daspletosaurus, slightly smaller than the tyranno. In Latin, its name means 'frightful lizard.'"

"Fascinating," Kane drawled dryly. "As I was saying before I was so irrelevantly interrupted, there are other dinosaur forms on the island, including things with wings. If the temporal dilator was running wild on automatic for God knows how long, snatching samples from all historical periods, there might be several different tyranno types on the island. And if they're as vindictive as Mama Monstro, we'll have a hell of a time making this place safe for habitation."

"A dinosaur is a dinosaur," Domi declared dogmatically. "We can handle 'em."

"Nobody knows how many different species of dinosaur existed," Brigid said. "But they certainly represented thousands of different life-forms that existed on land, in the sea and in the air. Any kind of mammalian life larger than shrews was suppressed by them for millions of years. If something hadn't wiped the dinosaurs out, mammals would still be suppressed by them. So don't be so quick to believe dinosaurs are just dumb animals that humans can outthink and outfight. Certain of the more advanced dinosaur species might experience complex thought processes and even emotions."

The group of people reached the foot of the wide concrete steps leading to the entrance of the Cube. Philboyd said apprehensively, "You mean if there is a father, he might come here looking to avenge his mate and children?"

Brigid smiled reassuringly. "That's a very remote possibility, Brewster."

Kane did his best to first repress a smile at the man's anxiety, then frowned when Brigid addressed him by his first name. Although he didn't care much for the émigré from the Moon, he didn't blame him for being less than fearless regarding the prospect of a male Monstrodamus running loose on the island. According to Philboyd, the female of the species had pursued him literally to the very steps they were now climbing. Shizuka spoke a few words in Japanese, and the quartet of Tigers of Heaven assumed parade-rest postures at the foot of the steps.

There was only a single doorway in the featureless face of the Cube. When they first saw the place months before, there hadn't been a door, only a twisted, blackened metal frame hanging askew on sprung hinges. Wegmann, the Cerberus engineer, had fabricated a door out of sheet metal. It opened easily.

The big plastic sign was still bolted to the wall on the right of the doorway. Despite two centuries' worth of chem storms, fallout and weathering, the words imprinted on it were still legible. It bore a familiar warning: Entry To This Facility Strictly Forbidden To All Personnel Below B12 Clearance. Below the legend was an unfamiliar symbol, that of a stylized hourglass, the top half of it colored red, the bottom black.

Kane pulled open the door and allowed Domi, Brigid, Shizuka and Grant to walk through. As Philboyd stepped forward, Kane released the handle and the astrophysicist was forced to jerk to a clumsy halt to avoid being struck in the face by the heavy door. Although he glowered at Kane, he said nothing. He dared not, for a couple of reasons.

First and foremost, the actions performed by Kane, Grant and Brigid on the Manitius Base had freed Philboyd and his fellow inhabitants from lives of unending terror and servitude. They were offered an alternative to dying unknown and unmourned on the isolated colony. But Kane's status among the Manitius émigrés sprang more from the fact he had single-handedly faced off against the fearsome Maccan and imprisoned the crazed Tuatha de Danaan in a stasis chamber. As far as the Manitius personnel were concerned, that particular accomplishment made him a blend of ghost, assassin and wolverine.

Only a couple of weeks before, Kane had overheard Philboyd discussing him with Brigid. He had said to her, "He went one-on-one with Maccan, who was completely insane. And he won. Since then, he gives me the feeling that he's like two steps from going completely psycho."

Kane had done little to try to convince Philboyd otherwise, intentionally so.

The six people entered a large lobby. The floor was thickly layered with cement dust. The walls were black-speckled marble, and showed ugly crisscrossing cracks. A litter of office furniture was half covered by broken ceiling tiles.

A big reception desk occupied the far wall, and it was nearly buried by plaster and metal electrical conduits. Although much of the damage was the result of the nukecaust, quite a bit more was due to the venting of energies when the temporal dilator reached critical mass.

On the left side of the room, a hallway stretched away, lined on both sides with wooden, card-keyed doors. On their right a glass-and-chrome door led to a murky corridor. The dim blue glow of the occasional fluorescent light provided the only illumination.

"What this place really needs is a cleanup crew, not a salvage team," Grant muttered.

Kane looked back over his shoulder at Philboyd. "Maybe some of your friends from the Moon can volunteer for the janitorial duty. Be one way of paying for your keep."

Philboyd regarded him resentfully. "I'd think providing you with transatmospheric ships and plasma rifles would be enough of a trade-off."

Brigid cast Kane a jade-hard stare. "Don't mind him, Brewster. Kane lives by the 'what have you done for me lately' credo."

Kane opened his mouth to voice a profane reminder that if debts were indeed owed, the Moon base personnel could spend the next twenty years paying off what he, Grant and Brigid had done for them without a measurable reduction in the principal.

It annoyed him that Brigid seemed so defensive of the lanky, myopic astrophysicist. He didn't understand what she found so appealing in him, even if she was drawn to his intellect. Philboyd wasn't a man of action, but he wasn't a coward, either.

At the same time that Kane was locked into brutal hand-to-hand combat with Maccan, the last of the Tuatha de Danaan, Philboyd and Brigid were facing Enki, the last of the Annunaki, the legendary Dragon Kings. According to Brigid, Philboyd's courage, although it cracked, hadn't completely crumbled, and Brigid had been glad to have a solid bulwark at her side on that terrifying night.

Kane found the notion she might be attracted to the man foolish, but not so foolish he didn't feel a twinge of angry fear that Brigid might prefer the astrophysicist to him. He knew he feared losing his credential.

He wasn't quite sure what that meant, but he knew he always felt comfortable with Brigid Baptiste, despite their many quarrels. He was at ease with her in a way that was similar yet markedly different than his relationship with Grant. He found her intelligence, her iron resolve, her well-spring of compassion and the way she had always refused to be intimidated by him not just stimulating, but inspiring. She was a complete person, her heart, mind and spirit balanced and demanding of respect.

Once, when Brigid was critically injured, Kane found the thought of losing her too horrifying to contemplate, not just because of the vacuum she would leave in the Cerberus personnel, but because of the void her absence would leave in his soul. The memory of the kiss he'd given her when they'd taken the jump back in time to the eve of the nukecaust drifted across his mind. It was no surprise that he should remember the kiss, but the intensity of emotion associated with it still shook him.

He also recalled with startling clarity what Sister Fand of the third lost Earth had whispered to him about Brigid Baptiste: "The lady is your saving grace. Trust the bond that belongs between you. The gift of the *anam-chara* is strong. She protects you from damnation—she is your credential."

In the dark hours between midnight and dawn, Kane had often wondered if he lost Brigid, lost his credential, would he become a damned soul, cruel, merciless and without any purpose in life except to kill?

After a number of turns, the corridor began to slant downward. It ended at a heavy metal door without a knob or a latch. Brigid waved to the lens of the vid spy-eye bracketed to the wall just above the frame. Machinery clanked, and with a prolonged hiss of pneumatics, the door slid to the right. They entered a room dominated by a huge flat-screen vid monitor. The screen was divided into twelve square sections, showing various views of the Operation Chronos facility and its exterior perimeter.

The six walked to another door, which opened automatically at their approach. As they stepped into a narrow accessway beyond, sensors in the walls reacted to their motion signature and overhead fluorescent strips flashed on, shedding a wavery illumination.

They walked down the passageway toward a brighter light glimmering in the murk just beyond a tall arch. As the corridor stretched through the arch, it became a catwalk overlooking a vast chamber that was shaped like a hexagon. A dim glow shone down from the high, flat ceiling, two faint columns of light beaming from twin fixtures, both the size of wag tires. Massive wedge-shaped ribs of metal supported the roof.

The shafts of luminescence fell upon a huge forked pylon made of some burnished metal that projected up from a sunken concave area in the center of the chamber. The two horns of the pylon curved up and around, facing each other. Mounted on the tips of each prong were jagged shards of what appeared to be blackened quartz crystal.

The pylon was at least twenty feet tall, with ten feet separating the forked branches. Extending outward from the base of the pylon at ever decreasing angles into the low shadows stretched a taut network of fiber-optic filaments. They disappeared into sleeve sockets that perforated the plates of dully gleaming alloy sheathing the floor. Many of them were buckled here and there, bulging and split. The faint odor of superheated and slagged metal still hung heavy in the air, even after three months. The pylon itself was canted forward, about ten degrees out of true.

As Kane, Brigid, Shizuka and Grant strode along the elevated platform, they couldn't help but recall the last time they had seen the temporal dilator functioning. It had been encapsulated, cosmic chaos with sparks sizzling through the facets of the prisms, crackling fingers darting from one sphere to the other and back again like snakes made of electrical current.

The pent-up energies built to critical mass and when they were vented, the floor supporting the pylon ruptured, rivets popping loose and the crystal spheres exploding. It could have been far worse—the Archon fusion reactor that powered the complex could have hit critical mass. The energy output of the generators was held in a delicately balanced magnetic matrix. When the matrix was breached, an explosion of apocalyptic proportions resulted—something they had witnessed twice before.

But fortunately only the temporal dilator's individual power source melted down and left the machine itself somewhat intact. It was composed of a blend of conductive alloys and ceramics that made it virtually indestructible. Sindri described the dilator as being essentially a giant electromagnet, creating two magnetic fields, one at right angles to the other. Both of the fields represented one plane of space, but since there were three planes of space, a third field was reproduced through the principle of resonance, or sound manipulation.

The catwalk led to a chamber full of instrument consoles with glass-covered gauges. Computer terminals lined the walls. Almost all of the consoles were dark, and only a few of the drive units of the computer hummed. At the far end of the room stood the familiar arrangement of armaglass slabs enclosing a mat-trans jump chamber. The semitranslucent armaglass was tinted a smoky gray, the hue of old lead.

The heavy counterbalanced door hung open, and they saw various boxes and parcels piled within it. Female voices were speaking in murmurs.

Loudly Grant announced, "We're back."

DeFore stepped out of the jump chamber. "Who needs stitching up this time?"

Kane threw her a grin. "A little bit of antiseptic, maybe a couple of squirts of liquid bandage are all we need this time, believe it or not."

"I tend not to believe it," she countered waspishly.

A stocky, buxom woman in her early thirties, Reba DeFore usually wore her ash-blond hair pulled back from her face and intricately braided at the back of her head. Its color contrasted starkly with the deep bronze of her skin and her dark-brown eyes. She always looked good in the one-piece white jumpsuit most Cerberus redoubt personnel wore as duty uniforms.

As a medic, even with the deliberately limited training she had received in her barony of birth, DeFore was one of the few exiles who acted as a specialist. The ten people who lived in the Cerberus redoubt, regardless of their skills, acted in the capacity of support personnel. They worked rotating shifts, eight hours a day, seven days a week. For the most part, their work was the routine maintenance and monitoring of the installation's environmental systems, the satellite data feed, the security network.

However, everyone was given at least a superficial understanding of all the redoubt's systems, so they could pinch-hit in times of emergency. Fortunately, such a time had never arrived, but still and all, the installation was woefully understaffed. Their small numbers had been a source of constant worry to Lakesh, but with the arrival of the Moon base personnel, there was now a larger pool of talent from which to draw.

Grant and Kane were exempt from cross-training, inasmuch as they served as the enforcement arm of Cerberus and undertook far and away the lion's share of the risks. On their downtime between missions, they made sure all the ordnance in the armory was in good condition and occasionally tuned up the vehicles in the depot.

Brigid Baptiste, due to her eidetic memory, was the most exemplary member of the redoubt's permanent staff, since she could step into any vacancy. However, her gifts were a two-edged sword, inasmuch as those selfsame polymathic skills made her an indispensable addition to away missions.

Nora Pennick, another émigré from the Moon, stepped out of the gateway unit. She looked nothing like the woman Grant, Kane and Brigid had met in the DEVIL control nexus only weeks before. Then, she was dirty, undernourished looking and her long dark hair was a tangle of uncombed Medusa snarls. Since her arrival in the Cerberus redoubt, she had been dipping into the supply of cosmetics left there by the female personnel of the installation before it had been abandoned in the days preceding the nukecaust.

The white bodysuit she wore clung tightly to her trim, small-waisted figure. Her hair was coiffed, neatly trimmed and the makeup she had applied to her face was evidently in fashion before the nukecaust.

By way of a greeting, she declared, "There's a lot of valuable tech here you've been overlooking. You just didn't recognize it for what it was."

"And how kind of you to point out our ignorance," Brigid retorted with icy sarcasm. "I don't think those of us who were born in the twenty-second century can be blamed for not being as familiar with artifacts manufactured in the twentieth century as the people who were alive at the same time.''

Nora flushed slightly in embarrassment and she ducked her head quickly. ''Sorry, I didn't mean to sound patronizing. You're right, of course.''

A thinly veiled attitude of superiority had been displayed by several of the recent Manitius Moon base transplants, particularly by a scientist named Neukirk. The base personnel seemed amused by the Cerberus exiles' ignorance of a number of twentieth-century events and items. Neukirk seemed to enjoy expressing himself in condescending tones.

However, still stinging from Brigid's defense of Philboyd, Kane said gallantly, ''Forget it, Nora. Nothing to apologize about.''

Smiling self-consciously, Nora said, ''I'm just sort of awed by this place, that's all. I heard rumors about black tech, experiments in time travel, of course…crazy things about the Montauk Project that were so over the top nobody could take them seriously. But this place—''

She broke off, gesturing helplessly, at a loss for words. Even Brigid couldn't blame her. Redoubt Yankee, the main Operation Chronos installation, was indeed awe inspiring. Before skydark its engineering and computer centers were second to none, and its accomplishments in the field of physics were never matched, much less exceeded.

''If we could get all the computers back online,'' Nora continued, ''there's really no telling the kind of data we'd find in storage.''

Musingly Philboyd said, ''We might be able to re-boot the dilator's basic diagnostic systems, providing the hardware failure isn't total.''

Grant's brow furrowed in consternation. ''Why in hell would we want to do that? Hasn't it caused enough problems—?''

A prolonged rumble of an earth tremor interrupted him. Shizuka had reported mild tremors for some time, and they had become so commonplace in the region of New Edo that her people were scarcely aware of them any longer. Even Kane, Grant and Brigid had experienced them a few times during their return trips to Thunder Isle.

But this one was much stronger. The Cube shifted around and under them, and a jagged crack appeared in the ceiling, showering them with dust. The crack intersected with an inset light fixture, and it shattered with a jangle of glass and a brief sputtering flurry of sparks.

Nobody cried out or even staggered, but the tense silence following the rumble was broken by Domi's murmur of ''Don't like this much.''

''Me, either,'' agreed Brigid. ''It would be helpful if we found some seismographic equipment to measure the severity and frequency of the tremors. They seem to come more often now.''

''They do,'' Shizuka confirmed. ''And the sea level is rising, as well...we've had some coastal flooding during high tide. Nothing major, but we may be looking at saltwater incursion into our freshwater supply if it keeps up.''

"Isn't Dr. Singh studying some sort of phenomena occurring in the Antarctic?" Nora inquired. "Something about the polar ice cap shifting?"

"That doesn't mean anything," retorted Kane dryly. "Lakesh is always studying some sort of phenomena."

"Still and all," Shizuka said, "something is causing seismic disturbances on the entire New Edo island chain."

Philboyd stated, "Since the islands are connected by an undersea ridge, it could be you're undergoing a tectonic shift due to a weakening in the fault lines. Maybe you ought to think about relocating…at least until it's over."

Shizuka's face locked in a cold, hard mask, and the slit-eyed glare she threw at Brewster Philboyd caused him to stop speaking almost instantly. Brigid, Kane and Grant could read the normally inscrutable woman's emotions easily. For better or for worse—and New Edo was certainly better than most of the Western Isles—the island was her home. Dangerous, but still hers. Moreover, she considered the well-being of its citizens her responsibility.

A few months before, during an attempted insurrection, Lord Takaun was grievously injured and the former captain of the Tigers, Kiyomasa, was slain. It fell upon Shizuka's slender shoulders to end the rebellion, and she did it in the only way that would satisfy the honor of both factions—by killing the seditionist leader in single combat, literally slicing him in two with her *katana*.

The rebels saw only two options—to continue to press their faltering coup and die to a man, or to swear loyalty to the samurai who had slain their leader. They decided to swear loyalty and to live. Ironically many of them did not live long after making their oaths. They perished repulsing the invaders dispatched from Baron Snakefish. Despite the losses New Edo suffered, Shizuka had led them to victory over a tactically superior force.

After that New Edo obeyed her every command, appeased her every whim with a kind of devotion different yet more powerful than that they would have given to a man. Shizuka was not viewed as a woman or even a Tiger of Heaven—she was revered almost as a goddess.

Scratching at the dried mud caked on her arms, Domi demanded impatiently, "Can't we talk about this back home? I want to get clean."

DeFore's full lips quirked in a smile. "We've already packed enough stuff to keep us busy inventorying and cataloging for a week. No reason to linger."

The medic stepped into the chamber, followed by Nora. Philboyd gazed uneasily at the eight-foot-tall gateway chamber, peering through its open door. The ceiling was patterned with interlocking, hexagonal raised metallic disks. The pattern was repeated in the floor. Although Philboyd had been alive when the mat-trans units were pressed into secret, limited service in the late twentieth century, he had only recently screwed up enough courage to travel by hyperdimensional pathways. He had muttered cryptic references to rematerializing with the head of a fly, but nobody bothered to question what that meant.

Kane was the last one to enter the jump chamber and when he realized Grant hadn't followed him in, he stepped to the heavy, counterbalanced door. Grant still stood at the base of the platform. "Well?" Kane challenged. "You waiting for a formal invitation or what?"

Grant's expression was unreadable. He drew in a long breath, released it slowly and said, "Well..."

Then he began to talk.

Chapter 8

Grigori Zakat stood on the foredeck of the *Fafnir* and drew in deep lungfuls of air. The smell of brine and kelp and the wet, wild wind sent shivers of excitement through him. The hull vibrated slightly as the dragon ship's turbines were notched up in order to continue the pursuit. The prow cleaved a foaming path through long, white-edged rollers, throwing up salt spray.

Zakat looked over the watch, impressed again with how the yellow-haired sailors knew their business despite the discomfort they felt from the heat and humidity. Most of them were stripped to the waist, and their pale skin was pink from the sun. Two armored guards stood at the bow and stern, their powerful hands gripping the hilts of heavy longswords that rested before them with the chapes of the scabbards on the floor. Snorri, the helmsman, kept his eyes on the compass and held the wheel with a practiced hand. If the blond, bearded giant seemed bored by the chase, he didn't show it.

First had come the cry from the lookout station and then the sighting of the distant sail, almost on the edge of the horizon. The chase had continued for the past two hours. The prey was a wooden vessel riding high above the waterline, its configurations suggest-

ing sharp angles, arches and buttresses. The sails
didn't look like broadcloth. They reminded Zakat of
window blinds made of a waxed and oiled paper. He
had seen a number of junks in the few weeks the
Fafnir had ranged the Cific coast, but he let them go
on their way.

According to Chaffee, most of the junks were part
of the Chinese Tong fleet out of Autarkic, their ships
identified by bright scarlet chops painted on the hulls.
Chaffee explained they weren't just the average Tong
pirates, either—judging by the Chinese characters
marked on their craft, they belonged to Wei Qiang.

Even the most ambitious trader and vicious free-
booter gave the Wei Qiang Tong crews wide berth.
As the warlord of Autarkic, more or less the capital
trading center in the Western Isles, Wei Qiang hand-
picked his men, and all of them were hardened killers.
Their chosen weapon for close-in fighting was a sin-
gle-bladed hand ax. They had invaded the Western
Isles many years in the past and had set up an empire
there.

Zakat and his crew made a port of call on the island. They had been entranced by the people of all
colors, with monkeys and parrots for sale. There were
vendors of magical charms for the healing of wounds
and curing of scurvy. There were sellers of maps who
offered charts of submerged predark cities and their
treasures—and there were tales of four outlanders
who had reputedly defeated Ambika, the Lioness of
the Isles. They spoke of how the she-devil of the seas
had found a mate, a pale-eyed, scar-faced man who

then turned on her when she threatened a woman with hair the color of sunset. The man's name was Kane.

Zakat learned what he needed to learn on Autarkic and didn't overstay. Besides, there was something a bit too poignant, too bittersweet about the exotic, barbaric place when he knew that in a short time, it would once more be beneath the waves, taking all the vendors, monkeys and parrots with it.

After the visit, Grigori Zakat settled for chasing down and scuttling trading craft from the mainland. The *Fafnir* had swiftly gained a fearsome reputation in the short time she hunted in the coastal waters. The crews of the trader ships shuddered at the tales of the serpentine craft that no vessel could outrun, manned by iron-clad warriors whose savagery could not even be equaled by great white sharks. They whispered also of the giant blond Amazon who wielded a sword like a cleaver.

Or so Zakat liked to believe. He really had no way of knowing the extent of his ship's reputation. But the junk the *Fafnir* had been pursuing certainly seemed to know something of them. It had veered sharply, running for the line of surf that boomed along the palm-fringed shore of a distant island. Zakat wouldn't have ordered a pursuit at all if it had borne the identifying Chinese characters of Wei Qiang. Since it didn't, the ship was fair game. However, since the vessel had managed to maintain a steady distance from the *Fafnir,* it was apparent it was outfitted with an engine and wasn't relying strictly on the wind.

At the sound of heavy footfalls thumping on the

deck behind him, Zakat didn't bother to turn. After the past few weeks of sailing with the man, he recognized the gait of Chaffee.

Life at sea didn't agree with the man. Grigori Zakat had learned that very little did, particularly Sif. His fractured left wrist was still tightly bound in a splint made of wood and leather. Zakat didn't feel sorry for the ex-Mag. Months ago he had learned that Sif always gave fair warning to the men who became overly familiar with her. Perhaps with the way romantic moonlight gleamed from her enormous bosom, Chaffee hadn't believed her or understood her words. Either way, she had broken his wrist when she removed his hand from her thigh.

"How long is this going to go on?" he rasped angrily. "We've wasted the better part of a day chasing after these goddamn slants."

Mildly Zakat inquired, "What else should we be doing, tovarich?"

Chaffee ran his hands over his gray hair, now cropped so short it resembled a gray skullcap of bristles. "Mebbe you should start living up to your end of the bargain and sail us to Thule."

Zakat studied the man for a silent moment, noting how the wrinkles in his leathery skin were caused more by exposure and stress than by advanced years. It was as though the ex-Mag had been cooked by the sun and leached by acid rain until only bone, muscle and sinew were left.

Both men were dressed similarly, in supple tunics of soft leather that left their arms and legs bare. Zakat wore a black glove on his right hand. Gesturing to the hold belowdecks, Chafee continued acidly, ''We've already have enough different kinds of seeds and plants for six farms. What makes you think that boat has anything more valuable aboard it than the last two or three we boarded and sank? This isn't part of the mission objective.''

Grigori Zakat smiled slightly at the use of the military vernacular. He distrusted soldiers as a general rule, even though by the strict definition of the term he had been one himself. Outside of bureaucrats, he had never met a more hidebound, dense, play-by-the-numbers bunch. Most of them had the imaginations of tree stumps.

Chaffee was incapable of visualizing anything unless it was within the pages of a manual. He was such a rigid thinker, Zakat found that just being near him for any length of time lowered his energy levels. Chaffee smelled of bad karma, and after everything was in place, he intended to put the man out of sight and out of mind.

''Need I remind you,'' Zakat said in a silky soft tone, ''that I informed you of the mission objective *I* intended to accomplish before we returned to Thule. You provided the initial intelligence of Kane sightings in the vicinity.''

Chaffee did a poor job of repressing a groan of frustration, but he did roll his eyes. ''If I'd known you planned to cruise all over this part of the fucking Cific after one standard-issue renegade—''

Grigori Zakat lost what was left of his patience, but

he kept his temper in check, even when he hit Chaffee. He drove his left fist into the man's diaphragm, just below his breastbone. He knew from his District Twelve training the blow, if delivered properly, was incapacitating, even paralyzing.

Chaffee fell, wheezing, his features squeezing together like a fireplace bellows. Zakat nudged him with a foot. "There is nothing standard issue about this particular renegade, I assure you. I explained to you the spiritual debt I owe this man and how I cannot simply write it off."

Watching the man writhing on the deck with his skinny arms folded over his middle, the two guards guffawed.

"You hear that?" Zakat asked. "My Thulians, my Norsemen. The best seamen on Earth, the best warriors—stubborn, superstitious, hard drinking and ill-tempered, but they're loyal to the last breath. Loyal to *me*. I expect the same loyalty from you, tovarich…or over the side you go—in chains."

Sif emerged from the small galley beneath the poop deck, shading her eyes with a hand. When she saw Chaffee twitching on the deck with Zakat towering over him, she laughed. She was nearly naked, clad only in a white linen shift that was little more than a T-shirt. Her heavy breasts pressed against the thin fabric. A thin silver diadem held her long blond hair away from her face.

Zakat smiled and he beckoned her over. Sweet, brave Sif who was stronger than even most men on the ship, whose long arms could clasp with passion or break bones. On bare feet, she padded over and in the ancient Teutonic tongue of the Ultima Thule, he asked her to take Chaffee below until he felt better.

Sif grinned, nodded and bent over the gagging Chaffee, sliding her huge hands under the man's armpits. She hummed softly as she effortlessly swung the lean man astride the wide yoke of her shoulders. Zakat recognized the tune. It was a snatch of Wagner's "Ride of the Valkyries." He wasn't surprised that she hummed it. He had taught it to her, after all.

The tune made him think back to another wild ride, but it was not romantic or operatic in nature, despite its inherent drama. Memories of that day's dawn, now feeling like a thousand years ago but in reality only two, swept through Zakat's mind in fragments.

When he awakened in the first gray light to the wild cries of the Mongols thundering into the Russian base on their war ponies, he didn't even wait to look out the barracks window before grabbing his side arm. In that same kind of dim light, three daybreaks before, his commanding officer Colonel Sverdlovosk, three Americans named Kane, Baptiste and Grant and four troopers had left the base, escorted by Boro Orolok and a handful of his Mongols. They were traveling to the main camp of the Tushe Gun's followers, some fifty kilometers away.

Neither the colonel, the soldiers nor the Americans had returned, but a quick glance showed him that almost all of the Tushe Gun's followers were storming across the compound, borne on their fleet, shaggy steeds.

It didn't matter that most of the horde's firearms consisted of single-shot, matchlock muzzle loaders and two-century-old handblasters—not only did they wield them with blood-chilling accuracy but they also outnumbered the base personnel by a five-to-one margin.

Although he was the ranking officer, left in charge by Sverdlovosk, Zakat saw little point in rallying the panic-stricken soldiers, most of whom were just roused from sleep and in states of undress.

He left the barracks and made for the huge Tu-114 cargo plane, the Mossback, which had carried him, the colonel, Captain Ivornich, the Americans and his inner circle of trusted aides from Russia to the Black Gobi.

The mounted Mongols rode down the troopers as they tried to escape, pursuing them like wolves, killing them with bullets, short swords or yard-long arrows loosed from bows made of yak horn and wood.

It was all screaming, dashing chaos as Zakat sprinted across the dim compound, struggling into his greatcoat as he ran. A few troopers set up widely separated pockets of resistance, knocking Mongols from their horses with controlled bursts of autofire from AKM subguns. They were too far apart to establish a solid fire zone. Zakat saw five of them literally pincushioned by a hail of arrows.

As he neared the runway, he heard the loud, vibrating drone of the Mossback's four engines powering up. In the cockpit, limned by the lights of the instrument panel, he glimpsed the head and shoulders of Kuryadin.

Zakat increased his speed toward the open cargo hatch in the aircraft's belly. He was so intent, so focused on the door to his escape he didn't see the Mongol warrior until he was literally on top of him.

The roar from the plane's engines and his own pounding footfalls masked the drumming hoofbeats. The warrior leaped from his pony's saddle and slammed him violently to the hard-packed sand.

Zakat managed to fire two rounds from his Tokarev at the swarthy face snarling above him, but not before he felt the ticklish, hot and cold kiss of the Bundhi dagger thrusting into his midsection.

Paying no attention to the pain, clapping a hand over the blood streaming from the wound, he regained his feet just as the Mossback began lurching down the runway. He saw a soldier trying to close the hatch, but when he caught sight of Zakat, he gestured frantically for him to hurry.

With the trooper's help, he managed to clamber into the ship's belly, but a spray of gunfire raked the fuselage and a stray shot caught the soldier in the chest.

Zakat couldn't tell how seriously he was wounded, but he fell, vomiting blood over the hatch's crank and winch control assembly. Zakat kicked him out and down onto the runway and hastily sealed the hatch.

As the plane picked up speed, bullets hammered like hailstones against the hull. Zakat remained in the cargo hold as the Mossback became airborne. He examined his wound, finding it more unsightly than critical. The blade had pierced the abdominal wall without slicing through his intestines. Still, he bled profusely as he used a first-aid kit to apply a field dressing and a pressure bandage. He didn't take any of the pain medications, assuming he would need to be alert and clearheaded for the immediate future.

When the plane leveled off, Zakat made his way forward. The two troopers in the passenger section were surprised to see him and not at all pleased, though they almost managed to conceal it. Their superior he might be, but they distrusted him and his placid facade. He had replaced far too many of their comrades and officers over the past few years.

He found Kuryadin in a state of terror, wrestling with the control yoke of the huge plane and constantly eyeing the fuel gauge. Bullets had ruptured the main tank, and the fuel sprayed out of it as through a wind-blown sieve. The reserve tank held only half the capacity and wouldn't carry the heavy, ungainly craft far, certainly not back to Russia.

Zakat knew little more than Kuryadin about the finer points of flying. Both of them had received a few hours of flight training as part of their District Twelve duties, but neither of them had soloed. Russia's military aircraft were far too rare to risk on a novice's education. Sitting in the copilot's chair, he allowed Kuryadin to fly while he tried, without much success, to make sense of the navigational charts.

Within two hours, the main fuel tank had drained

completely, and the reserve was pressed into service. An hour more, and snow-blanketed mountain peaks shouldered up from the horizon. Zakat was fairly certain they were in the Himalayas, and that was where the Mossback chose to nosedive.

He had survived the crash, but Zakat never did learn what had turned the followers of the Tushe Gun against the Russian garrison in the Black Gobi, but he suspected the three Americans who had accompanied Colonel Sverdlovosk were somehow responsible. Six months later, when facing those selfsame three Americans in the ruins of the Museum of Natural History in Newyork, he had asked Kane and Grant about the Tushe Gun and the fate of his former commanding officer. He wasn't too shocked to find out they took responsibility for killing both men.

The return of Sif brought him out of his ruminations. She gazed steadily at the distant junk, even though she carried a pair of binoculars in one hand.

"How is Chaffee?" Zakat asked in the Thulian dialect.

A bit absently, Sif replied, "Out of the breath. The worm is in terrible condition…nearly as bad as yours when we first met."

Almost involuntarily, Zakat touched his gloved right hand with his left one. "That's hard to believe," he replied.

Sif suddenly handed him the binoculars. "The ship is bypassing the island."

Zakat frowned and lifted the binoculars to his face,

squinting through the eyepieces. He saw that the island was actually the largest of a smaller string consisting of three islets. The main landmass reared out of the sea like a massive cube of black, volcanic rock, but he saw green vegetation on the summit of a small peak. Atop it he could barely discern the outline of a watch or bell tower. Castellated cliffs loomed at least a hundred feet above the surface of the Cific. Thundering waves crashed and broke on the bare rock, foaming spray flying in all directions.

He saw the junk swinging slowly around the headland of the islet closest to the larger mass. The strait between the two islands was a long, narrow channel, and the wooden vessel sailed for that. But the junk moved sluggishly, the hull dragging. The ship seemed to wallow in the shallows. Long slow waves rocked kelp and seaweed back and forth. To the junk's starboard, the dark outlines of the small jungled island rose from the surf. From astern curled up a corkscrew of smoke.

Zakat murmured, "His engine is out…overstressed."

Sif caught her breath in excitement. "He's turning to fight."

Zakat smiled thinly. He couldn't see the details of the activity on the junk, but he knew preparations for battle had begun as soon the *Fafnir* was sighted. The junk had been heading for a place to make a stand all afternoon.

He handed the binoculars back to Sif. Cupping his hands around his mouth, Grigori Zakat shouted in the

Thulian tongue, "Stand to battle stations! Stand to battle stations!"

His crew roared in approval.

"It's about time," Sif muttered before she rushed to her quarters to dress for the fun to come.

Chapter 9

Shields slid onto men's arms and fully armored warriors assembled on the quarterdeck as the *Fafnir* overhauled the junk. The hatch cover was heaved away from the hold, and a man passed up a selection of lances, grappling hooks, chains, ropes and the long hollow cylinder of the LAW 80 rocket launcher. Sif took it greedily, hefted it in her arms, then pulled apart the two sections to its full extended length. She unfolded the reflex collinator sight on its smooth upper surface. With her back to the breeze, her red cloak billowed open, revealing her chain-mail tunic, sword belt and ax hanging from it by a leather thong. Her eyes blazed cobalt with wild excitement.

All the Thulians moved with speed, determination and discipline. Zakat paced the poop deck, occasionally shouting orders. He wore gilded scale-mail and his feature-concealing dragon helmet. He bore a round embossed shield on his right arm. In his left he held a Ruger Redhawk revolver. The sunlight glinted from the brushed-satin finish of its seven-inch, stainless-steel barrel. A telescopic sight was mounted to the frame.

Although Breeze Castigleone and Chaffee had provided a hold full of death-dealing ordnance, the Thu-

lians scorned firearms as the weapons of cowards—
except for the rocket launchers. They likened them to
the power of Thor, hurling thunderbolts from afar,
and therefore they were acceptable.

Sif took up position by the port-side gunwales as
her fellow Thulians, fully armored now in horned and
winged helmets and brandishing swords and axes, ran
to their battle stations. She held the LAW as if it were
an infant. Zakat knew it was a one-shot disposable
weapon, designed specifically to take out armored vehicles. But the 94 mm high-explosive missiles had
proved devastatingly effective on seagoing vessels, as
well.

As the *Fafnir* bore down on its prey, Zakat absently
toyed with the phallic symbol hanging from his neck.
The emblem symbolized Rasputin's penis, cut off by
one of his assassins, then recovered and preserved in
a velvet container by his devoted followers. Upon his
initiation into the Khylsty priesthood, Zakat had been
permitted to glimpse the blackened, desiccated holy
relic, but not touch it.

No one, not even his superior officers, suspected
he was a Khylsty priest. The few members of his sect
who held high posts in the Russian government had
helped him to deceive the rigorous background
checks prior to his assignment to District Twelve, the
ultrasecret arm of the Internal Security Network.

Zakat was not his birth name, but his Khylsty
name, yet no one questioned it, even though it meant
"twilight." Even the people who had glimpsed the
pattern of wealed, raised scars on his back, the result

of numerous flagellation rituals, kept their curiosity in check. In the Internal Security Network, it was considered bad form to question a comrade, and even quite dangerous to make personal inquiries of an officer. It hinted at ambition. Grigori Zakat had advanced rapidly as a District Twelve officer under the command of Sverdlovosk, primarily because he didn't appear to be ambitious.

But of course he was. He couldn't be a Khylsty priest otherwise. But he approached the obstacles to his ambition differently than other men. An off hand comment made to a superior officer regarding rivals, or the discreet planting of black market contraband among their possessions or, if they were particularly impressionable, a campaign of subtle suggestions that they were being treated unfairly, passed over for advancement. When they filed their complaints, they tended to either disappear or be reduced in rank, and Zakat easily stepped into the power vacuum.

He had achieved the rank of major very quickly, after he arranged matters to make General Stovoski believe he had been seduced by his middle-aged, oversexed wife. Zakat managed to smile at the memory of Stovoski's face when he stumbled into the parlor to find his wife kneeling before him, clawing at his trousers, oblivious to his pious protests.

The stupid cow of a woman, her brain saturated with vodka, had been childishly easy to manipulate, never realizing that the strength of his will had been imposed over hers. And if his mind was exceptionally strong, his body complemented it. None of his comrades, or even the surprisingly perceptive Sverdlovosk, knew he had the strength in his delicate-appearing hands to throttle a man to death—something he had done as part of his ordination ceremony.

Much of his Khylsty training revolved around camouflage, infiltration and deception. Through years of long practice, he could make his gray eyes reflect nothing but a mild, dull disinterest in his surroundings. Infinite patience was one of the prime articles of Khylsty faith.

After all, Saint Rasputin had not been accepted by the family of the czar overnight. He had waited, performing trivial miracles to earn first the czarina's trust, then her bed.

It always amused Zakat to think about the haughty Alexandra spreading her legs for the unkempt holy man from western Siberia. Rumors of her affair with Rasputin had been one of the triggers for the October Revolution, when the starving Russian masses finally understood that the royal family were flesh and blood, not gods, goddesses and godlings.

Of course, those rumors led to Rasputin's assassination by royal retainers, but he had accomplished his mission nevertheless. In Khlysty texts, it was known as the power of causitry—persuasion and seduction to achieve an objective.

The very fact Grigori Zakat strode the poop deck of the *Fafnir,* with the half-savage Thulians obeying his every order, was proof of his powers, of his intimate understanding of causitry.

Men with Oriental features, their heads bound with strips of white cloth, appeared at the rail of the junk, all of them wielding bows. Even from such a distance, Zakat could tell the weapons were beautifully crafted, made of smooth, red-lacquered wood. The arrows were exceptionally long, the tips were steel and, like the bows, gave the impression of being lacquered. He wasn't intimidated, however. So few of the people he had encountered in the Western Isles were armed with anything other than the basics. Except on Autarkic, the only firearms he had seen were crude, home-forged muzzle loaders.

The archers aboard the junk nocked their long arrows, aimed and a dozen bowstrings hummed simultaneously as they loosed a flight of arrows at the dragon ship. Only a few landed on deck—most bounced away from the shields lining the rail or those on the arms of the warriors.

The junk began a port-side board turn just as the rocket launcher in the hands of Sif fired with an ear-knocking report. With a sound as of a gigantic piece of stiff canvas being ripped, the rocket screamed across the surface of the sea, a trail of sparks and smoke wavering in its wake.

The warhead detonated on the junk amidships, just above the waterline. The bowmen staggered backward, drenched by the geyser of water fountaining up over the side. Men went sprawling. Some stayed on their feet by clutching the deck rail.

Moving with swift, practiced moves, Sif loaded another rocket into the launcher, sighted and squeezed the trigger. The second rocket went into the forecastle, smashing wood, flinging jagged shards of broken timber through the air, slashing at the sailors in the vicinity.

A man wearing a short white jacket and an orange headband shouted stridently to the sailors, obviously trying to rally them. Zakat guessed him to be the captain, since the men nodded to him deferentially. Once again the archers took up position at the rail.

Zakat braced the barrel of the revolver on his left forearm, squinted through the Redhawk's scope and brought the man's head into target acquisition, framing it in the center of the crosshairs. He squeezed the trigger and a single shot cracked, like the snapping of a whip. The man's headband floated away, surrounded by a mist of blood. Twisting in a clumsy pirouette, he fell behind the rail of the junk and out of sight. Faintly he heard an outburst of shock and fear.

Zakat turned toward Snorri and gestured sharply. "Ram them!"

Snorri put the helm hard over, and the *Fafnir's* dragon figurehead snarled at the center of the junk. Beneath the ship's bow, just below the surface, stretched a long ramming sprit. It was about ten feet in length, made of sturdy oak and wrapped with hammered-out strips of metal riveted around it for reinforcement. The shaft terminated in a broad-bladed iron triangle, like a plowshare.

Zakat grasped the handrail as the dragon ship hove closer. Then, in a tumult of screams and splintering crashes, the hulls collided. The impact threw half of the Thulian warriors off their feet. They quickly regained their footing and raced to the bow. They drove long lances into the junk's side to serve as makeshift scaling ladders, since the ship rode eight or more feet higher in the water than the *Fafnir*.

Then, as a final volley of arrows arced down, the Thulians formed a multilegged tortoise by holding and locking their shields over their heads. They hurled their grapnels aboard the junk, the metal hooks biting and holding into the deck rail. With wild howls, they swarmed up the chains.

Zakat watched them board the junk and sighed heavily. The sound echoed hollowly within the confines of his helmet. He knew the power of causitry notwithstanding, he couldn't rest on his laurels and assume the Thulians would respect his decision to remain aboard the *Fafnir*. Thulian respect was not easily given and always required a booster shot of action and risk. That was one reason Chaffee was the butt of so many cruel jokes, since he never participated directly in their attacks.

Shouting to Sif to join him, Zakat scrambled to the bow and leaped over the gunwales and across the narrow space between the two ships. Once he gained the deck of the junk, he and Sif, in a flying wedge, struck the crew like a steel-shod avalanche. If the Thulians expected an easy victory, they were sadly mistaken.

The junk's crew made a crazed, animal-desperate charge against the invaders and for a few minutes, it was a confused, brutal, bloody battle on the decks.

The sailors were armed with flat, mirror-bright, curved swords and they used them well. Bragi, one of the youngest of the Thulians, had his neck sliced halfway through by one of the flat blades. Blood spouted from the half-severed stump, a fountain that splashed across Sif's face.

She licked her lips and the taste of the man's blood pushed her forward, shrieking and hacking with her battle-ax. The other warriors followed her screaming lead. The sailors were divided in broken groups and were chopped down or driven over the sides. Some closed ranks and fought back with their swords, but they were overwhelmed by the armored Thulians, most of whom towered a full head and shoulders over the tallest of the Asians.

Zakat glanced back at Sif and called to her, but she was unable to hear over the battle cries and screams of pain. The Valkyrie had gone berserker. Heaving a sailor's corpse aside, she leaped into a gap with the battle-ax. Three men fell to the weapon—three swipes that split them down the middle before they could think how to engage the fearsome giantess.

She used her ax to cut a bloody swath for Zakat to follow. Curved swords in the hands of terrified sailors menaced her, but they were less than useless. The swinging ax sheared through metal, flesh and bone, beating them to the deck by the sheer weight of the blows.

Zakat followed Sif, managing to fire accurate shots as he ran across the reeling deck. Two men went down, then three and four, knocked back over the stations they were assigned to defend. Zakat emptied the last of the weapon's cylinder into a sailor's face, shattering his head and blowing it back over an archer trying to get into position behind Sif.

Temporarily blinded by blood and flying brain matter, the bowman held his arrow, nocked but unloosed. Zakat went low, dropping the pistol and drawing a knife from his belt. He took the shock of hitting the man with his shield. The bowman dropped to the deck, and as the man's head snapped backward from the impact, Zakat slashed his throat with the knife. Scarlet rivered down the front of the tunic as he clutched at his neck.

Elbowing him aside, Sif screamed hoarsely and chopped off the man's head, the ax blade burying itself deeply into the deck planks. Her eyes were wild and glassy. As she struggled to wrench it loose, Zakat took advantage of the opportunity to strike her across the face. He had learned there was no other way to get her attention, to check her battle madness.

He pointed out the survivors of the junk's crew, how they had taken refuge on the quarterdeck. There were only a handful of them, less than a half dozen, but they were still armed with the longbows and equally long arrows, not to mention a few swords. Thulian warriors, under locked shields, stormed the quarterdeck, but they were driven back by a shower of arrows. Three of them hobbled out of the fray, tugging at the shafts protruding from various parts of their bodies.

Zakat saw a brass, tripod-mounted telescope bolted

to the quarterdeck. A man stood beside it, waving his arms in a strange, rhythmic manner. He held a pair of long-handled, flat, paddlelike fans in his hands. Zakat only glimpsed the complex symbols inscribed on their surfaces, but he knew the sailor was using them to signal to an observer.

Zakat whispered to Sif, then Zakat bellowed an order to the Thulians. They roared and made another concerted charge, milling below the quarterdeck with their shields raised. A salvo of arrows struck them with a series of semimusical gongs. Then Sif bounded forward, brandishing her unsheathed broadsword. Gracefully she leaped atop the massed shields and ran along them as if she were crossing a stream by jumping from rock to rock.

Shouting in fear and anger, the sailors met her as she alighted on the elevated deck housing. Feinting with the sword, Sif sent the sailor to her left stumbling to the side. Sif spun instead, facing a man with a heavy sledge lifted over his head, holding the long wooden shaft in both hands. Teeth bared in a fierce grimace, the sailor brought the hammer down.

Sif shifted position, a grim smile on her face, and the Thulians below her bellowed approval. Fighting was the one true art they knew, and by the skillful way she whipped her sword forward, Sif proved she was a master.

Already committed to the move, dragged by the weight of the heavy hammer, the sailor cried out in panic as he saw Sif step lithely out of the way, then swing her sword.

The blade bit into the man's midsection with a sound like a melon splitting. His intestines spilled out, flopping in all directions. Sif wheeled again, slashing backhanded with the sword. The keen edge sliced through the neck of a second man, popping the head free of its shoulders. Before she could move again, another sailor was on her. He swung a sword as hard as he could at her head.

Sif lifted her bloody sword, meeting the other blade edge-on. Steel rang against steel, and sparks jumped from the impact point. She moved again, instantly on the attack, her thrust with the sword was quick and sure, burying the point deep in the man's chest.

Incredibly the sailor managed to grab the sword blade impaling him in one hand, then pulled himself closer. The scream that issued from his throat was thin and piping, and his lips were flecked with blood. He raised his sword in one hand.

Sif lifted her foot and kicked the man contemptuously in the stomach, removing his last dying threat, as well as freeing her sword. Only two defenders remained on the quarterdeck. The man with the signal fans dropped them to the deck. Completely blank of expression, he moved to stand shoulder to shoulder with his comrade. They dropped to their knees.

Coldly smiling down at them, Sif cocked back her sword arm as if she intended to decapitate them both with a single scything swing. Before she moved, the two men produced small knives from their tunics and stabbed themselves, almost in unison, in the lower abdomen. As they bent forward in the direction of the pain, they jerked up on the handles of the knives. Blood and viscera spewed from the incisions as they toppled forward onto their faces.

Sif stared at them in dumbfounded silence, her face registering angry confusion as if she couldn't quite understand how her victims had put themselves out of the reach of her blade by the simple dint of suicide. Zakat had heard of seppuku, of course, even if Sif and the Thulians had not. Any doubts he might have had about the nationalities of the junk's crew dissolved. They were Japanese without a doubt.

With a snarl of frustrated fury, Sif lifted her sword high and slashed downward in two strokes. The men's heads rolled across the quarterdeck like awkward balls and fell from the edge, banging on the shields of the Thulians. As if the postmortem beheadings were a signal, the mailed warriors laughed uproariously. They kicked the heads around for a few moments, as if they were playing a game of soccer.

Then they shook their notched and dripping swords skyward, blood trickling down their arms as they stood above the mangled corpses of the junk's crew. A bestial howling arose from their lips, the cry of a rabid wolf pack baying its victory over the bodies of the prey. They bellowed ''Thoo-lee! Thoo-lee!''

Zakat removed his stifling helmet and wiped at the sweat pebbling his face. He waited until the warriors had no breath left to shout the name of their homeland and their religion and snapped orders to search the hold.

He removed his helmet and scaled the ladder to the

quarterdeck and patted Sif's shoulder. "Well done, my queen."

She looked nothing like royalty unless she was ruler of a slaughterhouse. Her face, arms and heaving bosom were splashed with blood, the ends of her long blond hair dabbed in crimson. She looked at him with a dazed, almost beatific expression, then grabbed him around the waist, kissing him violently. The film of Bragi's blood on her mouth salted her lips.

Zakat carefully disengaged, not wanting to offend her for fear of his life, but also knowing the Valkyrie expected a fuck dessert after a blood feast.

"Later," he said to her quietly, using a low yet vibrant and persuasive tone of voice. Khlysty training revolved around a form of psionics, of imposing the force of one will upon another.

Sif blinked, smiled and whispered huskily, "Later, my warlord."

She turned and marched off the quarterdeck, to join the search for loot. Zakat picked up one of the signal paddles, noting how the symbol inscribed on it was utterly unfamiliar, like a sunburst containing three geometric shapes. Although he had no way of knowing what it meant, he did know that the marking was called an ideograph, and as such would mean something to somebody. He wondered who that somebody might be.

On impulse, he shaded his eyes and scanned the distant island, at least a quarter of a mile away. He could barely make out a rocky sweep of beach and the outlines of a small, single-masted boat anchored there. He stiffened when he caught sight of movement shifting in the undergrowth.

Zakat went to the telescope and, bending, aligned it with the island, squinting into the eyepiece. A group of people was emerging from the perimeter of a jungle and walking down to the shoreline.

He saw several Japanese men wearing lacquered, laminated armor and flaring helmets that gave them a sinister, dangerous appearance. At their sides hung broad, curved swords in wooden scabbards.

A woman stood among them, dressed in a billowy kimono-like garment. Her face was of a startling Oriental beauty, but her dark eyes glinted with anger. A man dressed much like the sailors aboard the junk appeared to be speaking to her urgently, gesturing frantically toward the sea.

Zakat nudged the telescope up a fraction. Towering a full head over the other people was a mustached black man. He held his left arm immobile in a sling. There was something in the set of his grim features that touched a distant chord of recognition in the files of Zakat's memory.

Before he could pull out the file and examine it more closely, the man raised a pair of binoculars to his eyes and appeared to gaze directly at him. It took Zakat a moment to identify the bulky shape strapped to the man's forearm as a holster. Then, in a rush, he recalled where and when he had last seen such an item in tandem with the black man—and whom he had been with.

A thrill of elation surged through Grigori Zakat, so

powerful and exhilarating he felt his knees grow momentarily weak. He stood up from the telescope to allow Grant a clear and unobstructed view of him. After a few seconds, he bent back down over the telescope, peering through the eyepiece.

To his disappointment, Grant's expression remained neutral. But he watched as he lowered the binoculars and he saw his lips stir. He knew without knowing how he knew that Grant muttered, "Zakat."

Zakat stood again and grinned broadly, hands on his hips, his head cocked at a defiant, challenging angle. The spiritual debt was now in the process of being paid.

Chapter 10

Mohanduas Lakesh Singh seemed to black out and come to again repeatedly, swimming in and out of consciousness. In one of the brief moments of lucid wakefulness, he sensed he was lying on the floor of his quarters, grinding the side of his face into the carpet as he writhed in pain.

He felt deep, boring pains in his chest, in his legs, and a fire burning behind his eyes. With a certain amount of clinical detachment, he understood the curious fact that it was the waves of pain that made him lose consciousness. Even more intense pain had roused him again. Then his skill at analysis left him, usurped by agony again.

Lakesh heard a faint voice floating over his head, calling his name, echoing as if speaking down a well. He was fairly certain he was being summoned over the intercom, but he couldn't gather enough strength or resolve to answer. Everything was overwhelmed by agony, even the shocking realization that his body experienced the worst pain in areas where it had undergone surgeries in the distant past—his legs, where the knee joints had been replaced with polyethylene, his chest, where he had undergone a lung and heart transplant, and his head, where his glaucoma-afflicted brown eyes were switched out for bright new blue ones.

As it was, his heart thudded slowly, lurching in his chest. Breathing took such a deliberate, conscious effort that he didn't bother with it for what seemed like a long time. Lakesh laboriously reviewed the past few minutes of his life, trying to isolate the incident that had slammed him to the floor in blinding pain. All he could remember was sitting on the edge of his bed, zipping up his bodysuit and then standing. He presumed the onslaught of pain had been so sudden and overwhelming he had no recollection of falling.

Finally, by degrees the flaring fireballs of agony igniting in his body began to ebb. His mind slowly started working again. Sucking in a noisy rattling gasp, Lakesh clawed himself forward by the strength of his fingers. His head pounded, as if sharp hammers were beating on the inside of his skull, chipping away at the bone.

He fought, wrestled and cursed his way to all fours, then to his knees. The furniture of his quarters tilted and spun all around him. He forced himself to shamble erect, face glistening with sweat. His hands shook violently in a tremor. He stumbled and reeled and fell half on top of a built-in bureau, leaning his entire weight against it.

Lakesh gazed into the small mirror hanging above it, examining his reflection by the dim light. For more than fifty years, since his resurrection from cryo sleep, he had always experienced a moment of disoriented shock when he saw a wizened, cadaverous face gazing back at him. For the first three years after his awakening, he was always discomfited by the sight of blue eyes staring out at him from his own face.

The year before the nukecaust he had been diagnosed with incipient glaucoma, and although the advance of the disease had been halted during his century and a half in cryostasis, it had returned with a double vengeance upon his revival. The eye transplant was only the first of many reconstructive surgeries he underwent, first in the Anthill, then in the Dulce installation. None of the reconstructive surgeries or physiological enhancements had been performed out of Samaritan impulses. His life and health had been prolonged so he could serve the Program of Unification and the baronies.

After his brown eyes were replaced with blue ones, his leaky old heart exchanged for a sound one and his lungs changed out, arthritic knee joints had been removed and traded with polyethylene ones. By the time all the surgeries were complete, the mental image he'd carried of his physical appearance no longer coincided with the reality. From a robust, youthful-looking man, he had become a liver-spotted scarecrow. His glossy, jet-black hair became a thin gray patina of ash that barely covered his head. The prolonged stasis process had killed the follicles of his facial hair, and he could never regrow the mustache he had once taken so much pride in.

His once clear, olive complexion had become leathery, crisscrossed with a network of deep seams and creases that bespoke the anguish of keeping two centuries' worth of secrets. For a long time, Lakesh could take consolation only in the fact that though he looked very old indeed, he was far older than he looked.

But now he looked far, far younger than his chronological age. Still he felt a shock when he looked into the mirror, but it was different, stemming as it did from fear. At the temples of his thick, jet-black hair, he saw more and more gray threads, but his olive complexion was still unlined, holding few creases from either age or stress, although he certainly had a stockpile of both.

The vision in his blue eyes was still sharp. He glanced down at the pair of eyeglasses resting on top of the bureau. They were ugly, dark-rimmed things with thick lenses and a hearing aid attached to the right earpiece. For over a decade he had worn them, knowing he resembled a myopic zombie—or Jerry Lewis's portrayal of the nutty professor.

For the past six months, they hadn't been necessary, and he realized the prospect that they might be again shook him far more profoundly than he expected. Although he didn't see any signs of accelerated aging, he assumed the sleet storm of agony he had just experienced was an omen of far worse things to come.

Inhaling a deep breath, wincing at the ache in his lungs, Lakesh inspected his reflection with a more objective eye. His restored youth—or more accurately, his restored early middle age—was the only beneficial result of his encounter with Sam, the self-proclaimed imperator of the baronies. He still remembered with vivid clarity how Sam, who resembled a ten-year-old boy, had accomplished the miracle by the simple laying on of hands.

Lakesh knew the process was far more complex than that, but he could engage only in fairly futile speculation of how it had been accomplished. He would never forget how Sam laid his little hand against his midriff and how a tingling warmth seemed to seep from it. The warmth swiftly became searing heat, like liquid fire, rippling through his veins and arteries. His heartbeat picked up in tempo, seeming to spread the heat through the rest of his body, a pulsing web of energy suffusing every separate cell and organ.

He was aflame with a searing pain, the same kind of agony a person felt when circulation was suddenly restored to a numb limb. His entire metabolism seemed to awaken to furious life from a long slumber, as if it had been jump-started by a powerful battery.

He still remembered with awe that after the sensation of heat faded, he realized two things more or less simultaneously—he wasn't wearing his glasses but he could see his hand perfectly. And by that perfect vision, he saw the flesh of his hand was smooth, the prominent veins having sunk back into firm flesh. The liver spots faded away even as he watched.

Later Sam claimed he had increased Lakesh's production of two antioxidant enzymes, catalase and superoxide dismutase, and boosted up his alkyglycerol level to the point where the aging process was for all intents and purposes reversed. For the first few weeks following Sam's treatment, his hair continued to darken and more and more of his wrinkles disappeared. But then the entire process reached a certain point and came to halt. Lakesh estimated he had returned to a physical state approximating his midforties.

Lakesh assumed Sam possessed the ability to transfer his biological energy to other organic matter, which in turn stimulated the entire human cellular structure. Beyond that, he could only guess.

Regardless of how Sam had done it, Lakesh knew his youth and vitality was not bestowed without a price. At this juncture he didn't know what he would eventually have to pay out. The fact his hair showed streaks of gray after such a short time indicated he either needed regular treatments or the process had a definite time limit.

He recalled the words of the extremely skeptical DeFore: "If aging is controlled by a kind of biological alarm clock, a sort of genetic switching system and the hands of yours were turned back, it stands to reason they'll start moving in the normal fashion again."

She went on to say, "Just as different kinds of clocks and watches are designed to run for different lengths of time after being wound, so different kinds of bodies are genetically designed to run for different periods. The mainspring of your body's clock could break at any time or it could go haywire. You could age ten years in ten seconds."

Comparing his body to a clock with a malfunctioning mainspring did nothing to ease Lakesh's fears. He started to push himself up, then winced as pain crawled across his chest. Slowly he unzipped the front of his bodysuit. Outlined in blue and red against the deep olive tone of his skin, a spiderweb pattern of broken blood vessels and ruptured capillaries extended from his left pectoral across his chest. They radiated outward from the surgical scars of his heart and lung transplants. Even as he looked at them, the livid network seemed to pulse and expand.

As fingers of dread knotted in the pit of his stomach, Lakesh bent and undid the Velcro tabs on the bodysuit's left boot sock. Leaning against the bureau, he tugged up the leg, over his knee. He set his teeth on a groan of incredulous horror when he saw the same kind of blue-and-red pattern spreading across the skin, just under the kneecap. He didn't bother checking on his right leg.

Quickly he leaned toward the mirror, turning his head to and fro, inspecting the area around his eyes for any signs of lividity. Although he saw none, he did not feel relief. An inner voice warned him that it was only a matter of time.

An insistent rapping on his door commanded his attention. Carefully he pushed himself upright and called, ''Come in.''

The knocking continued. Lakesh cursed and, dragging a mouthful of air into his aching lungs, he shambled out of his bedroom, through the living room. He winced at the stabbing pains in his knees. All in all, he felt as if he had just run a three-minute mile with his limbs weighted down by anchor chains.

He reached the door and opened it. For an instant, he didn't recognize the woman standing on the other side of it with her fist poised to knock again.

"Dr. Singh," Mariah Falk said. "Are you all right?"

Lakesh forced a smile to his face. "Of course," he replied, noting how hoarse his voice sounded. "Why wouldn't I be?"

Mariah eyed him a little suspiciously and Lakesh continued to smile at her engagingly. The woman wasn't beautiful or young. Her face was pale and angular. Her chestnut hair, frosted here and there with gray, was cut painfully short to the scalp. Deep creases curved out from either side of her nose to the corners of her mouth. Dark-ringed brown eyes gazed at him from beneath long brows that hadn't been plucked in years, if ever. Her teeth, though white, were uneven.

Like Brewster Philboyd and Nora Pennick, Mariah Falk was an astrophysicist and another recent immigrant from the Moon colony. Lakesh had also found her to be brilliant, pushy and abrasive. He liked her very much.

"You didn't answer the comm when I called you, for one thing," Mariah responded. "And I heard what I thought was a cry of pain."

Lakesh kept the smile on his face, even though it was an effort. The trans-comm units in the private quarters of the Cerberus redoubt were sound activated, so when she had comm-called him his involuntary groans had been transmitted.

"I'm fine," he said. "I was taking a nap. Maybe you heard me snoring."

She nodded, her mouth quirking in a mirthless smile. By the tone of her drawled "Right," Lakesh knew she didn't believe a word he said.

"Do you need me for something?" he asked.

Mariah lifted a shoulder in a negligent shrug. "I've fine-tuned the thermal signature in-feed from the Vela and I've been observing the area of the South Pole you pointed out to me."

Lakesh angled a challenging eyebrow. "And?"

She angled an equally challenging eyebrow in response. "And I think you'd better take a look at this for yourself."

Lakesh closed the door behind him and walked with Mariah along the twenty-foot-wide corridor made of softly gleaming vanadium alloy. Great curving ribs of metal and massive arches supported the high rock roof. From the main corridor, side passages and lifts led to a well-equipped armory, bunk rooms, a cafeteria, a decontamination center, an infirmary, a gymnasium with a pool and even a detention area.

"How do you like our little sanctuary here?" Lakesh asked conversationally, hoping to keep his attention diverted from the pain in his chest and knees.

"It's much roomier than the Manitius base," the woman replied. "A good deal more high-tech, too…which I wouldn't have expected."

Constructed in the mid-1990s, no expense had been

spared to make the redoubt, the seat of Project Cerberus, a masterpiece of concealment and impenetrability. The redoubt had housed the Cerberus process, a subdivision of Overproject Whisper, which in turn had been a primary component of the Totality Concept. The researches to which Project Cerberus and its personnel had been devoted were locating and traveling hyperdimensional pathways through the quantum stream. Once that had been accomplished, the redoubt became, from the end of one millennium to the beginning of another, a manufacturing facility. The quantum interphase mat-trans inducers, known colloquially as gateways, were built in modular form and shipped to other redoubts.

Most of the related overprojects had their own hidden bases. The official designations of the redoubts had been based on the old phonetic alphabet code used in military radio communications. On the few existing records, the Cerberus installation was listed as Redoubt Bravo, but the handful of people had who made the facility their home for the past few years never referred to it as such.

The thirty-acre, three-level installation had come through the nukecaust with its operating systems and radiation shielding in good condition. When Lakesh had reactivated the facility some thirty years before, the repairs he made had been minor, primarily cosmetic in nature. Over a period of time, he had added an elaborate system of heat-sensing warning devices, night-vision vid cameras and motion-trigger alarms to the surrounding plateau. He had been forced to work in secret and completely alone, so the upgrades had taken several years to complete. However, the isolated location of the redoubt in Montana's Bitterroot Range had kept his work from being discovered.

In the generations since the nukecaust, a sinister mythology had been ascribed to the mountains, with their mysteriously shadowed forests and hell-deep, dangerous ravines. The range had been referred to as the Darks for nearly a century. The wilderness area was virtually unpopulated. The nearest settlement was nearly a hundred miles away in the flatlands, and it consisted of a small band of Sioux and Cheyenne.

Planted within rocky clefts of the mountain peak and concealed by camouflage netting, were the uplinks with an orbiting Vela-class reconnaissance satellite, and a Comsat. It could be safely assumed that no one or nothing could approach Cerberus undetected by land or by air—not that anyone was expected to make the attempt, particularly overland. However, there had been a recent exception.

The road leading down from Cerberus to the foothills was little more than a cracked and twisted asphalt ribbon, skirting yawning chasms and cliffs. Acres of the mountainsides had collapsed during the nuke-triggered earthquakes nearly two centuries earlier. It was almost impossible for anyone to reach the plateau by foot or by vehicle; therefore Lakesh had seen to it that the facility was listed as irretrievably unsalvageable on all ville records.

The redoubt had been constructed to provide a comfortable home for well over a hundred people.

Although there were far fewer than that now, there were still more than there had been in the past two centuries. Lakesh and Mariah passed a number of people in the passageway, nodding to them and speaking words of greeting. He wasn't accustomed to seeing more than one or two people in the corridors, although he was gratified by it.

Even after Grant, Domi, Kane and Brigid had arrived at the installation two years before, there had been only a dozen permanent residents. For a long time, the Cerberus personnel were outnumbered by shadowed corridors, empty rooms and sepulchral silences.

Over the past month or so, the corridors had bustled with life, the empty rooms filled and the silences replaced by conversation and laughter. The immigrants from the Manitius base had been arriving on a fairly regular basis ever since the destination-lock code to the Luna gateway unit had been discovered. Whether they intended to remain in the installation, try to make separate lives for themselves in the Outlands or relocate to the installation on Thunder Isle was still an open question.

As they approached the operations center, Mariah went on, "I'm a little jealous, I have to admit. I thought all the best toys were reserved for us up on the Moon."

Lakesh smiled slightly. "It helps if you're one of the toy makers. Then you get first choice of what to play with."

Mariah laughed. ''Being in government service for twenty years, how well I know that.''

The two people walked through the open doorway into the central control complex, the command center, essentially the brain of the installation. A long room with high, vaulted ceilings, the walls were lined by consoles of dials, switches and readout screens. A double row of computer stations formed an aisle. Circuits clicked, drive units hummed, indicator lights flashed.

A Mercator projection map of the world spanned one wall. Pinpoints of light glowed on almost every continent, and thin, glowing lines networked across the countries, like a web spun by a rad-mad spider. The map not only delineated the geophysical alterations caused by the nukecaust, but it also displayed the locations of all functioning gateway units the world over. At present, none of the lights flickered, which signified no activity in the network.

Through an open doorway at the far end of the center in a separate antechamber stood the redoubt's gateway unit. The brown armaglass walls atop the elevated emitter array housing gleamed dully. Lakesh usually felt a small flush of pride whenever he looked at this particular unit, since it was the first fully debugged matter-transfer inducer built after the prototypes. It served as the basic template for all the others that followed.

A number of people were in the control complex sitting at various computer stations—shaved-headed, goateed Farrell, chunky, crew-cut Neukirk, who was a Moon base refugee and a couple of other Manitius émigrés whom Lakesh didn't know. If he had been introduced to them, he had already forgotten their names.

Quavell, seated in a chair at the medical monitor station, turned slightly when they entered. The hybrid female was small, smaller even than Domi. Her huge, slanting eyes of a clear, crystal blue gave Lakesh and Mariah a silent appraisal. They dominated a face of chiseled, elfin loveliness. If not for the grave austerity of her expression, she would have been beautiful. White hair the texture of silk threads fell from her high, domed-skull and curled inward at her slender shoulders.

Her compact, tiny-breasted form was encased in a silvery-gray, skintight bodysuit. It only accentuated the distended condition of her belly, even though the fabric provided adequate support. The material of the one-piece garment was a synthetic polymer with a high-degree of elasticity, so one size did indeed fit all.

"Status?" Lakesh inquired almost automatically.

Quavell indicated the monitor screen near her right elbow, which displayed a number of pulsing icons representing the heart rate, brain-wave activity and blood pressure of the Cerberus personnel.

"For approximately ten to fifteen minutes, Kane's and Domi's readings were spiking rather high," she replied. Her tone was crisp, but sounded almost child-like despite the fact she was sixty-seven years old. "But I suppose that's natural while engaged in a dinosaur hunt. The readings have been back to normal levels for the past half an hour.''

''Good.'' Lakesh turned to the man seated at the main ops console. ''Report, Mr. Bry?''

''Holding steady,'' Bry answered. A small man with rounded shoulders and coppery curls, his white bodysuit bagged on him.

Lakesh and Mariah stood behind Bry and gazed at the image on the main VGA screen, a four-foot square of ground glass.

''Satellite transmissions are still clear,'' Bry continued, sounding very pleased with himself. ''No fluctuations.''

In many ways, Lakesh couldn't really blame the man for preening a little. After all, it was his year's worth of hard work—as well many failures—that allowed Cerberus to at long last gain control of the two still functioning satellites in Earth orbit.

Although most satellites had been little more than free-floating scrap metal for well over a century, Cerberus had always possessed the proper electronic ears and eyes to receive the transmissions from at least two of them. The Vela reconnaissance class satellite carried narrow-band multispectral scanners. It could detect the electromagnetic radiation reflected by every object on Earth, including subsurface geomagnetic waves. The scanner was tied into an extremely high resolution photographic relay system.

The other satellite to which the redoubt was uplinked was a Comsat, which for many months was used primarily to keep track of Cerberus personnel when they were out in the field. Everyone in the installation had been injected with a subcutaneous transponder, which transmitted heart rate, respiration, blood count and brain-wave patterns. Based on organic nanotechnology, the transponder was a nonharmful radioactive chemical that bound itself to an individual's glucose and the middle layers of the epidermis.

The signal was relayed to the redoubt by the Comsat and directed down to the redoubt's hidden antenna array on the mountain peak, which in turn transferred it to the Cerberus computer systems. Sophisticated scanning filters combed through the telemetry using special human biological encoding. The digital data stream was then routed through a locational program to precisely isolate an individual's position in space and time.

The image transmitted from the Vela dominated the big screen. It showed only a primeval wilderness of white, broken here and there by jagged, fanglike shorelines, rimmed by ice. The sea was barely visible between cracks in the ice floes. In the low country, snow had blown away from the round knobs of small outcroppings. It was a vista of desolation not even matched by hellzones.

"The Antarctic," murmured Bry. "The literal bottom of the world."

Lakesh repressed a shiver. He had been born in the tropical climate of Kashmir, India, and even after 247 years, his internal thermostat was stuck there. Although he had spent a century and a half in a form of cryogenic suspension, and though it made no real scientific sense, he had been very susceptible to cold ever since.

"Show me what caught your interest, Mariah," he said.

She reached over Bry and touched a key on the board. The image changed, shades of bright color blooming up from underneath the snowscape, like the petals of an unimaginably huge blossom. Hues of white, red, yellow, green, cyan, blue and even violet spread out across the screen.

"This is a thermal line-scan filter of the area," she said. "The spectroscopic analysis indicates exceptionally high levels of thermal radiation."

"Is it a signature from a naturally occurring geothermal source, like a volcano or a hot springs?" Lakesh asked.

She shook her head. "No. It's too localized. The signature is confined to a radius of about twenty square miles."

Lakesh nodded but he said, "That's really nothing when we're talking about a continent the size of Antarctica."

"I realize that. Fact of the matter is, the localized area is a key one, near the apex point of the ice sheet. From the readings we're getting, it apparently varies in thickness from one mile to a thousand feet."

Bry turned in his chair to stare at her blankly. "And?"

"And," stated Lakesh, "normally the sheet is as much as three miles thick in some places."

Frowning, Bry repeated, "And?"

Mariah sighed wearily. "Mr. Bry, we're talking about a single ice sheet that is larger than the entire European continent. Think what would happen if it slipped into the sea."

"You'd get a big splash?" he asked acidly.

"You'd get that, all right," answered Mariah grimly. "The splash would be so big we might even get our feet wet way up here. And we'd get a hell of a lot more besides. Essentially it would trigger an event that would plunge us into a new ice age. More than likely, one from which the Earth would never recover."

Lakesh started to speak but closed his mouth at the sound of a fierce, rushing wind erupting from the emitter array concealed within the raised platform of the gateway unit. It swelled in volume, climbing in pitch.

"Incoming jumpers," Farrell announced unnecessarily.

Chapter 11

Although the mind didn't sleep during gateway transit, it dreamed.

Brigid Baptiste dreamed of her past, the world's past, humanity's past, buried beneath the rubble of war and deliberately concealed by a cunningly contrived belief system.

Judgment Day, the long-prophesied apocalypse, scorched the earth clean late in the first month of the first year of the twenty-first century. For nearly thirty years the judgment continued in the form of skydark, the nuclear winter. It was a period of Nature gone amok. The hundreds of very nearly simultaneous nuclear explosions propelled massive quantities of pulverized rubble into the atmosphere, clogging the sky and blanketing all of Earth in a thick cloud of dust, debris, smoke and fallout.

For nearly two decades it was as if the very elements were trying to purge the earth of the few survivors of the atomic megacull. The exchange of nuclear missiles did more than slaughter most of Earth's inhabitants—it distorted those ecosystems that weren't completely obliterated. The entire atmosphere of the planet was hideously polluted by the nukecaust, producing all manners of deadly side effects in the ecosphere.

After eight generations, the lingering effects of the nukecaust and skydark were more subtle, an underlying texture to a world struggling to heal itself, but the side effects of the war still let themselves be known from time to time, like a grim reminder to humanity to never again take for granted the permanence of the earth.

Shortly after skydark, a group of families who had taken the measures to survive the nukecaust and its resulting horrors emerged from their shelters, their caves, their refuges. The North American continent was a Deathlands, but they believed they had inherited it, by the divine right that they survived when most others did not.

The families and their descendants spread out and divided the country into little territories, much like old Europe, which had been ruled over by princes and barons. Though the physical world was vastly changed, they were determined to bend it to their wills, to control it, to crawl back to the top of the food chain.

After skydark, the wastelands of America were up for grabs, and as usual, power was the key. Pioneers who tried to rebuild found themselves either shoved off their lands or facing bandits who killed with no pretense of ethical or moral right.

The alternatives were few. One could live the life of a nomad, join the marauding wolf packs or set up robber baronies. Whichever option was chosen, lives tended to be brutal and short. The blood that had splattered the pages of America's frontier history was a mere sprinkling compared to the crimson tide that flooded postnuke America. It took the nine barons and the unified villes to clean it up the only way it could be cleaned up—with an iron-fisted rule.

In the century following skydark, baronial territories were redefined, treaties struck among the barons. The city-states became interconnected points in a continent-spanning network. Nine baronies survived the long wars over territorial expansion and resources. Control of the continent was divided among them. The pretenders, those who arrogantly carved out their own little pieces of empire, were overrun, exterminated and their territories absorbed.

A Program of Unification was ratified and ruthlessly employed. The reconstructed form of government was still basically despotic, but now it was institutionalized and shared by all the formerly independent baronies.

Unity Through Action was the rallying cry that had spread across the Outlands by word of mouth and proof of deed. It offered a solution to the constant states of worry and fear: join the unification program and never worry or fear—or think—again. Humanity was responsible for the arrival of Judgment Day, and it had to accept that responsibility before a truly utopian age could be ushered in.

All humankind had to do to earn this utopia was follow the rules, be obedient and be fed and clothed. And accept the new order without question.

For most of the men and women who lived in the villes and the surrounding territories, this was enough, more than enough. Long sought after dreams of peace and safety had at least been transformed into reality. Of course, fleeting dreams of personal freedom were lost in the exchange, but such abstract aspirations were nothing but childish illusions.

Synchronized with this forward step in social engineering came technical advances. Technology, most of it based on predark designs, appeared mysteriously and simultaneously with the beginning of the reunification program. There was much speculation at the time that many previously unknown Continuity of Government Stockpiles were opened up and their contents distributed evenly among the barons.

Although the technologies were restricted for the use of those who held the reins of power, life overall improved for the citizens in and around the villes. To enjoy the bounty offered by the barons, all anyone had to do was to surrender his or her will.

The barons' legions of black-armored Magistrates were charged with the task of encouraging people to surrender their wills. Formed as a complex police machine, the Magistrate Divisions demanded instant obedience to their edicts, to which there was no possible protest. In a little under a century, both the oligarchy of barons and the Mags that served them had taken on a fearful, almost legendary aspect. The unification program established a social order by which generations of Americans were born into serfdom, slavery in everything but name.

The doctrines expressed in ville teachings encouraged humanity to endure a continuous hardship before a utopian age could be ushered in. Because humanity had ruined the world, the punishment was deserved. The doctrines ultimately amounted to extortion—obey and suffer, or disobey and die.

The dogma was elegant in its simplicity, and for most of her life, Brigid Baptiste had believed it. Then she stumbled over a few troubling questions, and when she attempted to find the answers, all she discovered were many troubling questions. The attempt to find answers to those questions had turned her, Kane and Grant into exiles on the planet of their birth.

Brigid had been in a unique position to seek out the answers and often she found the mysteries far more disturbing than any possible solutions. As a trained archivist in Cobaltville's Historical Division, she knew misinformation often began with half-truths, then grew into speculative translations as someone worked to record the event.

Despite a common misconception, the ville archivists weren't bookish, bespectacled scholars. They were primarily data-entry techs, albeit ones with high security clearances. A vast amount of predark historical information had survived the nukecaust, particularly documents stored in underground vaults. Much more data was digitized, stored on EMP-resistant computer diskettes.

No information was sometimes better than half information, but the archivists couldn't make that judgment call. Their primary duty was not to record predark history or evaluate the veracity of the data, but to revise, rewrite and often completely disguise it. The political causes leading to the nukecaust were well-known. They were major parts of the dogma, the doctrine, the articles of faith, and they had to be accurately recorded for posterity.

As Brigid rose up the ranks, promoted mainly through attrition, she was allowed greater access to secret records. Though these were heavily edited, she came across references to something called the Totality Concept, to devices called gateways and to projects bearing the code names of Chronos and Cerberus, which hinted at phenomena termed "probability wave dysfunctions" and "alternate event horizons."

Once she read a long, confusing scientific dissertation that dealt with the deliberate creation of mutations, years before the nukecaust. Like everyone else, Brigid assumed the muties were the result of widespread chemical warfare and radiation induced during the nuclear conflict. The document suggested otherwise, and was fraught with devastating implications regarding genetic engineering.

She wasn't foolish or disturbed enough to voice her concerns. Archivists were always watched, probably more than people working in other divisions. She had worked hard at perfecting a poker face. She wondered if some of the material handed to her was a test to gauge her reaction. Because of that suspicion, she had gained the reputation of being cool, calm, unflappable and immutable.

Then, toward the end of her sixth year as an Archivist, she read the *Wyeth Codex*. Some thirty years before, a junior archivist in Ragnarville had found an old computer disk containing the journal of one Mildred Winona Wyeth, a specialist in cryogenics. She had entered a hospital in late 2000 for minor surgery, but an idiosyncratic reaction to the anesthetic left her in a coma, with her vital signs sinking fast. To save her life, the predark whitecoats had cryonically frozen her.

After her revival nearly a century later, she joined a wandering band of survivalists. At one point during her travels, she found a working computer and recorded her thoughts, observations and speculations regarding the postnukecaust world, the redoubts and the wonders they contained.

Although the *Wyeth Codex* contained recollections of adventures and wanderings, it dealt in the main with her observations of postnukecaust America.

She also delved deeply into the Totality Concept and its many different yet interconnected subdivisions. Despite her exceptional intelligence, and education, Wyeth had no inkling of the true nature of the Totality Concept's experiments, but a number of her extrapolations that they were linked to the nukecaust came very close to the truth.

In the decades following its discovery, the *Wyeth Codex* had been downloaded, copied and disseminated like a virus through the Historical Divisions of the entire ville network.

That particular virus had infected Brigid also, when

she found a disk containing the *Codex* at her workstation in the archives. After reading and committing it to memory, she had never been the same woman again.

The *Wyeth Codex* began her secret association with the Preservationists. This was the name given by the barons to a suspected underground-resistance group of insurgents operating in the villes. The Preservationists were alleged to be an elite group of historians who possessed a greater understanding of the "true" history of the pre- and postnukecaust world.

The Preservationists were, in fact, a fiction created by Lakesh as an adversary to occupy the attention of the Magistrate Divisions and the barons while the real insurrectionist work proceeded elsewhere.

A whine vibrated within Brigid's head, then against her eardrums, and a dazed part of her mind realized the gateway transit had been successful. From the hyperdimensional nonspace through which she had traveled, she seemed to fall through vertiginous abysses. There was a microinstant of nonexistence, then a shock as her senses returned.

Enduring a matter-transfer jump could be very disorienting. Intellectually she knew the mat-trans energies transformed organic and inorganic matter to digital information, transmitted it through a hyperdimensional quantum path and reassembled it in a receiver unit. Emotionally the experience felt like a fleeting brush with death, or worse than death. It was nonexistence, at least for a nanosecond.

Brigid opened her eyes, struggling against a spasm

of nausea, striving and straining for inner balance after a mat-trans jump. She blinked against vision-clouding vertigo. She saw the silvery shimmer fading from the hexagonal disks on the ceiling and felt the pins-and-needles static discharge from the metal floor plates, and beneath them she heard the emitter array's characteristic hurricane howl fading away to a high-pitched whine.

Her head swam dizzily. The vertigo was routine by now, a customary side effect of rematerialization. She knew better than to sit up until the light-headedness went away completely. All things considered, temporary queasiness and dizziness were small prices to pay in exchange for traveling hundreds, sometimes thousands of miles.

Occasionally the toll exacted was terrible, as when she, Kane and Grant jumped to a malfunctioning unit in Russia. The matter-stream modulations couldn't be synchronized with the destination lock, and all of them suffered a severe case of debilitating jump sickness, which included hallucinations, weakness and vomiting.

Hearing a rustle of cloth behind her, Brigid gingerly eased herself up on one elbow, looking around slowly. Domi, Kane, Philboyd, Nora and DeFore stirred from their supine positions on the platform. One of the most baffling features of mat-trans jumps was how a subject could start it standing up and end it by lying flat on his or her back. The floor plates had already lost their silvery shimmer, and the last wisps of spark-shot mist disappeared even as she looked at it. Lakesh once explained that the vapor wasn't really a mist at all, but a plasma wave form brought into existence by the inducer's "quincunx effect."

Brigid was the first to sit up, making sure the armaglass walls enclosing the jump chamber were tinted brown, which meant they had reached their destination. The six-sided chambers in the Cerberus gateway network were color-coded so authorized jumpers could tell at a glance into which redoubt they had materialized.

It seemed an inefficient method of differentiating one installation from another, but Lakesh had once explained that before the nukecaust, only personnel holding color-coded security clearances were allowed to make use of the system. Inasmuch as their use was restricted to a select few of the units, it was fairly easy for them to memorize which color designated what redoubt.

One by one, the six people climbed to their feet. Both Nora and Philboyd gazed around uneasily, then looked themselves over, flexing their fingers and touching their faces. They showed considerable relief at finding themselves whole and in one piece.

"It's going to take me a long time to get used to traveling like this," Philboyd murmured.

"Try the interphaser," Brigid suggested wryly. "That's really a smooth ride."

Philboyd smiled dourly. "I'll take your word for it."

No human being, no matter how thoroughly briefed

in advance, could be expected to remain unflappable on a hyperdimensional trip through the gateway.

Brigid glanced toward Kane. "How do you feel?"

Kane didn't appear to have heard the question. He lifted up on the wedge-shaped handle and pushed the heavy door open on its counterbalanced hinges. He stepped down off the platform into the ready room. In the process of picking up the boxes of material that had been salvaged from Thunder Isle, DeFore called out with some asperity, "Hey, why don't you help me cart this stuff to the infirmary?"

Kane didn't even bother looking around. "Since it's mostly medical stuff, get Auerbach to help you."

Auerbach was DeFore's main aide and not one of Kane's favorite people in the redoubt.

Sighing, Brigid picked up a couple of the smaller boxes and followed Kane out of the ready room into the adjoining command center. She wasn't surprised to see Lakesh standing over the main ops console with Mariah Falk by his side. She saw other Manitius personnel present, as well—Eduardo Vega, a man slightly below middle height, with a dark complexion and long black hair that framed a deeply scarred face, gave her a welcoming grin. Neukirk, a short, chunky man with weather-beaten features and a white crew cut, sat at one of the consoles and ignored her. Brigid didn't mind—she didn't like Neukirk much.

Lakesh stood behind Bry and gazed at the big VGA monitor screen, and seemed only mildly interested in their return. He couldn't have been surprised, since the Mercator index map would have registered a mat-trans unit going online when the dematerialization process began. Brigid noticed how his eyes narrowed to slits as if he were experiencing twinges of pain.

As the six people trooped through the command center, Lakesh did a double take when Domi drew abreast of him. He noted the multitude of abrasions on her muddy arms and legs and started to reach for her. Then he quickly drew his hand back, surreptitiously glancing toward the ready room.

"Don't worry," Domi said. Her voice was sweetly mocking. "Grant didn't come back with us, so it's all right to touch me in public."

Brigid had no idea to what she was referring, but Lakesh obviously did. Angry embarrassment glinted in his eyes, but it was almost instantly replaced by confusion. Brow furrowed, he demanded, "Why didn't Grant come back? Explain."

Domi stalked past him without answering. When no one else seemed inclined to answer, Lakesh turned before Kane could leave the room. "Kane! What is going on?"

With a sharp, dismissive gesture of his right hand, Kane said, "Grant is staying with Shizuka on New Edo. 'Till death do they part' and all that shit. He's quit on us."

Lakesh's "What?" was loud, ragged and incredulous.

Kane didn't bother to respond or even look around. Followed by Domi, he strode through the door and out into the corridor.

Lakesh turned toward Brigid. "Will you tell me what is going on?"

Brigid bristled at his autocratic tone. She stared into Lakesh's bright-blue eyes, but the man never flinched. She still hadn't grown accustomed to dealing with a relatively youthful Lakesh whose eyes weren't covered by thick lenses and whose voice no longer rose to a reedy rasp. "There's not much to tell," she replied. "Right before we gated back here, Grant dropped the bomb on us. He's standing down. Retired."

Bry swung his head up and around to gape at Brigid in astonishment. Lakesh opened and closed his mouth several times before he was able to husk out, "What reason did he give?"

Brigid eyed him speculatively. "What do you think his reasons were, Lakesh?"

He pursed his lips and shook his head in either weary exasperation or stunned disbelief. He dabbed at the film of perspiration on his forehead. Brigid could guess the kind of thoughts wheeling through his head. Grant, like Kane, had been through the dehumanizing cruelty of Magistrate training, yet had somehow almost miraculously managed to retain his humanity. But vestiges of their Mag years still lurked close to the surface, particularly in Grant. Superficially Grant had handled his status as a renegade better than Kane, the man was always stoic in the face of physical and emotional pain. He presented a dour, closed and private persona rarely showing emotion. He was taciturn and slow to genuinely anger.

''What exactly did he say?'' Lakesh demanded.

With her extraordinary memory, Brigid could have quoted Grant's statement word for word, imitating even his cadence of speech. Instead, she told Lakesh how Grant felt, not what he said. The man was not known for being loquacious or erudite, but he could definitely make a point.

He told Kane, Brigid, DeFore and Domi and whoever else was in earshot that the exile years had been hard and desperate, but they'd been good ones, too. But still and all, he owed Cerberus nothing. He had put in his time, shed his blood, lost his pound of flesh for the cause. It was no longer enough for him to wish for a glorious death as a payoff. His latest brush with mortality, which resulted in his partial paralysis, proved something he had known for years but never admitted to himself—when death came, it was usually unexpected and almost never glorious.

More than that, he was simply emotionally and spiritually drained. He had witnessed many violent deaths, and been responsible for bringing dozens of them about during his Mag days and after. Why he wanted to bring it all to an end wasn't very complicated. The most obvious answer was the correct answer: he was getting old.

Brigid wasn't overly surprised by Grant's decision, but she was disturbed by how calmly Kane took it. He accepted everything Grant said without a flicker of emotion or a single question. Lakesh was actually experiencing a more extreme reaction, and she supposed it had something to do with losing one of the enforcement arms of Cerberus.

She remembered Kane's cynical remark of years ago regarding the man's reasons for recruiting him and Grant: "Lakesh wants me and Grant here because we're Mags. We're the professional guns he never had, the killer instincts he could never bring into play."

"So you and Kane just let him go?" Lakesh asked angrily. He snapped his fingers. "Just like that?"

Brigid ran her hands through her mane of red-gold hair, knowing the anger wasn't truly directed at her. Lakesh always had problems dealing with the whims of chance, of cruel circumstance, of situations beyond his immediate control. In spite of the fact the Cerberus personnel ultimately worked toward the same goals, those objectives were for the most part chosen by Lakesh, regardless of who actually implemented the action to achieve the goals.

Rather than engage him in an argument, Brigid simply said, "Yes. Just like that."

DeFore spoke up, her tone bleak and just a little bitter. "It's not like we could stop him, Lakesh. He's not a machine who has a worn-out part that can be repaired or replaced. He is a human being, a man who has done his duty. More than done it."

Philboyd cleared his throat nervously. "I don't want to interfere in a family squabble…but it's not been that long ago since Grant basically saved the entire solar system from entropic reversal. And from what I've heard since I've been here, that's the capper of some pretty hairy situations over the last couple of years. I'd say he's earned a rest.''

Lakesh tugged absently at his nose, a habit that carried on even into his restored youth. Brigid noticed a slight tremor in his hand. ''Haven't we all,'' he muttered darkly.

Exhaling an unsteady breath, he turned toward DeFore, repeating in a harsh whisper, ''Haven't we all.''

Then Lakesh clutched at his chest and his knees buckled.

Chapter 12

"Goddammit, Kane—wait up!"

Kane shortened his long-legged stride enough for Domi to catch up to him in the corridor. Her bare feet slapped softly on the vanadium sheathing of the floor, muting the sound to little more than a series of pats.

"Where are you going?" she asked.

He hefted the USAS-12 shotgun and patted his holstered blaster. "To turn these back in, as per procedure."

"Oh." She fell into step beside him. "You don't seem too surprised by Grant bailing out on us."

Kane only grunted in response. They passed the workroom and the vehicle depot and entered the armory. He pressed the flat toggle switch on the door frame, and the overhead fluorescent fixtures blazed on, flooding the armory with a white, sterile light.

The big square room was stacked nearly to the ceiling with wooden crates and boxes. Many of the crates were stenciled with the legend Property U.S. Army, and others bore words in Russian Cyrillic script.

They moved along the aisles, past glass-fronted cases holding M-16 A-1 assault rifles, SA-80 subguns, and Heckler & Koch VP-70 semiautomatic pistols, complete with holsters and belts.

Lining the walls were bazookas, tripod-mounted M-249 machine guns and several crates of grenades. Mounted on frameworks in a corner were two full suits of Magistrate body armor, standing there like black, silent sentinels. Every piece of ordnance and hardware, from the smallest-caliber handblaster to the biggest-bore M-79 grenade launcher, was in perfect condition.

All of the ordnance was of predark manufacture. Caches of matériel had been laid down in hermetically sealed Continuity of Government installations before the nukecaust. Protected from the ravages of the environment, nearly every piece of munitions and hardware was as pristine as the day it rolled off the assembly line. Over a period of years Lakesh had smuggled out all of the weaponry from the largest COG facility, the Anthill, assuming wrongly that everyone he recruited to his cause would gleefully snatch up all the ordnance.

Most of the exiles had never so much as touched a blaster until they arrived at Cerberus. All of them were expected to become reasonably proficient with guns, and they had spent some time on the indoor and outdoor firing range under Grant's tutelage. The lessons were restricted to the use of the SA-80 subguns, lightweight "point and shoot" autoblasters even the most firearm-challenged person could learn to handle.

Domi paused at an open gun case where nearly a dozen Sin Eaters in their forearm holsters hung from pegs. Kane and Grant had appropriated the spares a short time before from a squad of hard-contact Mags dispatched from Cobaltville.

The squad's mission was to investigate Redoubt Bravo and ascertain if it was inhabited. The Magistrates were stopped and soundly defeated by Sky Dog's band of Amerindians in the flatlands bordering the foothills. Grant and Kane were instrumental in the victory, although they managed to keep their involvement concealed from the invading Mags.

The survivors of the engagement were disarmed and allowed to go on their way, believing the Indians alone were responsible for their humiliation. Kane and Grant took their discarded Sin Eaters, since they were murderous weapons and almost impossible for a novice to manage. Mag Division recruits were never allowed live ammunition until a tedious, six-month-long training period was successfully completed.

As the Indian warriors were unaccustomed to blasters of any sort, Grant and Kane feared they would wreak fatal havoc by experimenting with them.

"I guess I'll have to learn to use one of these now," Domi commented.

"I suppose so," Kane replied disinterestedly.

He hung his holstered blaster on a hook inside the gun case and then carried the shotgun to another case that stood behind the two suits of Magistrate armor. He glanced at them and felt his heart jerk within his chest. The armor served as a symbol of his and Grant's pasts, when the two men served as enforcers of the ville laws and Baron Cobalt's edicts, legally and spiritually sanctioned to act as judges, juries and executioners.

All Magistrates followed a patrilineal tradition, assuming the duties and positions of their fathers before them. They didn't have given names, each taking the surname of the father, as though the first Magistrate to bear the name were the same man as the last.

As Magistrates, their lives had been charted before their births. They were destined to live, fight and die, usually violently, as they fulfilled their oaths to impose order upon chaos. By a strict definition, Grant and Kane had not only betrayed their oaths, but as Lakesh was wont to say, "There's no sin in betraying a betrayer."

The bromide was easy enough to utter, but to live with the knowledge was another struggle entirely. Two years before, when they broke their lifetimes of conditioning, the inner agony was almost impossible to endure. The peeling away of their Mag identities, their Mag purpose, had been a gradual process but now, when Kane thought of his years as a Magistrate, it brought only an ache, a sense of remorse over wasted years.

But old Mag habits died very hard. Kane managed to push most of them to the back of his mind, storing them with his memories of all the other things that were past and he wasn't particularly anxious to think about.

Coming to stand beside him, Domi murmured, "Turn the page."

Kane snorted out a rueful laugh, knowing what she meant. "He might have the right idea, you know."

Domi nodded in agreement. "I don't hate him, you know. I never did."

"I know you didn't, Domi. He knew you didn't, too."

She gave a questioning look. "How?"

Kane grinned, but it looked forced. "Because when you found out about Shizuka, you didn't do a Guana on him."

Kane employed a bit of personal vernacular, referring to Guana Teague, the former Pit boss of Cobaltville. Teague was crushing the life out of Grant beneath his three-hundred-plus pounds of flab, when Domi expertly slit his throat.

After that, Domi attached herself to Grant, viewing him as a gallant black knight who had rescued her from the shackles of Guana Teague's slavery, even though in reality quite the reverse was true.

For more than a year, she made it fiercely clear that Grant was hers and hers alone, even though Grant fought hard to make sure there was nothing but friendship between him and the albino girl. He tried to make the gap in their ages the reason he didn't want to get involved with her, sexually or otherwise. Domi had been patient and understanding until she grew tired of waiting.

Grant knew he had hurt Domi dreadfully when she spied him and Shizuka locked in a passionate embrace. He didn't speak to her about it at first. Part of his reluctance was due to shame, another part due to pride, but more than anything else, fear made him hold his tongue.

Finally, when he did reveal to Domi his feelings for Shizuka, the outlander girl accepted it with the same pragmatic stoicism as when she was informed of being time trawled.

For his part, Kane wasn't sure how he felt about Grant's decision to stay on New Edo. He felt resentment and a certain anger, and he was embarrassed by both reactions. His life as a Mag and an exile had left him hard and solitary. Mag training had taught him that any personal bonds he made with his comrades compromised his worth and loyalty to his unit. Caring about someone else made a warrior weak. It was one thing to go into battle prepared to die, but watching someone else die when feelings were involved was distracting.

The Mag command had seen the bonds growing between Kane and Grant back in Cobaltville, which was why the decision had been made to break them up. But that bond had kept Kane alive as much as it had Grant.

Conversely, Kane reflected, the bond Grant shared with Domi had almost gotten them killed. He remembered Domi's wild behavior when she believed Grant had rejected her love in favor of Shizuka. Without Grant as the mitigating influence, the authority figure, what little self-restraint the girl ever practiced was completely discarded. All her bottled-up passions were unleashed, but turned from love to violence. Her shame, her mad desire for vicarious revenge against

Grant, had been unbottled during the mission to Area 51 and set in motion a dramatic sequence of events, the fallout of which Cerberus was still dealing with.

Area 51 was the predark unclassified code name for a training area on Nellis Air Force base. It was also known as Groom Lake, but most predarkers preferred to call it Dreamland.

Contained in the dry lake bed was a vast installation, extending deep into the desert floor. Only a few of the buildings were aboveground. Area 51 was more than just a military installation; it served as an international base operated by a consortium from many countries. Two centuries later, its operation was overseen by a consortium of barons.

After the destruction of the Archuleta Mesa medical facilities, the barons were left without access to the techniques of fetal development outside the womb, so both the baronial oligarchy and the entire hybrid race were in danger of extinction.

Baron Cobalt occupied Area 51 with the spoken assumption of taking responsibility to sustain his race—but only if he was elevated to a position of high authority, even above his brother barons. It wasn't a matter of making an incursion into another baron's territory, since most of Nevada was an Outland flat zone, not a part of an official baronial territory, certainly not Baron Cobalt's.

Since Area 51's history was intertwined with rumors of alien involvement, Baron Cobalt had used its medical facilities as a substitute for those destroyed in New Mexico. Of course, he couldn't be sure if the aliens referred to by the predark conspiracy theorists were the Archons, but more than likely they were, inasmuch as the equipment that still existed was already designed to be compatible with the hybrid metabolisms.

In any event, Baron Cobalt reactivated the installation, turning it into a processing and treatment center without having to rebuild from scratch, and transferred the human and hybrid personnel from the Dulce facility—those who had survived the destruction there, at any rate.

Still and all, the medical treatments that addressed the congenital autoimmune system deficiencies of the hybrids weren't enough to insure the continued survival of the race. The necessary equipment and raw material to implement procreation had yet to be installed. Baron Cobalt had unilaterally decided that the conventional means of conception was the only option to keep the hybrid race alive.

Kane and Domi had penetrated the Area 51 and been captured. Domi was found by a little group of insurgents led by the hybrid female Quavell, and she and Kane were sentenced by Baron Cobalt to what amounted to stud service.

During his two weeks of captivity, Kane was fed a steady diet of protein laced with a stimulant that affected the renal blood supply, increasing cardiac output without increasing the need for cardiac oxygen consumption.

Combined with the food loaded with protein to speed up sperm production, the stimulant provided

Kane with hours of high energy. Since he was forced to achieve erection and ejaculation six times a day every two days, his energy and sperm count had to be preternaturally high, even higher than was normal for him.

Although Kane was supposed to be biologically superior, he knew the main reason he was chosen to impregnate the female hybrids was simply due to the fact male hybrids were incapable of engaging in conventional acts of procreation, at least physically. Their organs of reproduction were so undeveloped as to be vestigial.

Kane wasn't the first human male to be pressed into service. There had been other men before him, but they had performed unsatisfactorily due to their terror of the hybrids. At first the females selected for the process donned wigs and wore cosmetics in order to appear more human to the trapped sperm donors. The men had to be strapped down and even after the application of an aphrodisiac gel, had difficulty maintaining an erection.

Such a problem wasn't something a hybrid, baron or no, was likely to ever experience. What made the barons so superior had nothing to do with the physical. The brains of the barons could absorb and process information with exceptional speed, and their cognitive abilities were little short of supernatural.

Almost from the moment the barons emerged from the incubation chambers, they possessed IQs so far beyond the range of standard tests as to render them meaningless. They mastered language in a matter of weeks, speaking in whole sentences. All of Nature's design faults in the human brain were corrected, modified and improved, specifically the hypothalamus, which regulated the complex biochemical systems of the body.

They could control all autonomous functions of their brains and bodies, even to the manufacture and release of chemicals and hormones. They could speed or slow their heartbeats, increase and decrease the amount of adrenaline in their bloodstreams.

They possessed complete control over that mysterious portion of the brain known as the limbic system, a portion that predark scientists had always known possessed great reserves of electromagnetic power and strength.

But since they were bred for brilliance, all barons had emotional limitations placed upon their enormous intellects. They were captives of their shared Archon hive-mind heritage, captives of a remorseless mindset that didn't carry with it the simple comprehension of the importance to humans of individual liberty.

Visceral emotions didn't play a large part in the psychologies of the so-called new humans. Even their bursts of passion were of the most rudimentary kind. Although the tissue of their hybridized brains were of the same organic matter as the human brain, the millions of neurons operated a bit differently in the processing of information. Therefore, their thought processes were very structured, extremely linear. When they experienced emotions, they only did so under moments of stress, and then so intensely they were almost consumed by them.

Therefore, Kane was surprised when Quavell, during one of their scheduled periods of copulation, confided to him that not every hybrid agreed with the baronial policy toward humanity. He was even more surprised when she helped him and Domi escape. He was forced to reassess everything he thought he knew about the barons, about the hybrids.

With the advent of Sam the imperator and the siege of Cobaltville, everything was different—yet, strangely still the same. The imperator's stated intent was to end the tyranny of the barons and unify both hybrid and human and build a new Earth, but Lakesh didn't believe him. Kane saw no reason to do so, either. But if it turned out that female hybrids could conceive offspring by human males, then a continued division between the so-called old and new human was pretty much without merit. And without that division, the barons could no longer rule. A child conceived by an old and new human represented a future wherein the baronial oligarchy was no longer unique or superior.

Now there appeared to be no question about whether offspring could be produced by hybrid and human. Kane still recalled with shocking clarity his first sight of a pregnant Quavell sitting in Lakesh's office, when he entered to brief him about the events that had occurred on the Moon.

Kane repressed a sigh and turned to leave the armory. As he did so, he asked Domi, "What was the meaning of that crack you made to Lakesh?"

She lifted a mud-stained shoulder in a shrug. "He wanted to keep our relationship secret from Grant."

"Why?"

Again came the shrug. "Afraid he'd get mad, come gunning for him, I guess. Do you think Grant would have?"

Kane considered the possibility for a moment, then shook his head ruefully. He hadn't considered it likely Grant would decide to give up his life in Cerberus to live with Shizuka, either. "I really couldn't say."

He and Domi walked along the corridor to the wing that held the apartments and dormitories. At the door to his quarters, Domi, with an impish grin asked, "Want me to come in and scrub your back?"

"I usually do that myself, thanks."

"Want to scrub mine, then?"

Kane gave her a dour smile. "I'd hate to have Lakesh come gunning for me."

His smile widened to a grin to show her he was flattered by her offer, then he entered his four-room suite. It was substantially larger and better appointed than his old flat in the residential enclaves of Cobaltville.

In the bathroom, he stripped out of his dirty clothes and stepped into the shower, adjusting the water so it was as hot as he could stand it. He soaped himself up, and dirty brown puddles formed at his feet, swirling down into the floor drain. He stayed beneath the shower longer than was necessary, wanting to scrub every microscopic bit of the swamp from his pores.

When his fingertips wrinkled and turned pink, he decided he was as clean as he was likely to be. He rinsed himself with jets of cold, clear water.

He felt much better when he stepped out of the shower. Toweling his hair dry, he walked into his bedroom. At the same time, Brigid Baptiste walked in. When she saw his total state of undress, she uttered a wordless murmur of surprise and swiftly turned her back.

"I knocked," she said, "but when no one answered, I let myself in."

Although he quickly wrapped the towel around his waist, Kane growled, "It's not like you're looking at anything you haven't seen before, Baptiste."

Her shoulders stiffened and she turned to face him. In a neutral voice she retorted, "That's right. I guess I forgot."

"Ha, ha." Kane went to the closet and took out one of the white bodysuits. It wasn't his first choice of attire, but it was easy to get into. Behind him, he heard a faint, startled intake of breath from Brigid.

He knew she was reacting to the sight of the swirling pattern of scar tissue between his shoulder blades. It was from the injury he had received in the Black Gobi, when he rescued her from the Tushe Gun's genetic mingler. He had shielded her unconscious body from the machine's wild energy discharges with his own. Only the tough, Kevlar-weave coat he'd worn at the time prevented the wound from being fatal.

As it was, she had suffered wounds of her own, far subtler and far more devastating. Her exposure to both the energy discharges and an unknown type of radiation had rendered her barren.

As Kane thrust his arms into the suit, he asked, "What brings you here?"

Matter-of-factly, she answered, "Lakesh collapsed in the command center. He's been taken to the infirmary."

"What's the matter with him?"

Brigid shook her head. "Reba is examining him now, but she suspects it has something to do with his restoration or revitalization or whatever you want to call it."

Kane paused in zipping up the front of the bodysuit. "You mean he's getting old again?"

"We don't know yet."

"Does he want us in the infirmary?"

"No—before he was taken there he asked us to meet with Mariah for a briefing."

Kane's eyebrows arched in surprise. "Why? About what?"

Brigid sighed. "According to her, a huge section of the Antarctic ice sheet is on the brink of slipping off into the sea."

"And what does that mean to us, more or less?"

One corner of Brigid's mouth lifted in a humorless smile. "The end of civilization as we know it, more or less."

Chapter 13

Flat on his back in a darkened examination room, Lakesh closed his eyes, fighting off unconsciousness. He set his teeth against groans dragged out of him by the excruciating pain in his chest. It had crept up to his head, making his skull feel like a huge hollow filled with knives. Auerbach had administered analgesics, but they had yet to take effect.

"I'm going to take a blood sample, Lakesh," DeFore's voice said curtly.

"Get on with it, please."

He felt the cold swab of alcohol at the soft area of his right arm below the bicep, then the jabbing sting of a needle. He didn't move, refusing to allow the fierce pain in his chest to show on his face as DeFore withdrew blood from his arm. Within a few moments, the needle withdrew and a new voice, high and lilting, almost childlike, said, "Relax your arm, Dr. Singh."

Lakesh opened his eyes to see Quavell bending his arm at the elbow, pressing a square of absorbent gauze over the hypodermic puncture.

"I didn't realize you knew anything about medicine," he said to her, dismayed by how raspy his voice sounded.

"I learned very quickly after the destruction of the

Archuleta Mesa installation. I had no choice." Her tone of voice wasn't cold, but it wasn't particularly warm.

Swallowing with difficulty, Lakesh said, "I suppose you did. Just like my people did after January 20, 2001. They had no choice, either."

"Yes." Quavell said nothing more, and he wasn't inclined to engage her in further conversation.

A jumble of images raced through his mind: the fresh spring morning in Kashmir when he had received his acceptance letter from MIT; the plea of his widowed mother to stay in India; his promise, later broken, that he would return when he received his doctorate; his terrible bewilderment, his suffocating sense of betrayal when he glimpsed an Archon and learned the true magnitude of the Totality Concept experiments and the true origin of the technologies at work.

A century before the nuclear megacull of January 20, 2001, enlightened nineteenth-century minds found it fashionable to speculate that Earth's nearest alien neighbors would be found right next door, on the planet Mars.

A hundred years after Victorian era scientists expounded on their theories, Lakesh discovered that not only were extraterrestrial neighbors much closer than the theorists dreamt, but also they had lived on Earth for a very, very, *very* long time.

The mystery of humankind's interaction with another species had haunted Lakesh for more than two hundred years, ever since he first heard about the Archon Directive. He had heard whispers of the existence of aliens, of course. Lakesh at the time was the overseer for Project Cerberus and even he wasn't immune to urban legends and conspiracy theories regarding aliens, mysterious animal mutilations and of Area 51, where captured extraterrestrial spacecraft allegedly underwent retroengineering. But he was a scientist, and he discounted just about every rumor that filtered back to him.

Lakesh subsequently learned that contact with the Archons' forebears had begun literally at the dawn of Earth's history, a relationship and communication that continued unbroken for thousands of years, cloaked by ritual, religion and mystical traditions.

All of them in Cerberus had learned that much of what they had accepted as gospel about the Archons, the Totality Concept and the nukecaust itself was all a ruse, bits of truth mixed in with outrageous fiction. The Archons didn't exist except as a vast cover story, created in the twentieth century and embellished with each succeeding generation. The only so-called Archon on Earth was Balam, the last of an extinct race that had once shared the planet with humankind.

After three years of imprisonment in the Cerberus redoubt, Balam finally revealed the truth behind the Archons and the hybridization program initiated centuries before. Balam claimed that the Archon Directive and later the Directorate existed only as appellations created by the predark government agencies as a control mechanism. Lakesh referred to it as the Oz effect, wherein a single vulnerable entity created the illusion of being the representative of an all-powerful body.

Balam himself may have even coined the term Archon to describe his people. In ancient Gnostic texts, *Archon* was applied to a parahuman world-governing force that imprisoned the divine spark in human souls. Lakesh had often wondered over the last few months if Balam had indeed created that appellation as a cryptic code to warn future generations.

For many years, Lakesh had clung to the belief that the global megacull wasn't humanity's fault at all, but due to the deceptions of Balam's people over the long track of centuries. Now he knew the so-called Archon Directorate hadn't really conquered humanity—it had tempted humanity with the tools to conquer itself.

Ambition, naked greed, the desire for power over others, those were the carrots snapped up gleefully by the decision makers. In order to survive, Balam and his people had deceived humankind, but it was humankind's choice whether to do live down to its worst impulses.

He was still suspicious of Balam's version of the story, but he didn't know if that was due to pragmatism or a denial of accepting the truth.

Suddenly he realized the pain in his body had made a considerable recession. It was no longer as all consuming and he tentatively lifted his head, looking around the dimly lit examination room. A pale shape shifted on a chair near him. "Quavell?"

"No," Domi said. "It's me."

She came to stand by his side, looking down into

his face. He blinked up at her, wondering why she looked so foggy, so blurred around the edges. "Darlingest one," he husked out. "Did I fall asleep?"

"Yes," she answered. "But not for long, maybe half an hour. How are you feeling?"

"Better. A bit better."

"Good," she said softly. She nibbled at her underlip nervously. "We need to talk."

Lakesh didn't care for the implications of her statement, but he said only, "I think I'm ready to be discharged."

DeFore announced from the doorway, "Not yet, you're not."

She strode to the other side of the bed, opposite Domi, the posture of her stocky body telegraphing tension, her dark eyes glinting with worry. More than just worry, Lakesh noted. Outright fear.

Striving for a bantering tone, Lakesh asked, "What has gotten you so agitated today, Doctor?"

DeFore lifted a small capped test tube, holding it between thumb and forefinger. "*This* has, Lakesh."

He squinted at it. At first glance, it appeared to be empty, then he could barely discern tiny, almost invisible specks on the inner wall of the tube, like a scattering of dirt particles.

"This was in your blood sample," DeFore continued grimly. "I used the centrifuge to separate them from the plasma."

Lakesh said nothing for a long tick of time. He exchanged a mystified glance with Domi then ventured, "Dirt? Dirt was in my blood?"

Too stressed out to become really irritated, DeFore declared, "I can't be sure, Lakesh, but I think these are nanites. And since I found millions of nanites in one blood sample, it stands to reason there are billions all through your body."

Lakesh gaped at her in astonishment, too shocked to speak.

Domi demanded, "How did they get there?"

Reba DeFore shook her head. "I have no idea in hell. I was hoping Lakesh might have a theory how they got into his body."

Squeezing his eyes shut, Lakesh heard his voice say, echoing as if from the bottom of a well, "There's only one theory and one solution. Sam, the imperator."

Chapter 14

Mariah Falk sat before the VGA monitor screen, her fingers playing the keyboard with the skill of a concert pianist.

Across the right side of the screen scrolled a constant stream of figures, symbols and numbers. The screen showed a limitless panorama of a gray, angry sea. Then the ocean gave way to glistening, towering cliffs of ice and interminable plains of snow, broken by yawning abysses and jutting peaks. Tiny networks of cracks spread across the crust of snow and ice fields.

Tapping one pattern of cracks with a forefinger, Mariah commented, "The view is from about twenty-three thousand miles up. You can imagine the size of the fault lines to be visible at all. Antarctica must be shaking itself to pieces."

Kane only grunted. He still remembered his reaction of surprise when he learned that Cerberus was uplinked with a pair of satellites. Like everyone bred in the villes, he had been taught that the few satellites still in orbit were free-floating pieces of scrap metal.

From a pocket in her shirt, Brigid took out the badge of her former office as an archivist, a pair of wire-framed, rectangular lensed spectacles, and slipped them over her eyes. Years of inputting predark data and documents, staring at columns of tiny type in Cobaltville's Historical Division had resulted in a minor vision problem.

Still, she squinted at the screen, first leaning down close to it, then moving back. Kane briefly wondered if her vision hadn't been further impaired by the head injury she had suffered several months before, ironically enough in the Antarctic. The only visible sign of the wound that had laid her scalp open to the bone and put her in a coma for several days was a faintly red, horizontal line on her right temple. Her recovery time had been little short of uncanny. Kane was always impressed by the woman's tensile-spring resiliency.

However, he couldn't help but notice how she needed her glasses more and more in the months following her release from the infirmary.

"How can we be so sure that we're not seeing a natural geological phenomenon?" Brigid asked. "After all, geology—the science of the earth itself—was based on catastrophism, the belief that the world was formed from chaos."

Mariah smiled at her, but there was very little humor in it. "In my day, the consensus among scientists was that the next glacial period would come sooner rather than later. Before the nuclear holocaust, the world was already about one-sixth of the way toward average ice-age temperatures. There remained only one final trigger to be pulled to catapult the planet all the way into a major ice age—the great Antarctic ice sheet. Keep in mind the polar cap represents about ninety percent of the world's ice surface.''

''I can understand the dangers of tidal waves and coastal flooding,'' Kane commented. ''But predicting another ice age seems a little extreme.''

''The ice sheet wouldn't melt,'' replied Mariah. ''It will cover some two million square miles of ocean. Ordinarily the world's oceans are poor reflectors of sunlight, but covered with the shield of the massive ice sheet, the seas would divert so much solar energy back into space that the entire atmosphere would be chilled, glaciers would begin to form and a new, perhaps the longest, ice age would begin.''

''Why the longest?'' inquired Kane.

''Once an ice age begins, it can continue growing by a process of positive feedback. More snow and ice increases the albedo of the earth—the proportion of sunlight it reflects back into space, so the climate cools even further.''

''And therefore there's yet more snow and ice,'' Brigid observed. ''On and on in a terminally vicious circle.''

Mariah nodded as if satisfied. ''Exactly.''

Brigid frowned, her expression skeptical. ''But is such slippage likely? I mean, if the nukecaust didn't trigger it—''

''The nuclear winter, what you call skydark, held it back,'' Mariah broke in. ''The seismic disturbances caused by all the atomic explosions certainly loosened the sheet, but the long winter chilled it back into place. The glaciers actually grew and expanded. Now they're thawing again.''

Kane smiled sourly. ''So I suppose that's one thing we can thank skydark for.''

Mariah shook her head in annoyance. ''It was only temporary, a holding action. Your skydark actually made the situation worse. There's more ice to deal with now, and the global cooling will manifest in all sorts of bizarre weather fronts. Masses of warm air will run head-on into entrenched polar air and cause thunderstorms, hail and tornadoes all over the world.''

''But is all of the Antarctic ice so unstable?'' Brigid inquired.

''Antarctica once had a temperate climate with forests and swamps,'' stated Mariah, ''but it changed radically about seventy thousand years ago. Evidence suggests that two separate ice sheets, beginning in two structurally different mountain areas, gradually covered a subsurface trough. The trough separated the main areas of Antarctica by mountain ranges. That's the area of greatest instability.''

''I was under the impression,'' Kane said, ''that ice ages were gradual things.''

''It all depends,'' the woman retorted. ''Many scientists believed that surprisingly quick climatic changes are possible, especially if human tampering disturbs the balance of the average mean temperature.''

''True,'' agreed Brigid. ''Rapid climatic flips might explain the flash-frozen mammoths found in Siberia a couple of hundred years ago. They were so well-preserved, some of them had fresh, undigested grass in their stomachs.''

Mariah gave her an appreciative smile. "Exactly. Studies by the Geological Survey of Canada revealed that the mile-thick blanket of ice that covered central Canada over eight thousand years ago thawed in less than two centuries.''

Kane snorted. "If it takes that long now, I don't see why we should get so fused-out about it. We'll all be long gone before the first snowflake falls.''

"That time frame was for fairly normal circumstances,'' Mariah argued. "As the geologists reconstructed the event, the Canadian ice sheet lay on land that was below sea level. As the bottom layers of ice grew warmer, the sheet began to slip into Hudson Bay, where it broke up into smaller icebergs. Soon a channel formed into which more of the main ice sheet poured, broke up and dispersed. Once the center of the bay had been cleared, the ice sheet to the west slipped into the gap, followed by an equally massive surge of ice from the east.''

Kane looked at her blankly. His "So?'' was intentionally challenging.

Mariah sighed. "Conditions in east Antarctica are currently very similar to those of central Canada nearly nine thousand years ago…much of the land is below sea level.''

Her bright gaze flicked from Kane to Brigid. "I consulted the database on this,'' she said defensively. "I'm not theorizing in the dark.''

The central control center had five dedicated and

eight shared subprocessors, all linked to the mainframe behind the far wall. Two hundred years before, it had been the most advanced model ever built, carrying experimental, error-correcting microchips of such a tiny size that they even reacted to quantum fluctuations. Biochip technology had been employed when it was built, protein molecules sandwiched between microscopic glass-and-metal circuits.

The information contained in the main database may not have been the sum total of all humankind's knowledge, but not for lack of trying. Any bit, byte or shred of information that had ever been digitized was only a few keystrokes and mouse clicks away.

"We're not doubting you," Brigid said reassuringly. "Something is causing the seismic events and coastal flooding on the New Edo island chain."

From the enviro-ops station Bry spoke up, "Samariumville territories are noticing a rise in the water table, too. I've been listening to chatter about it for the past couple of weeks. They're starting to get worried."

Kane and Brigid knew Bry referred to the eavesdropping system he had established through the communications link with the Comsat satellite. Bry had worked on the system for a long time and had managed to develop an undetectable method of patching into the wireless communications channels of all the baronies in one form or another. The success rate wasn't one hundred percent, but he had been able to eavesdrop on a number of the villes and learn about baron-sanctioned operations in the Outlands. He monitored different frequencies on a daily basis.

"What are they so worried about?" Brigid asked him.

Bry ran a hand through his coppery curls. "Actually it doesn't have much to do with the coastal flooding. Apparently somebody ambushed a Mag squad a couple of months ago and they haven't found the perps yet. There's also a report that the main Samariumville arsenal was looted of some pretty big-time weapons. Right at the moment, the Mag Division there is trying to track down some pirates."

Kane shrugged. "No big surprise. That part of the Cific is crawling with pirates."

Bry grinned bleakly. "Yeah, but this bunch supposedly travels around in a dragon ship—"

"Can we get back to the matter at hand?" Mariah broke in with some asperity. "This is a little more important."

Kane smiled and nodded to her graciously. "Pray proceed, Professor Falk."

Mariah said flatly, "In the 1990s, at Byrd Station, a hole drilled 7200 feet into the ice uncovered a layer of lubricating slush. Depending on the internal strength of the ice, a slush-filled crevasse just fifteen to fifty feet deep could fracture through a two-hundred-yard-thick ice shelf. The remains are probably held together by bridges between crevasses until a combination of winds, tides and another season of melting leads to a breakup."

Mariah gestured with her hands to emphasize her

words. "The extra outward pressure of the meltwater counteracts the internal pressure holding the ice together. Crevasses routinely form at the landward side of the shelf as glacial ice pushes past coastal features and flows into the floating ice. The crevasses slowly travel seaward as the ice shelf grows."

"What's the primary cause of the melting?" Kane asked.

"Radar probes made from low-flying aircraft revealed the presence of numerous lakes beneath the ice surface," answered Mariah, "warmed by the heat radiating up from deep within the planet. So if the melting continues at its current accelerated rate, a confluence of catastrophic events—earthquakes, volcanic eruptions and violent storms in the Pacific, all working to tip the globe's spin axis only slightly or even to increase the wobble by a few degrees, would be enough to send the ice sheet crashing into the ocean."

Brigid nodded contemplatively. "So the glacier could reflect back enough sunshine to cause a global cool down, huge tidal waves would roar down on almost every coastal area on Earth?"

"That would be the most immediate effect," Mariah stated grimly. "Hundreds of thousands of lives would be lost instantly, and those who survived to pick up the pieces would find they lived in an ice-covered world with only the lands around the equator warm enough to raise crops. Even in the twentieth century, scientists and military strategists feared that some hostile nation or terrorist group might use nuclear weapons to shake loose the Antarctic sheet and send it plunging into the sea.''

Kane frowned. "Why would anybody want to do that?"

Mariah chuckled but it had no mirth in it, only scorn. "Even with Dr. Singh here to spin yarns, I see you still don't know everything about the twentieth century. We had reached a point in history that might be called a knowledge crisis…we learned to move mountains without knowing where to put them or whether they should even be moved in the first place. In other words, we learned how to turn on the machine, even control a few of its basic functions, but we had no idea at all of how to turn it off.

"We of the scientific community didn't use our knowledge to avert catastrophe—instead, we brought it down upon us. When we used our technologies to move mountains, we ignored nature's reasons for placing them there in the first place. From what Dr. Singh told me about the Totality Concept technology, my fellow scientists were like greedy children set free in a candy store. They stuffed their faces and didn't take into consideration the inevitable consequences of gluttony. They—we—built toward the catastrophes of too much knowledge and not enough wisdom.''

Deliberately trying to sound condescending, Kane said, "Well, maybe now humanity can take a different direction. We won't begin the drive to destroy ourselves again.''

Mariah brushed his observation away with a dismissive gesture. "Cultural evolution will inevitably lead to a similar crisis of knowledge, even though its course and time of development will be different. The knowledge crisis is that every cultural species on every habitable planet in the universe must transcend a critical point in its evolution or become extinct. I mean, it took the planet Earth 4.5 billion years to discover that it was 4.5 billion years old.''

Although Brigid smiled at the remark, Kane only scowled. ''Let's get back to the matter at hand. Assuming the Antarctic ice sheet is about to slip, what can we do about it?''

Mariah looked up at him. ''If it's a natural occurrence, nothing. But if it's being intentionally triggered, like I suspect, through some means of heating underground lakes and such, then conceivably it can be stopped.''

Kane shook his head wearily. ''Who or what would intentionally do something like that? There's nothing down there to work with.''

''We don't know that for sure,'' Brigid pointed out. ''It's one of the most isolated and unexplored regions on Earth.''

''I know,'' he countered sarcastically. ''I've been there, remember?''

''Then you'll remember that underground redoubt we found. We know now a last battalion of high-ranking Nazi officers and scientists escaped to Antarctica on submarines in the last days of World War II. Where there's one base, there may be another.''

Kane uttered a snort of disdain. ''Not even freeze-dried Nazis would benefit by uprooting the polar cap.

Besides, how could you possibly heat a body of water the size of a lake enough to melt three miles worth of ice?''

Mariah answered, ''Believe it or not, there could be several ways to arrange it, but—''

Suddenly lights flashed and needles wavered on the consoles. All of them looked up as a humming tone vibrated from the gateway chamber.

''Incoming jumper,'' Bry announced.

Kane looked behind him at the Mercator map spanning the wall. Only one light blinked and it took him a moment to place its location. ''Redoubt Yankee,'' he said, not bothering to hide the surprise vibrating in his voice.

Mariah swiveled in her chair to look. ''Where is that?''

''Thunder Isle,'' Brigid bit out. ''Where we left Grant.''

Then she and Kane ran through the command center and into the anteroom. They came to a stop facing the armaglass door. Both people refused to speculate on who was gating into Cerberus from Thunder Isle, or the reasons why. Bright flares, like bursts of distant heat lightning, arced on the other side of the armaglass barrier. Manufactured in the last decades of the twentieth century from a special compound that combined the properties of steel and glass, armaglass was used as walls in the jump chambers to confine quantum energy overspills.

The droning hum climbed rapidly in pitch to a hurricane wail, then dropped down to inaudibility as the device cycled through the materialization process.

Kane moved swiftly to the jump platform. Grabbing the handle of the door, he wrenched up on it. He was nearly bowled off his feet by the door flying open, pushed by Grant's shoulder. The big man leaned against it for a moment, eyes glassy and unfocused, breathing heavily. His face and shirt were damp with sweat, and by his labored breathing it was apparent he had been exerting himself before he made the gateway transit.

However, he appeared uninjured, so Kane ventured, "This must hold top honors for being the shortest retirement on record——"

Grant's angry, agitated voice cut through the rest of Kane's words like a cleaver. "It's Zakat. I don't know if he's back from the dead, but wherever he came from, he didn't come alone."

Chapter 15

Grant was as upset as Kane had ever seen him since the day they had embarked on their first Magistrate patrol together, nearly fifteen years before.

His agitation didn't show on his dark face. Grant was one of those men who had the ability to keep his emotions from registering on his features. His emotional control was something that not even his closest associates in the Mag Division had ever been able to fathom, including his partner. Grant could have had mutie borer beetles turned loose on his bare ass, and he would have endured the torture without so much as an "Ouch."

Although to Mariah, perhaps even to Brigid, Grant appeared inscrutable, Kane recognized the naked fear in his eyes, heard it in the timber of his voice, in the way he moved.

As it was, the mention of the name Zakat sent shivers of dread streaking up and down Kane's and Brigid's spines. Their breath caught in their throats.

Incredulous, Kane half snarled, "Zakat? *Grigori* Zakat?"

"The one and only," Grant rumbled, stepping clumsily off the platform, careful not to bump his left arm on the jump-chamber door. Curtly he reported what he had seen from the shore of Thunder Isle.

"Are you sure it was Zakat?" Brigid demanded. "You only saw him in Newyork, in bad light—"

"Not only am I sure," Grant snapped, "I exchanged pleasantries with the son of bitch no more than an hour ago. He recognized me at the same time I recognized him. Shizuka sailed back to New Edo just in case he and his crew tried making a raid."

Grant stalked into the command center, favoring his left leg. "I came back through the jungle to the installation to gate here."

"What was Zakat doing?" Brigid asked.

"He cut and run," Grant answered. "Or that's what it looked like. Maybe his crew suffered too many casualties for them to want to mix it up with even a handful of Tigers." He shook his head in frustration. "I really don't know."

Stopping near the enviro-ops station, Grant glared at Kane accusingly. "You told me he was dead...that you threw his ass off a cliff."

"No, I didn't," Kane shot back. "I said he fell into a chasm. I didn't say I saw his body."

"You didn't say you didn't, either," Grant countered, the anger now very pronounced in his voice. He advanced on Kane. "That was one of the first things drilled into us in the academy—make sure of your kills."

Kane's jaw muscles knotted. "I wasn't about to climb down God only knew how far to check the bastard's pulse! You wouldn't have, either."

Grant scoffed, a sneer twisting his lips and turning his features into something ugly. The two men stood almost toe-to-toe. Grant opened his mouth to voice a profane rebuke, but Brigid insinuated herself between the two men. She was very aware of all eyes turned to the confrontation. She had witnessed Kane's and Grant's disagreements before, but generally it never went beyond an insult or two.

Now the two men glared at each other, eyes locked and unblinking, tension crackling between them like static electricity before a thunderstorm. She knew the source of the tension—Kane was angry about Grant's decision to stay in New Edo, and Grant was angry that one of Kane's unfinished bits of business from the past threatened the new life he hoped to build there.

"Let's knock it off," Brigid murmured to them in a warning, whispering singsong. "We've got a lot of matters to contend with, which won't be solved by sniping at each other. We've got a couple of missions to perform—what we need to do now is find out which one takes the higher priority."

Grant and Kane glanced down at her, then they stepped away. Anger still glinted in their eyes, particularly in Grant's, but a bit of the dangerous energy in the room ebbed. The words *mission* and *priority* struck responsive chords with them, reminding both men of Magistrate Division briefing sessions. Years of conditioning died hard. Though neither man replied, Brigid could easily guess the kind of thoughts spinning through their minds.

Magistrates were a highly conservative, duty-bound group. The customs of enforcing the law and obeying orders were ingrained almost from birth. The Magistrates submitted themselves to a grim and unyielding discipline, because they believed it was necessary to reverse the floodtide of chaos and restore order to postholocaust America.

Magistrates were proud that each of them accepted the discipline voluntarily, so by nature their rigid self-control won out over raw emotions, at least temporarily.

Taking advantage of the respite from the hostilities, Mariah asked, "Who is this Zakat?"

"That's a good question," Kane replied. "Even after all this time, I still haven't made up my mind."

Although he, Brigid and Grant had briefly crossed paths with Grigori Zakat in Russia, they hadn't been formally introduced until they contended with him over possession of the facets of the Chintamani Stone, also known as the Shining Trapezohedron.

They were pieces of an inestimably ancient artifact predating humanity's rule of the earth. The existence of the black stone had been hinted at through all the ages of humankind, whispered about since the dawn of recorded history, to the near annihilation of the human species in the nukecaust nearly two centuries before.

The stone had been known by many names, by many peoples, of civilizations both primitive and advanced—Lucifer's Stone, the *kala,* the Kaa'ba, the Chintamani Stone, the Shining Trapezohedron. Al-

ways it was associated with the concept of a key that
unlocked either the door to enlightenment or madness.
As humanity climbed up the ladder of evolution, the
stone was treasured by them, worshiped. It crossed
strange lands and seas that no longer existed, and it
sank with Atlantis and was recovered by the forerunners of the Egyptians. It rested in an underground
crypt between the paws of the Sphinx before the
Flood. It was found aeons later, split by priests and
scattered across the earth.

It served as the centerpiece, the spiritual focal point
of Balam's people, the First Folk, even after it had
been fragmented and the facets scattered from one
end of the earth to the other. He claimed that through
it, they glimpsed all possible futures to which their
activities might lead.

But the Black Stone was far more than a calculat-
ing device that extrapolated outcomes from actions.
Balam had said, "It brings into existence those outcomes."

He had referred to the stone as a channel to "si-
dereal space," where many tangential points of reality
lay adjacent to each other, the parallel casements of
the universe. He had also called it something else, a
doorway to "lost Earth," and the memory of those
two words still sent a chill down Kane's spine. Even
now he found it almost impossible to grasp the concept of a multitude of realities coexisting with his
own. He couldn't wrap the fingers of his mind around
it. The notion turned to smoke and drifted away.

Grigori Zakat hadn't understood it, either, but that

ignorance hadn't prevented him from embarking on a quest to recover all the pieces of the stone, following a path so many others had trod before him. His life was dedicated to the accruing of personal power, according to an esoteric religious tenet he practiced.

The Russian assumed if there were people of great power, then it stood to reason there were objects of equally great power, perhaps far older than humanity itself, swirling with forces that defied any attempts to measure or evaluate them.

Kane had believed for over a year that Zakat's dreams of power lay entombed with him in the eternal darkness of a subterranean abyss, deep beneath the mountains at the border of Tibet and China.

Forcing a smile to his lips, Kane turned to Mariah. "He's an acquaintance, an old enemy. I never expected to hear from him again, especially not in the company of—"

He trailed off and directed a puzzled glance toward Grant. "Did I hear you right? He was with a boatload of Vikings?"

Grant nodded brusquely. "They looked like pictures I've seen."

Mariah eyed him suspiciously. "Where would he find Vikings?"

Grant looked at her with angry impatience. "How the hell do I know? I can only tell you what I saw— a bunch of men in armor carrying shields with swastikas on them."

"Swastikas?" echoed Brigid in disbelief. "Are you sure?"

Growling deep in his throat, Grant limped over to a desk. Absently Kane realized Grant favored the same leg Zakat had caused to be fractured in the Museum of Natural History. He had also suffered from strained ligaments, abrasions and internal bruising. The injuries had been inflicted, by of all things, the preserved carcass of a blue whale.

Grant snatched up a pen and a notebook from the desk and hastily scrawled a design on the paper. He handed it to Brigid. "That's what I saw. Is that or is that not a swastika?"

Brigid stared at the drawing for so long and so silently Grant almost repeated the question. When she finally spoke, her voice was a hushed, hoarse whisper. "Yes and no. It is a swastika but not of the type we associate with Nazi Germany. It's something a lot worse."

She swept her jade-hard gaze over the people in the command center. "We need to have a briefing, stat. Somebody find out if Lakesh can attend. Either way, whoever wants to be involved in this, convene in the cafeteria in ten minutes."

THE CERBERUS REDOUBT had an officially designated briefing room on the third level. Big and blue walled, it was equipped with ten rows of the theater-type chairs facing a raised speaking dais and a rear-projection screen. It was built to accommodate the majority of the installation's personnel, back before the nukecaust when military and scientific advisers visited. It hadn't been used since Lakesh reactivated the installation except to watch old movies on DVD and laser disks in storage.

Because the briefings rarely involved more than a handful of people, they were always convened in the more intimate dining hall. Grant, Brigid, Mariah, Philboyd and Kane sat around a table, sharing a pot of coffee. Access to genuine coffee was one of the inarguable benefits of living as an exile in the redoubt. Real coffee had virtually vanished after the skydark, since all of the plantations in South and Central America had been destroyed.

An unsatisfactory synthetic gruel known as "sub" replaced it. Cerberus literally had tons of freeze-dried packages of the authentic article in storage, as well as sugar and powdered milk.

By way of a preamble, Brigid declared, "Lakesh is still undergoing examination and won't be joining us. Domi elected to stay with him, to sit this one out unless we need her."

Kane noticed that Brigid had not arrived in the dining hall loaded down with sheaves of computer printouts, maps, diagrams or other visual aids. "I guess you don't need any reference material," he commented.

She cast him a slightly reproving glance. "Not this time. I've had this information in my head for months, ever since we found that Nazi installation in the Antarctic. I never could quite figure out why it was there, but now hearing about the melting of the ice sheet and the reappearance of Zakat in a dragon ship…" She trailed off and shrugged.

"Now you think you've figured it out?" Grant demanded.

"I do," Brigid replied confidently. "And it fits in with all the long hours of research at the computer."

As a historian by training and career, she didn't find research to be a labor. Rather, it was the breath of life itself. Unlike her years spent cataloging and revising selected pieces of human history, in Cerberus she had unrestricted access to everything and anything in the main database. If nothing else, the freedom to dip her probing intellect into that well-spring of information made her exile worth a termination warrant hanging over her head.

Due to her eidetic memory, anything she read or saw or even heard was impressed indelibly on her mind. She supposed simply possessing an encyclopedic memory made her intellect something of a fraud, at least compared to the staggeringly high IQ of Lakesh. Although Kane often accused her of using her photographic memory to make herself appear far more knowledgeable than she actually was, she viewed her ability as a valuable resource that had nothing to do with ego.

Linking her fingers together on the tabletop, Brigid announced, "I think Grigori Zakat somehow found Ultima Thule, a nation of Aryan superbeings, progenitors of the Teutonic peoples."

Philboyd's forehead wrinkled in consternation. "I never heard of that place."

"I'm not surprised," Brigid responded smoothly,

"since it was allegedly underground, located in the so-called hollow earth."

"What?" Mariah demanded. "There's no such thing. That was disproved many times. It's crackpotism."

Recalling his and Brigid's travails in the subterranean kingdom of Agartha, Kane said, "Hear her out."

Brigid threw him a quick smile. "I won't disagree the theories of a hollow earth were pretty much discredited, but not all the questions about the structure of our planet were ever satisfactorily answered, either.

"The British astronomer Edmund Halley—of comet fame—proposed that the earth might consist of several concentric spheres placed inside one another in the manner of a Chinese box puzzle. Halley proposed his theory in the seventeenth century, when scientific knowledge about Earth was still primitive.

"As time went on, the improbability of a hollow Earth became apparent to most scientists and scholars, but Halley's theories inspired an American eccentric named John Cleves Symmes. Like Halley, Symmes thought the earth was made up of five concentric spheres, but he postulated huge openings, popularly called 'Symmes Holes,' at each of the poles."

Philboyd and Mariah snorted in disdain almost at the same time. Grant favored them with scowls, but they ignored him.

Mariah said, "I know a little bit about this, due to my training in geology. In 1926, Admiral Richard Byrd made his first flight over the North Pole, and in 1929 he performed the same feat at the South Pole.

As history records, Admiral Byrd did not find any gaping holes. As I recall, the Symmes Holes were supposed to be over one thousand miles in diameter, so they would have been pretty hard to overlook. They never showed up in any satellite photos, either.''

Brigid nodded agreeably but said, ''There was a school of thought that insisted Byrd actually *did* discover the big hole at the South Pole and actually flew a good way into the interior of the earth. But these ideas had some influence on Nazi Germany. They sent out several expeditions in the hopes of finding these polar holes and thus making contact with Ultima Thule.''

''And what is this place exactly?'' Grant demanded.

''In ancient lore, Ultima Thule was known as the capital of Hyperborea, a kingdom in the polar regions. Tradition has it that Hyperboreans were in contact with various nonhuman cultures. Descendants of the Thulians who emigrated to other areas of the planet became the templates for the Norse religions, their pantheon of gods and demigods like Odin, Frey, Thor and others. One of the tenets of the Nazi party was that the Germanic peoples were citizens by descent of Thule. In fact, the forerunner of the Nazi party, perhaps even the power behind it, was the Thule Gesellschaft.''

''The what?'' Grant asked, a dangerous edge in his voice.

''The Thule Society,'' Brigid answered, completely unperturbed. ''It was actually a front for a whole web of secret societies that had similar racist and anti-Semitic occultist roots. Among the members of these groups were a number of influential people. If the Thule Society was a cult, then Adolph Hitler was its high priest.

"Most historians are entirely ignorant of Hitler's occult background. The Nazis were being manipulated, through Hitler, by the Thule Society. Everything Hitler did revolved around ancient prophecies concerning Ultima Thule. He viewed the Third Reich as the force by which to bring about Ragnarok, the final conflict of fire and ice. After that, the Frost Giants would reign over the earth. This, of course, ties in with another belief of the Thule Society and the Nazis...the doctrine of Eternal Ice."

Philboyd squinted at her. "What kind of doctrine is that?"

"Essentially a ridiculous one," Brigid retorted. "The doctrine of Eternal Ice postulated that the world would be destroyed by vast blocks of ice that fill outer space. They will slow down Earth's orbital rotation, freeze the world solid, then another cycle of planetary evolution will begin."

"That's absolutely absurd," Mariah muttered in disgust. "No scientific basis at all."

"You'll get no argument from me," replied Brigid. "When World War II ended, Hitler and a battalion boarded a submarine and escaped first to Argentina, then to an already established base at the South Pole."

Almost unconsciously, Brigid lifted a hand and

with a fingertip traced the scar on her right temple. "Which, of course, some of us have visited. When the Allies learned what had happened, they dispatched Admiral Richard Byrd and a scientific expedition…this expedition was in fact an army to attack the Nazi base, but they were no match for their superior weaponry."

Brigid took a deep breath, then slowly exhaled it. "As far as the Nazis were concerned, they were the outer-earth representatives of the inner earth, which accounted for their racial superiority."

"What does this have to do with Zakat, exactly?" Kane asked.

"I think it's pretty obvious," Brigid said calmly. "Grigori Zakat somehow found Ultima Thule and was accepted into their society."

Mariah and Philboyd stared at Brigid wide-eyed as if she had just sprouted a third eye in the middle of her forehead. "Oh, come *on!*" exclaimed Philboyd, sounding scandalized. "You can't really believe any of this. You can't expect us to believe any of it!"

Kane narrowed his eyes, saying coldly, "None of us really gives much of a shit if you believe it or not. One thing I've learned not to believe is a chain of coincidence—Zakat returning from the dead in the company of Vikings who, according to legend hail from the Antarctic, at around the same time disturbances going on there come to our attention."

He turned toward Brigid. "But—and this is a big but—how in the hell did Zakat get from the bottom of an underground cliff in Asia to the South Pole?"

Brigid shrugged. "I can only speculate. He obviously survived the fall and made his way back to the Trasilunpo monastery. There was a gateway unit there, remember?"

Kane nodded. "I almost forgot. It was part of the old Sverdze project. The only aspect of the Totality Concept fully shared with the Soviet Union. So from there, he gated to the mat-trans unit outside of the Nazi base in Antarctica. Fits the facts, I guess."

"What facts?" Mariah shrilled angrily. "For God's sake, all I've heard so far is specious science, two hundred-year-old crackpot conspiracy theories and a lot of conclusion jumping!"

Grant slammed the flat of his hand on the table with such force coffee jumped and sloshed out of cups. Between clenched teeth he grated, "Fact one—an evil bastard the three of us faced before is sailing around a place I want to make my home. He's already shown his willingness to kill and rob the people of New Edo. Fact two—if Brigid says the warriors I saw him with are from Ultima Thule and Ultima Thule is in the South Pole, that's good enough for me."

He paused and glared accusingly at Philboyd and Mariah. "And what she says should be good enough for you, too."

The two scientists did not meet the man's furious gaze. They cast their eyes downward in shame.

"Fact three," interjected Kane. "You, Mariah, are the one who theorized that someone was trying to trigger a new ice age. I asked you who would have the nerve and wherewithal to pull off something like that. Now we know.''

"We may have a suspect,'' Philboyd said, a less argumentative note in his tone, "but not a method. That would be pretty big order even for a hostile nation.''

Thoughtfully, Mariah said, "Not necessarily. In the mid-1990s Russian scientists using ground radar and artificial seismic waves discovered a vast warm water lake under the Antarctic. It lay under five thousand feet of solid ice and was approximately three hundred miles long by forty miles wide.''

"Why wasn't it frozen?'' Kane asked.

Mariah's eyes acquired a troubled glint. "Two theories were proposed—first was that heat from the earth's interior has kept it from freezing, and the second was that the lake hadn't time enough to freeze after a more temperate period that ended about five thousand years ago.''

"In that case,'' Kane said, "couldn't some sort of incendiary agents like HDX or phosphorus be dumped in the lake to raise the temperature even higher?''

Mariah nodded reluctantly. "That's very possible.''

"Yes, it is,'' Brigid agreed. "And now that we know, what are we going to do about it?''

Chapter 16

As was the Thulian custom and the Valkyrie's right, Sif chose the warrior who had made the most kills to join her and the warlord in the captain's cabin.

For Zakat it was a less a victory celebration than a confirmation of his devotion to the thesis of causitry. For Volstag, it meant an end to several celibate months at sea. As for Sif, it was a chance to once again practice an ancient goddess tradition—and plunge into carnality with the same wild abandon she had plunged into battle.

Naked, she knelt between an equally naked Volstag and Zakat, with her unbound hair and large breasts dangling. Groaning, Volstag pumped his hips slowly, sliding his erect organ back and forth into her warm, wet mouth.

Zakat stood behind her on wide-braced legs, firmly gripping her flaring hips and thrusting into her with deep, practiced strokes. He kept his eyes on Volstag, a fair-skinned giant of a man whose weather-bleached yellow hair hung to his shoulders. The Russian found him as attractive as Sif did.

Part of Grigori Zakat's duties as a Khylsty priest was to oversee and participate in so-called communal sin, which was simply a euphemism for an indiscriminate sexual orgy among the male and female apostles. He had been delighted to learn that the Thulians practiced a similar ritual, although their views on bisexuality were a bit more restricted.

Like other elements in their culture, the conceptions of their gods underwent constant growth and development. Zakat had learned that among the earliest historical knowledge of the Teutonic peoples were the primitive fertility practices associated with a goddess called Nerthus—who, unsurprisingly, was still a favorite deity in Ultima Thule. This goddess enthusiastically engaged in coitus with multiple male partners on the eve of every planting season.

As if she were an incarnation of Nerthus, Sif groaned around the mouthful of Volstag's hard flesh as Zakat's steady strokes rocked her entire body, causing her to butt the man's lower belly with her head. The experience was enormously exciting for the young warrior, and he orgasmed quickly, crying out hoarsely to Odin.

Volstag withdrew from her mouth as Zakat increased the speed and depth of his thrusts. Sif shivered, trembled and spasmed. With a high-voiced keening, she shuddered through one climax, then another. When her third orgasm shook her, she dropped her upper body writhing onto the sleeping pallet and Zakat allowed himself his own release. He clenched his teeth, not allowing any sound to escape as he poured his sperm into her.

Zakat made eye contact with Volstag and the slight smile of triumph never left his lips. Volstag stared at him, face sheened with sweat, but eyes full of admiration. Still implanted deeply inside the gasping Sif, Zakat gestured imperiously toward the door with his gloved right hand. "You may go now."

The warrior ducked his head deferentially, gathered his clothes and left the cabin. Slowly, Zakat withdrew from Sif's sodden sheath and ran his left hand over her ample flanks. Sighing, she stretched out on the pallet, a faint smile of utter satisfaction visible at the corners of her mouth.

Until the gray-eyed Russian had come into her life, the Valkyrie had easily dominated all her men. But Grigori Zakat could not be dominated—his will was as unyielding as iron, and though he wasn't as tall or as strong as even the smallest Thulian warrior, Sif found he could give pleasure beyond all her previous experience.

Leaving her to sleep, Zakat rose and pulled on a leather jerkin and left the cabin. He went to the quarterdeck of the *Fafnir* and stood at the taffrail. The moonlight danced in arabesque luminosity from the waves, delicate dabs of white light that shifted with the movement of the sea.

The American coast had long fallen away eastward. Only open ocean lay on all sides. Far to the south, thunderheads massed in the sky. The night was full of the sounds of the sea—the faint hiss and slap of prow-cleaved water, the creak of planks and tackle, the distant splashing of waves, the boom of taut sails and the humming vibration of the wind singing through the rigging.

The crew slept or spoke in hushed whispers. The Thulians were superstitious, always on the alert for good or bad omens, but even their fears of goblins, Frost Giants and trolls could not dim their courage. Even the prospect of death did not so much frighten them as inspire them. They believed that a hero's death on Earth would mean immortality in Valhalla.

Zakat had ordered the diesel engines to be allowed to rest while maintenance was performed on them, at least for the first leg of the journey. He and the Thulians would begin the return trip home as their Norse ancestors had done—driven by the winds of the gods.

Gods. He whispered the word beneath his breath and smiled sourly. The Thulians were not gods, but some of them didn't know that. When he had first met them, he hadn't been sure himself. Once he learned the language of Ultima Thule, in actuality an archaic Germanic dialect, he realized why there was confusion regarding their status as deities or humans.

Norse mythology was never a unified body of doctrine, but a composite of legends that varied from age to age. The Thulians believed the ancient creation tale of their origin, which was described as the spontaneous result of a union between fire and ice in a chasm called Gin-nungagap. From that elemental conflict arose the pantheon of Nordic gods, the Frost Giants, even humanity.

All fell under the leadership of Odin, who had been known as Wotan, Wodan and Wothenjaz. The latter designation had been adopted as hereditary title of chieftainship in Ultima Thule.

Odin was the particular protector of warriors, and he sent his Valkyries, the choosers of the slain, to bring him heroes who had died on the battlefield. In Valhalla, the Hall of the Slain, they fought and feasted until the day of the final world battle, when they rode forth as Odin's host. This was Ragnarok, a veritable Armageddon that would result in the destruction of the universe by fire. Then a new world would rise out of the sea, and a new age would begin.

Zakat had heard it all during his first few weeks in Ultima Thule, but he interpreted the gods as being heroic men who were elevated to divinity, a race of people who became the basis of the Nordic religions. He theorized that the entire Niebelung cycle of legends was derived from the tales of Thule and the advanced civilization existing there. The Norse myths themselves were coded sacred knowledge of the kingdom and its people, passed down to Teutonic and Scandinavian tribes.

But thousands of years ago, a cataclysmic event caused a shifting of the continents and Ultima Thule vanished, except as a collection of distorted myths and legends. Historians, academics and folklorists managed to revive an interest in the old tales. And as Zakat had reason to know for certain, the Nazi interest in the lost land of Ultima Thule was far more than academic.

Zakat rolled his shoulders, wincing slightly at the tightness of the scar tissue. He had learned about the Nazis' deep connection with the Thulians the hardest way possible—with his own pain and blood. He easily recalled the day Wothenjaz—old, white bearded and one eyed, yet still powerful—administered the final ordeal of acceptance.

After tying him to a timber, the warlord of Ultima Thule announced he himself would deliver two times ten lashes to the interloper's back. That way he could be sure none of the people Zakat had swayed with his magnetic eyes and persuasive words would show him mercy.

With tears in her eyes, Sif handed Wothenjaz the whip, its tip weighted with a stone the size of a plum. Small, sharpened bones were knotted into its plaited length. Wothenjaz flexed the whip, cracked it in the air above his head and made everyone jump.

The huge man delivered ten lashes to Zakat's bare back, then stopped to rest. Zakat uttered no outcry, nor did he even appeared to notice how the flesh from his shoulders to his hips was sliced and slashed. As an ordained Khylsty priest, he knew pain was only of the body, and the body was the servant of the mind and the spirit. Pain could thus be controlled.

Wothenjaz delivered ten more lashes. Despite the frigid temperatures, he was drenched with sweat when it was over, panting and shaking. Zakat remained so motionless that he overheard murmurs from the onlookers that he was dead. When his hands were untied, he took a savage satisfaction in turning away from the post and hearing the gasps of astonishment from the crowd.

Even Wothenjaz's single, cobalt-blue eye glinted with apprehension when Zakat calmly approached him. "You understand why this had to be done," the chieftain said.

Zakat nodded. "And you understand why I will do what has to be done."

A faint, scraping sound from behind him pulled Grigori Zakat back to the present. He didn't turn away from the rail, but his spine stiffened.

"How do you do it, Zakat?" The voice was soft, low, barely above a whisper.

As Chaffee stepped up behind him, Zakat asked calmly, "Do what, tovarich?"

"Get these barbarians to obey you, to kiss your ass, to do anything you want." The man's voice was raspy with resentment, his tone brittle and bitter.

"I thought I made that clear to you when you joined us," Zakat replied. "The Thulians worship strength and force of will. Their culture demands it. They have no place in their philosophy for kindness, because they consider it a sign of weakness. They know no other way of life."

"That's not what I mean," Chaffee growled. "You're not one of them, so they shouldn't be following you. You're nothing but a skinny, scheming Russkie."

"I told you I am a Khylsty priest, did I not?" Zakat sounded inoffensive, almost bored. "The deity of my religion is power, and the way one communes with such a god is to recognize and accept one's destiny. We are all agents of it. What is happening now is supposed to happen. That is the law of power."

"What the fuck does that mean?" Chaffee asked sneeringly.

Zakat laughed, as if he found the question truly funny. "If you obey the law of power you therefore shall gain more. It is a cumulative effect, known in my religion as causitry."

Chaffee snorted. "You're so full of shit, Russkie. I think you're more than a Russkie—I think you're a goddamn mind-mutie and you put the whammy on them. They're simple-minded so it worked on them. It didn't work on me."

"Even if that's true, what difference does it make? We had an agreement, a bargain. You wished a new life, I wished a method by which to bring about the prophecies of Ragnarok. Afterward we both will be men of power and influence."

"There's about one hundred kilos of HDX in the hold," Chaffee snapped, his voice rising. "And other incendiary agents. Not to mention weapons, ammo and about six tons of dried food and seeds. That's all pretty much due to me."

Zakat sighed, as if weary. "Did I ever say otherwise? When your friend Breeze first proposed you and I might be of some use to each other, you were more than willing to leave your old life behind."

"That's because you convinced me if I wanted to save my life and start a new one, then throwing in with you was my only option."

"You no longer believe that?"

Chaffee didn't step closer. He remained standing behind Zakat. Moonlight flashed dully from metal in

Chaffee's right hand. "I don't know what to believe," he replied in a gravelly whisper. "Convince me all over again. What are the prophecies?"

In a flat, matter-of-fact voice, Zakat stated, "As the end draws nigh, there will be famine and strife. This final period is called Ragnarok, which means 'the twilight of the gods.' Brother will slay brother and son will not spare his own father."

He paused. "Has this not been happening as a result of the war between your country's barons?"

When Chaffee didn't respond, Zakat continued, "Three continuous years of deadly winter will then ensue, after which mountains will crumble and every bond between man and Earth will be broken. The Fenris wolf will finally be loosed and will run around the world with jaws agape. Its lower jaw will drag along the ground—its upper jaw will touch the clouds. Its eyes will burn with a strange fire, and its nostrils will breathe flames. Loki, too, will be freed. He will rig a ghastly vessel, *Naglfar,* a ship made of dead men's flesh.

"With ragged sails and a crew of rotting corpses, he will sail up from his daughter's realm of the dead. And the Midgard serpent will slither ashore, winding its way over fields and meadows. To the south the heavens will be torn asunder.

"From the country beyond—the frightening, unknown Muspellsheim, land of fire that existed long before Odin and his brothers created the world—will come a mighty host of riders clad in shining vestments, armed with fiery swords. Everything will burst into flame and burn as they charge forward, and the great rainbow bridge will collapse under their weight. The final, decisive and bloody battle will be fought at a place called the Plain of Vigrid.

"Odin will be devoured by the Fenris wolf. Thor and the Midgard serpent will slay each other, as will Heimdall and Loki. The whole world will go up in flames. Even Yggdrasil, the great world tree, will burn. When the flames die down, the world will be a smoking ruin. The charred remains will sink below the surface of the sea and disappear."

After a long period of silence, Chaffee grunted, "Will that be the end?"

"No," Zakat replied. "Out of the sea a new earth, green and lovely, will grow, fertile as a dream. With fields that sow themselves, and an abundance of fish and game. No one will go hungry anymore, nor will anyone suffer from the cold. An end has been put to all evil. The earth has been washed clean. A new life may begin! The old world is no more. Not a single stone remains of the old fortress of the gods."

Chaffee laughed, a sinister, sibilant hiss. "You don't believe this prophecy, do you?"

Zakat shrugged. "Why not?"

"Because you have to bring all of it about. That's not a prophecy."

"Then what is it?" Zakat asked with studied indifference.

"A conspiracy."

"Is that really so important? Thule will resettle in the lands around the equator…the Green Belt, I call it. The climate zones of the rest of the world will shift southward, degrading their ability to feed themselves. They will war with each other for scraps of food, for parcels of dry land. Ragnarok will come true. What difference does it make if it is prodded?''

"It makes a difference to me," growled Chaffee. He took a shuffling step forward. "With you dead, these barbarian bastards will lose interest in making it come true."

"Thule is still their home," Zakat reminded him. "And you complained about not liking cold weather."

Zakat felt the kiss of a gun bore pressing into the back of his neck.

"We can go someplace else," Chaffee replied.

"With you in charge?" Zakat asked mildly.

"Why not?"

Zakat started to shrug, then thought better of it. "A moment ago you accused me of being a mind-mutie. I am not, although I will admit to having a degree of psionic influence over the Thulians."

"I knew it," Chaffee spit, digging the tip of the pistol harder into Zakat's neck.

"One Thulian in particular," Zakat went on, unperturbed.

Chaffee snorted out a contemptuous laugh. "Sif? I'm not worried about that giant whore of yours. She can die from a slug just like any other gaudy slut."

"Providing you can get the drop on her, tovarich."

Chaffee started to snort again—then he heard Sif's low laugh, as merciless and hard as the ring of steel against steel. Her hand closed around his right wrist, tightening so swiftly it felt as if the jaws of a vise crushed tendon against bone.

Sif bore him backward, away from Zakat, grasping both his wrists, shaking him like a terrier would shake a rat. The Ruger Redhawk revolver fell from Chaffee's nearly numb fingers and thumped loudly to the deck. Zakat bent to pick it up. "Threatening me with my own weapon," he murmured musingly. "How uncivil."

Sif held him easily, arms stretched wide, his wrists trapped within her hands. Moonlight gleamed in satiny highlights on the curves of her heavy breasts, sleek thighs and long, muscular legs. She smiled in adoration at Zakat.

Chaffee snarled in fearful anger. "Tell this oversize slut of yours to let me go—"

"What an ugly thing to say," Zakat said to him with quiet reproach. He waggled the gun barrel under Chaffee's nose. "I abhor ugliness. And so does Sif." He spoke a word of Thulian to her.

The knuckles of her hands distended as she tightened her grip. The crunch of bone came faintly as she crushed Chaffee's splinted left wrist, only half healed of its fracture. He screamed in pain and wrenched and heaved in frenzied motion, trying to tear himself free of Sif's agonizing grasp.

When he realized he couldn't struggle loose, he sagged, face gleaming with sweat, panting laboriously through an open mouth. He croaked, "Go ahead, then. Shoot me and be done with it."

"Shoot you?" Zakat shook his head, smiling sadly. "Bullets are costly."

Carefully he laid the revolver on the deck and toed it away. He stepped very close to Chaffee. "I've spoken to you about my Khylsty training, but I didn't mention to you one of my priestly duties."

He held up his hands before Chaffee's eyes. "I was trained in the art of making sacrifices with my hands. When I was first indoctrinated, I was given an infant to strangle, then a young boy...then women, old men and finally a man of my own age and stature."

His voice dropped to a crooning whisper. "I offered many sacrifices over the years, snapped many necks between these fingers...but now, because of one man, a man named Kane, I can no longer perform that priestly duty."

Zakat slapped Chaffee lightly on the cheek with his gloved right hand. "This hand is dead. I feel nothing in it. It was broken, you see...crushed, all the nerves severed. I can no longer function fully as a priest, and therefore I owe Kane a great spiritual debt."

Chaffee swallowed hard. "Then why are we going back to Thule?"

A smile stretched Zakat's lips, and his teeth gleamed in the moonlight. "Kane will come soon enough. That I do know. It is always best to meet an enemy on your home ground."

"And what about me?"

Zakat regarded him contemplatively. Then his left hand darted to Chaffee's neck. His fingers and thumb dug into the man's throat muscles, grinding them against the windpipe and the jugular vein.

Chaffee made a choked cry between his teeth. Terror flooded his eyes, and he threw himself back and forth. With a sudden lunge, Grigori Zakat put his right arm around Chaffee's head, shoving the back of his neck into the crook of his elbow.

To Sif he grunted, "Let him go."

Sif obliged, and Zakat whirled the man around until the small of his back bent over the rail. Chaffee's eyes bulged, his face purpling. Exertion caused the veins at the sides of Zakat's head to stand out in throbbing relief.

Chaffee snatched at Zakat's hand, his wrist, trying to prise his fingers from his throat. With a savage wrench, Zakat twisted Chaffee's head until his contorted face leered over his left shoulder. The snapping of vertebrae sounded like the breaking of a rotten tree branch.

Breathing heavily, Zakat straightened and let the twitching body slide over the rail into the sea. Chaffee entered the water with barely a splash. Sif leaned over the rail, watching the widening ripples, breathing heavily as if aroused. With her eyes bright, she husked out, "My darling...when this man Kane comes under your hand, I will help you kill him in the same way."

Zakat chuckled. "Thank you, sweet Sif. But such a death for Kane is too undignified...and far too merciful."

Chapter 17

The thing on the slide kicked its triple-jointed legs feebly. They didn't have the strength to propel its bulbous, dark gray body in either direction, even though the legs could swivel forward and backward in the sockets perforating both sides of its torso.

Lakesh straightened from the eyepieces of the electron microscope and rubbed the bridge of his nose. "So that's a nanite." He wasn't asking a question; he was making a statement.

"A type of one, anyhow," Reba DeFore said. "I've found several different kinds floating around in the blood sample."

Domi took Lakesh's place at the microscope. Bending her white-haired head, she said, "It looks like a bug, like a dust mite or something."

She stepped away and looked at DeFore with an intent, ruby-eyed gaze. "What the hell are nanites, anyway?"

Before the medic could formulate a response, Lakesh answered, "Toward the end of the twentieth century, engineers developed nanotechnology—or machines built from 'small' technology." He crooked his fingers when he said "small" to indicate quotation marks.

"Just how small is small?" Domi asked.

Lakesh nodded toward the microscope. "Obviously *very* small. Microscopic. The prefix *nano* refers to one-billionth of a part. By the beginning the twenty-first century, nanites were even smaller than one-billionth."

Domi frowned skeptically. "How could they make machines that tiny?"

Lakesh smiled at her affectionately. "The best way to miniaturize computer parts was through a process known as photolithography. New advances in that process produced an entire host of microscopic devices. I remember when the world's smallest battery was created that way—one hundred of them fit into a single human red blood cell."

DeFore crossed her arms over her bosom. "You certainly had at least that many in your blood cells—and now, finally, I understand how your youth was restored." She paused and added darkly, "And why you can't take it for granted."

Lakesh didn't respond to her oblique reference about his physical condition. Both of them had talked the matter to death over the past few months. Even after five years, he and DeFore still disagreed on a wide variety of matters. She had accused him of being overdemanding and high-handed, and sometimes he was sure she outright distrusted him, particularly after supplying Balam with the destination-lock codes of the redoubt's gateway. Quite possibly she thought he was lying about the means of restored youth.

He couldn't blame her about that, not really. She

didn't even pretend to understand how it had happened. The process Lakesh described flew so thoroughly in the face of all her medical training—as limited as it was—he might as well have attributed the cause to an angelic intervention.

All DeFore really knew was that six months earlier she had watched Mohanduas Lakesh Singh step into the gateway chamber as a hunched-over, spindly old man who appeared to be fighting the grave for every hour he remained on the planet.

A day later, the gateway chamber activated and when the door opened, Kane, Brigid Baptiste, Grant and Domi emerged. A well-built stranger wearing the white bodysuit of Cerberus duty personnel followed them. Lakesh still remembered how DeFore gaped in stunned amazement at the man's thick, glossy black hair, his unlined olive complexion and toothy, excited grin. She recognized only the blue eyes and the long, aquiline nose as belonging to the Lakesh she had known the previous five years.

Lakesh hadn't tried to convince DeFore or anyone else his condition was permanent. He claimed he had no idea how long his vitality would last. Whether it would vanish overnight like the fabulous One Horse Shay and leave him a doddering old scarecrow again, or whether he would simply begin to age normally from that point onward, he couldn't be certain. However, he told her he wasn't about to waste the gift of youth, as transitory as it might be. DeFore didn't know who One Horse Shay had been, or what was so fabulous about him, but she did notice Lakesh surreptitiously eyeing her bosom in a way he had never done before.

Although Lakesh didn't respond to DeFore's comment, Domi demanded, "What do you mean?"

"The introduction of the nanites into Lakesh's body was responsible for turning back his clock," replied DeFore. "Nanotechnology was believed to be a fundamental breakthrough in all sorts of predark scientific fields, particularly medicine. Molecular machines directed by nanocomputers were designed to combine sensors, programs and molecular tools to form systems able to examine and repair the ultimate components of individual cells."

"Exactly," Lakesh said.

"But how could teeny-weeny machines make you young again?" inquired Domi dubiously.

"That's a good question," Lakesh said, turning to DeFore. "Do you have an answer?"

A bit sarcastically DeFore retorted, "Believe it or not, I do. Natural repair enzymes function by detecting and repairing certain kinds of damage to DNA. These repairs help cells survive, but existing repair mechanisms are too simple to correct all problems, either in DNA or elsewhere. So, biochemical errors mount, contributing to the aging and death of cells— and of people.

"What you have in you are cell-repair nanites. They traveled through your tissue like white blood cells do, and entered cells as viruses do—then they sized up the situation by examining the cell's contents and activity, and then took action. By working along molecule by molecule and structure by structure, the nanites repaired whole cells.''

Lakesh tugged at his nose thoughtfully. ''Interesting. But how were the nanites programmed? Wouldn't they need guidance from a larger computer network?''

''I have a theory about that, too,'' replied DeFore. ''Obviously the repair nanites would have to be connected to a larger computer by means of mechanical data links. The devices pass along information, and the governing computer passes back general instructions.''

Lakesh nodded. ''I see. If we think in terms of hardware and software, the machine could repair my body's hardware while neither understanding nor changing its software.''

DeFore nodded. ''Something like that. But I also think the nanites put your metabolism in a form of biostasis. The natural aging process was slowed, maybe even frozen. And now—'' She broke off, compressing her lips as if not wanting to say anything further.

''And now?'' Lakesh prodded.

Sighing, DeFore declared, ''I think the nanites are running amok and damaging tissues on a molecular level. They're concentrating on the weakest areas of your body, where the transplant surgeries were performed.''

Although his belly did a cold flip-flop of fear, Lakesh kept his voice steady. ''Are you suggesting that the nanites are now destroying what they originally repaired?''

DeFore hesitated before saying, ''I don't know if I'd go so far as to make the diagnosis that they're ripping you up on the molecular level, but they're definitely having an adverse effect on your metabolic functions. Whether it's accidental or part of a program I don't know. But I'm certain of one thing—if Sam introduced the nanites into your body by a laying on of hands, it's pretty obvious he's not the flesh-and-blood avatar he claimed to be.''

Domi's eyes narrowed to slits. ''You mean he's a machine?''

Lakesh repressed a shudder. ''So that's your theory about the control computer for the nanites? It's Sam?''

DeFore shook her head. ''I have no idea if Sam is a machine or controlling the machine that controls the nanites. I saw him…he looked human enough to me.''

''I saw him, too,'' Domi put in. ''He was like a little boy. A *nasty* little boy, but still just a kid.''

''That kid,'' remarked Lakesh, ''is now the single most powerful entity on the continent. Maybe even the world.''

''Quavell says that not all the barons have thrown in with him,'' DeFore pointed out.

''The ones that haven't,'' Lakesh replied, ''are afraid to cross him. And the ones who resent his authority won't take action because they're putting their lives at stake.''

"A nasty little boy," intoned Domi, "and a damn clever one."

Neither Lakesh nor DeFore could disagree about that, but by the same token, none of them felt particularly good about an imperator controlling the villes instead of a group of hybrid barons. The ancient Roman Empire was governed by a senate, but ruled by an emperor, sometimes known as an imperator. This person served as the final arbiter in matters pertaining to government. The villes acted independently, unified in name only. The arrival of the so-called imperator changed all of that.

Months before, Lakesh first learned about a mysterious figure called the imperator who intended to set himself up as overlord of the villes, with the barons subservient to him. That bit of news was surprising enough, but it quickly turned shocking when they found out that Balam, whom they had thought was gone forever, was the power behind the imperator.

The introduction of the imperator was shocking and dramatic. After the destruction of the Archuleta Mesa medical facility, a council of the barons was convened in Front Royal. Baron Cobalt put forth the proposal to establish a central ruling consortium. In effect, the barons would become viceroys, plenipotentiaries in their own territories. They were accustomed to acting as the viceroys of the Archon Directorate, so the actual proposal in and of itself didn't offend them. Nor was there much of a familial spirit about the barons.

Although all of the fortress cities with their individual, allegedly immortal god-kings were supposed to be interdependent, the baronies still operated on insular principles. Cooperation among them was grudging despite their shared goal of a unified world. They perceived humanity in general as either servants or as living storage vessels for transplanted organs and fresh genetic material.

The barons were less in favor of Baron Cobalt's proposal than his intent to be recognized as the imperator. However, they really didn't have much of a choice—Cobalt had arranged matters that way. The hybrids may have been extremely long-lived, but cellular and metabolic deterioration was part and parcel of what they were—hybrids of human and Archon DNA. Just like the caste system in place in the villes, the hybrids observed a similar one, although it had little do with parentage. If the first phase of human evolution produced a package of adaptations for a particular and distinct way of life, the second phase was an effort to control that way of life by controlling the environment. The focus switched to a cultural evolution rather than a physical one.

The hybrid barons, at least by their way of thinking, represented the final phase of human evolution. They created wholesale, planned alterations in living organisms and were empowered to control not only their environment, but also the evolution of other species. And the pinnacle of that evolutionary achievement was the barons, as high above ordinary hybrids bred as servants as the hybrids were above mere humans.

But because of their metabolic deficiencies, the barons lived insulated, isolated lives. The theatrical trappings many of them adopted not only added to their semidivine mystique, but also protected them from contamination—both psychological and physical.

When Baron Cobalt dangled the medical treatments before his fellow barons like a carrot on a stick rather than offering to share them freely, war was the inevitable result—particularly after Sam, supported by none other than Balam, hijacked Cobalt's plan and the title of imperator.

The war hadn't lasted very long, but when it was over Baron Cobalt's forces were routed from Area 51, his ville and his territory overrun and the baron himself had disappeared. Still, judging by what Lakesh had heard by listening into the Cerberus communications scanner, there wasn't much reaction from the rank-and-file ville citizen to the rule of the imperator. Most probably knew very little about it, but they had picked up signals confirming reports of civil unrest in some of the baronies.

"Maybe enough barons will get sick of Sam and join forces against him," DeFore suggested hopefully. "So, if he's behind what's happening to you, Lakesh, it'll be stopped that way."

Lakesh smiled without humor. "You dream, Doctor."

For the majority of the ville-bred citizens, the concept of living outside a narrow, structured channel would be akin to insanity. Lakesh knew the people of the baronies wouldn't be as resilient as Kane, Grant and Brigid Baptiste when their entire belief system collapsed.

Quavell, before she fled from Area 51, claimed that she hadn't heard of a baronial alliance forming against Sam. Even if all the baronies united against the imperator, months would be required to prepare any kind of military campaign and to do so the dissenting barons would have to act in secret, else they would not have access to the medical facility in Dreamland.

First and foremost, they would be faced with subduing the growing civil unrest in the villes, secretly supply their forces and integrate the infrastructure necessary for a full-scale war—all without revealing themselves to the imperator.

"Is there any way those bugs can be flushed out of him?" Domi asked.

Lakesh started to chuckle at the girl's naiveté, then got himself together and fixed a questioning gaze on DeFore. "Is there?"

"I considered that," the medic replied. "Even if we gave you a complete blood transfusion and filtered all of your bodily fluids through dialysis, there are millions in the soft tissues of your cellular structure. We might be able flush out one hundred million, but twice that number would still be in you. It wouldn't be an efficacious treatment."

Lakesh nodded in reluctant agreement. "Whatever treatment you did use, Doctor, I thank you. I feel much better and my vision has improved."

Reba DeFore's forehead creased in consternation.

"I didn't treat you. All I did was administer a pain-killer. It made you sleep for a little while."

Frowning, Lakesh unzipped the front of his body-suit and looked down at his chest. The pattern of lividity was still there, but barely visible, like the residue of a mostly healed bruise. Half to himself he murmured, "This is madness."

DeFore leaned forward and touched his skin. "There doesn't seem to be any sign of subcutaneous rupturing. It's almost like the nanites went haywire for a while, then repaired any damage they might have caused."

"So it could have been an accident?" Domi ventured.

Lakesh and DeFore exchanged a long, meaningful stare, then Lakesh zipped himself up. Dolefully he said, "I'm afraid not, darlingest one. I think it was a demonstration, a display of power. Sam was showing me what he could do to me."

"How could he show you anything?" Domi demanded. "He's way over in China!"

"If he can manipulate the Heart of the World," Lakesh countered, "exerting long-distance control over nanites wouldn't present much of a problem to him."

Buried beneath the ancient Xian pyramid in China, the Heart of the World was a convergence of electromagnetism that contained the energies released in the first picoseconds following the big bang. It channeled the matrix of protoparticles that swirled through the universe before physical, relativistic laws fully stabilized. The Heart therefore existed slightly out of phase with the human concept of space-time. From its central core extended a web of electromagnetic and geophysical energy that covered the entire planet.

Domi's lips peeled back over her teeth in a silent snarl. "Why would he want to interfere with the nanites in the first place?"

Lakesh tugged again at his nose, then said quietly, "It's a way of summoning and warning me. Either I come to him…or I die horribly."

It was impossible for Domi to turn pale, but her face took on a strained, almost congested appearance. Forcing a smile to his lips and a cheery note into his voice, Lakesh asked, "Now, darlingest one, I recall you saying there was something we needed to talk about?"

Chapter 18

Lakesh and Domi left the infirmary together. As they walked along the broad corridor, he asked, "What was it that you wanted to talk to me about?"

With no inflection in her tone, Domi answered, "Grant came back about two hours ago. There's an emergency of some kind."

Startled, Lakesh inquired, "Of what nature?"

Domi shrugged. "I'm not sure. I just heard a little bit of intercom chatter. Something to do with Vikings and the South Pole."

Lakesh was too surprised to say anything for a moment. They reached a T intersection in the passageway, and without a word Domi turned toward the residential wing. Lakesh gazed after her, then followed swiftly. Before she reached the door to her quarters, he caught up with her and blocked her path.

He met her stony gaze with a smile. "Vikings and the South Pole, as intriguing a combination as that sounds, is not the topic of the conversation you wished to have with me."

Domi tried to sidle around him. "This isn't the time or place."

Lakesh experienced a flash of anger and put out a hand to restrain her. Instantly he regretted it when she pivoted on a heel and slapped his hand away. Her eyes seethed with crimson fury. "Don't put your hands on me like that, Lakesh!"

He held it up in a conciliatory gesture. He knew her reaction was restrained. Despite her petite frame, Domi's reflexes and tensile-steel strength were little short of inhuman. "Fine, darlingest one. I apologize. But I'm fairly certain I know what you want to talk about."

She stared at him expectantly, defiantly, but didn't speak.

"You're upset that our relationship is a secret."

"Not anymore it isn't," she bit out. "I told Kane."

Lakesh's eyes widened. "Indeed?" He struggled to tamp down a surge of apprehension, then embarrassment. "And what was friend Kane's reaction?"

"About like I figured." She shrugged. "No big deal. So why do you think it is? I thought you loved me."

Lakesh sighed heavily, started to reach for her, then thought better of it. "You know I do, Domi."

"If I did, we wouldn't be having this conversation."

He ducked his head, in acceptance of her charge. "I suppose you're right."

"I think you're ashamed to admit to anyone that you're involved with me—a piece of outlander trash." Her words were delivered without heat, but they stung him nevertheless.

"That's not the reason."

"Then what is?"

Lakesh groped for words. In truth, he did love the girl. Her upbringing in the Outlands was one of the reasons he loved her. Outlanders were the expendables, the free labor force, the cannon fodder, the convenient enemies of order, the useless eaters. Brigid, Grant, Kane and all of the exiles in Cerberus were outlanders by circumstance. Only Domi was one by birth, so in the kingdom of the disenfranchised, she was the pretender to the throne.

Humankind, at least those who were ville bred, had been beaten into docility long ago. In the Outlands, a fragile, disorganized freedom remained among the pockets of Roamers, half-feral mutants who had survived the purges and tribes of Amerindians who had returned to their traditional way of life.

But the population of hybrids swelled even as the small pool of truly human beings on Earth diminished, killed and bred and co-opted out of existence.

Lakesh fought back a surge of guilt. It wasn't an emotion he was used to grappling with, and certainly not one he enjoyed. Nevertheless, the guilt was neither neurotic nor misplaced. He and other twentieth-century scientists had willingly traded in their human heritage for a shockscape of planet-wide ruins. After all, they had been selected to survive in order to re-shape not only Earth, but also humankind in a new image, and if that meant planning the eventual extinction of the old humans, the outlanders, then that was simply part of summoning the future.

Domi's people had been exterminated by the forces of the barons in furtherance of that new order, and that was another source of guilt. As for Domi herself, Lakesh had been fond of her since the day they first met and over the past couple of years that affection had grown to love. He hadn't been able to demonstrate his feelings for her until recently. It was still a source of joy to him that Domi reciprocated his feelings and had no inhibitions about acting on them, regardless of the bitterness she still harbored over her unrequited love for Grant.

Lakesh guessed his reluctance to let anyone know about his affair with Domi derived mainly from the habit of keeping two centuries' worth of secrets. As it was, he had lived daily with the fear that he would anger Grant or Kane over some matter or another and they would expose his biggest secret—of how and why there were any exiles in Cerberus in the first place.

In the twentieth century he had been a major player in the conspiracy that led to the nuclear holocaust. After that, he became instrumental in establishing the baronial society and served as a trusted member of Baron Cobalt's inner circle. However, all that he'd seen and lived through and everything he remembered from the past altered Lakesh's alliances.

Instead of remaining a key facilitator of the unification program's aims and goals, he'd become its most dangerous adversary. His former role as senior archivist in Cobaltville's Historical Division was a front. As far as the baron was concerned, his true purpose was to ferret out any and all information regarding humanity's long relationship with the Archons and report it. The information would then either be suppressed or acted upon if there was any material gain to be had from it. The same was true of Totality Concept technology.

In reality, Lakesh had used his position to choose likely prospects to join his underground resistance movement. Over the past forty years he'd put his plans to build an active resistance into action and manipulated the political system of the baronies to secretly restore the Cerberus redoubt to full operational capacity. But having a headquarters for a resistance movement meant nothing if there were no resistance fighters.

The only way to find them was through yet more manipulation. Using the genetic records on file in villes, Lakesh selected candidates for his rebellion, but finding them and recruiting them wasn't the same thing. With his authority and influence, he set them up, framing them for crimes against their respective villes.

It was a cruel, heartless plan with a barely acceptable risk factor, but Lakesh believed it was the only way to spirit them out of their villes, turn them against the barons and make them feel indebted to him.

To his everlasting regret, Lakesh had never married or fathered children. The closest he came to producing offspring was when he rifled the ville's genetic records to find desirable qualifications in order to build a covert resistance movement against the baronies. He used the baron's own fixation with genetic purity against them. By his own confession, he was a physicist cast in the role of an archivist, pretending to be a geneticist, manipulating a political system that was still in a state of flux. Kane was one such example of that political and genetic manipulation, and the last thing Lakesh felt toward him was fatherly.

Nearly two years before, Lakesh's machinations had been exposed. Grant, Kane and Brigid had staged something of a minimutiny over the issue, but nothing had been decisively settled. However, Lakesh was on notice his titular position as the redoubt's administrator was extremely weak.

Under Domi's steady, unremitting stare, Lakesh felt all of his previous objections and fears dispelling. "There really is no sound reason," he declared. "It was force of habit, that's all. And you suffered for it. But no longer."

Reaching out, he took her by the hand and tugged her down the corridor. She resisted, digging in her heels, but the vanadium sheathing didn't afford much friction and she dragged along for a few feet. "Where are you taking me?"

"We're going to find out about Vikings and the South Pole," he announced confidently. "And we're going to walk into the command center, hand in hand."

She stared at him uncomprehendingly for a moment. "What will that prove?"

"To the people here? Very little. To you, I hope a great deal."

Domi's lips compressed and she wrested herself

free. "I don't feel like being put on display, La-kesh...I'm not an exhibit."

Lakesh reached for her again, but she evaded his touch. Falteringly he said, "Darlingest one, please don't be angry."

"I'm not." She started back toward her quarters. Over her shoulder she said, "You have another emer-gency to deal with, and I have some things to think over. We'll talk more when things aren't so hectic."

Lakesh stood in the corridor and watched her go, feeling foolish, inadequate and bewildered. His ex-perience with women was extremely limited, so he wasn't sure how to feel or react. His single purpose in life had been devoted to science, to dispelling the unknown, reasoning that was the only way to save the half-insane world from itself.

For that purpose he had studied most of his life, learned twelve languages and then left the country of his birth to work for what he truly believed was a way to restore sanity on Earth. His devotion and be-lief had been as utterly and thoroughly betrayed as it was possible for a human being to be and not commit suicide out of despair. He prayed he hadn't evoked similar feelings of betrayal in Domi by his reticence to reveal their relationship.

Squaring his shoulders, stiffening his spine, Lakesh marched more or less pain free into the command center. Grant, Kane and Brewster Philboyd were clus-tered around Brigid, who sat at the main monitor screen. As he drew closer he saw they were studying the satellite imagery of Antarctica.

"I'm sorry I missed the excitement," Lakesh said as he joined them. "I was otherwise occupied."

"So we heard," Grant replied. "Are you better now?"

"The worst of it seems to have passed, thank you. Friend Grant, your period of retirement must be one of the shortest on—"

"I heard that already," snapped Grant.

Lakesh caught the slight smile creasing Kane's lips and he nodded in understanding. "Of course you have. So, bring me up to date. What's all this about a Viking ship off the coast of New Edo?"

In terse, unadorned language, Brigid provided a detailed overview of everything that had transpired since his collapse. When she was done, all a stunned Lakesh could think of to say was a lame "Interesting."

Kane angled an ironic eyebrow at him. "Isn't it just. We've been discussing how much more interesting it's liable to get."

"How so?"

Brigid nodded to the monitor. "We've triangulated the position of the Antarctic mat-trans unit relative to the most intense areas of heat."

Lakesh eyed the pattern of glowing CGI lines and coordinates superimposed over the white starkness of the polar terrain. "It appears to be in comparatively close. Within five or six kilometers."

"A little less," Philboyd said. "As the crow flies anyway. But we don't know the lay of the land, what the terrain is like. Besides, comparatively close is strictly subjective if you're tramping through below-zero temperatures.''

A bit alarmed, Lakesh asked, ''You're planning to gate there? How can you be sure Ultima Thule is within reasonable proximity to the areas of heat?''

''Seems to be a logical step,'' Grant rumbled. ''If Ultima Thule actually exists in some form or another, it makes sense the Nazis would build their installation as close to it as possible.''

Lakesh nodded in reluctant agreement. ''So you're all going there?''

Brigid looked up at him. ''Shouldn't we?''

Lakesh didn't respond for a moment. If the decision had been left up solely to him, as all decisions had once been, he would have ordered more of an investigation before undertaking such a mission. But now a more democratic process was observed. No mission could be assigned or undertaken unless everyone involved was in agreement.

Glancing toward Grant, he asked, ''And you, too?''

As if in answer, Grant slowly slid his left arm free of the canvas. Wincing, he flexed his fingers. They moved, but stiffly and sluggishly. ''Yeah…if for no other reason than to make sure that goddamn Russian maniac is dead once and for all.''

Kane threw him a slit-eyed glare. ''What makes you so sure we'll find him there? He could still be cruising around, checking out New Edo for all you know.''

''He could be,'' admitted Grant. ''But from what I saw of his ship and crew, he doesn't have the firepower or the personnel to make an incursion into New Edo and live to get off the beach. Besides, I told you I watched him sail away.''

A little impatiently, Philboyd said, ''In my opinion, Grigori Zakat is the least of our worries. It's the condition of the ice sheet, not some old enemy of yours.''

Kane transferred his glare from Grant to Philboyd. ''Shut up, Brewster.'' He mockingly stressed the syllables of the man's name so it came out as Brooster. ''If you'd ever met the son of a bitch, you'd know 'some old enemy of ours' has a great deal to do with the condition of the ice sheet.''

Philboyd flushed in shamed anger and turned toward Brigid for support.

She said calmly, ''I have to agree with Kane on this. Zakat is our main concern, assuming he's under way back to Antarctica. Grant claimed his ship was engine powered.''

Grant nodded. ''Sounded like twin diesels to me.''

''There's no way to tell how long it will take him to return,'' Lakesh ventured.

Brigid indicated the screen again. ''If he follows old shipping lanes, it might take him weeks. If there's a route known only to the Thulians, we could be talking only a matter of days.''

''According to history,'' Philboyd pointed out, ''the Vikings were inveterate explorers. As I recall, few people in Western Europe even knew Norsemen existed until their dragon ships swarmed out of the north. So it's possible they knew of routes that remained secret for a thousand years.''

"Even so," said Grant. "There's no way he can get back to the Antarctic by tomorrow. If we get there ahead of him, we can lay a trap."

"Why tomorrow?" asked Kane.

"That's the earliest we can leave," Grant replied. "We have to get a lot of cold-weather equipment together. And if the weather is bad, we might have to sit it out in the mat-trans compound until it clears."

"What about the interphaser?" Lakesh suggested. Perhaps there's a set of nearby Parallax points that can be activated and you can circumvent the jump chamber altogether."

The interphaser, or to be technically precise, a quantum interphase matter-transmission inducer, was Lakesh's latest creation. It was actually a newer version that evolved from the Totality Concept's Project Cerberus. Nearly two years before, Lakesh had constructed a small device on the same scientific principle as the mat-trans inducers, an interphaser designed to interact with naturally occurring quantum vortices. Theoretically the interphaser opened dimensional rifts much like the gateways, but instead of the rifts being pathways through linear space, Lakesh had envisioned them as a method to travel through the gaps in normal space-time.

The interphaser hadn't functioned according to its design, and due to interference caused by Lord Strongbow's similar device, the so-called Singularity, its dilated temporal energy had sent Kane, Brigid, Domi and Grant on a short, disembodied trip into the past.

Although the interphaser had been lost, its memory disk had been retrieved, and using the data recorded on it, Lakesh had tried to duplicate the dilation effect by turning the Cerberus mat-trans unit into a time machine.

Such efforts were not new. Operation Chronos, a major subdivision of the Totality Concept, had been devoted to manipulating the nature of time, building on the breakthroughs of Project Cerberus. During development of the mat-trans gateways, the Cerberus researchers observed a number of side effects. On occasion, traversing the quantum pathways resulted in minor temporal anomalies, such as arriving at a destination three seconds before the jump initiator was actually engaged.

Lakesh found that time couldn't be measured or accurately perceived in the quantum stream. Hypothetically constant jumpers might find themselves physically rejuvenated, with the toll of time erased if enough "backward time" was accumulated in their metabolisms. Conversely jumpers might find themselves prematurely aged if the quantum stream pushed them farther into the future with each journey. From these temporal anomalies Operation Chronos had its starting point, using the gateway technology, to develop time travel.

Therefore, the interphaser was more than a miniaturized version of a gateway unit, even though it employed much of the same hardware and operating principles. The mat-trans gateways functioned by tapping into the quantum stream, the invisible pathways that crisscrossed outside of perceived physical space and terminated in wormholes.

The interphaser interacted with the energy within a naturally occurring vortex and caused a temporary overlapping of two dimensions. The vortex then became an intersection point, a discontinuous quantum jump, beyond relativistic space-time. The Parallax Points program was actually a map, a geodetic index of all the vortex points on the planet. Decrypting the program was laborious and time-consuming, and each newly discovered set of coordinates was fed into the interphaser's targeting computer.

For the first time in two hundred years, the Cerberus redoubt reverted to its original purpose—not a sanctuary for exiles or the headquarters of a resistance against the tyranny of the barons, but a facility dedicated to unfathoming the eternal mysteries of space and time.

Kane, Grant and Brigid had endured weeks of hard training in the use of the interphaser on short hops, selecting vortex points near the redoubt—or at least, near in the sense that if they couldn't make the return trip through a quantum channel they could conceivably walk back to the installation. Only recently had they begun making jumps farther and farther afield from Cerberus. So far, the interphaser hadn't materialized them either in a lake or an ocean or underground, since an analogical computer was built into the interphaser to automatically select a vortex point above solid ground.

"I already reviewed the log," Brigid answered. "I

didn't find any coordinates that corresponded with either of the poles. It doesn't mean they're not there—they just haven't been decrypted yet.''

Grant started toward the ready room and the jump chamber. "I'm going to gate back to Thunder Isle and tell the Tiger stationed there what we have planned. He'll let Shizuka know. I'll be back shortly.''

Kane grinned at him. "Got to let the little lady know why you won't be home for supper?''

Grant glowered at him. "I've got to let the little lady know why she and her samurai won't be cutting off Viking heads anytime soon. Is that all right with you?''

Without waiting for a response, Grant strode toward the mat-trans unit, trying to minimize his limp.

Under his breath, Kane growled, "Is he hard to get along with or what?''

Brigid chuckled. "Mr. Pot, I'd like to introduce you to Mr. Kettle.''

"What?'' Although Kane was accustomed to her enigmatic remarks, he could still be irked by them, particularly since they all seemed to center in on dead zones in his education. He always felt that he was playing straight man to one of her academic performances.

"She means you're in no position to judge Grant's behavior,'' Philboyd explained, doing a very poor job of repressing a grin. "Or anybody's for that matter.''

Kane forced a duplicate of Philboyd's grin to his face. "You know, Brewster, it's a shame you're not going with us, I'd give you a hands-on lesson about what it's like to walk on thin ice." The grin fled his face. "Because you sure as hell don't seem to get it otherwise."

Although Philboyd's complexion seemed to pale, he met Kane's steely gaze resolutely. "I guess you'll be able to teach me that lesson, Kane…because I intend to go with you."

Chapter 19

Kane struggled against dizzy nausea, and his vision was clouded. A pain throbbed in his temples, like a hangover or the first symptoms of his heatstroke. His stomach muscles fluttered and quivered. Slowly his vision cleared, and he found himself slumped in a half-prone position against a wall. Below and above him, the glow faded from the hexagonal metal disks. He heard a faint curse.

Kane pushed himself up, looking around, seeing his three companions stirring dazedly on the floor. Brigid stared around unfocusedly for a moment, then turned to Philboyd. He hiked himself to his elbows, breathing heavily.

"You feel all right?" Brigid asked.

Philboyd looked at her, opened his mouth as if to answer, then bowed his head and dry-heaved violently for a moment. Nothing was ejected, except a few strings of bile-laced saliva. Kane would have felt more sympathy for him if he didn't feel like vomiting at the moment himself. Irrationally he held the man responsible for his own surge of queasiness.

Dragging in a harsh breath, Philboyd said hoarsely, "I feel awful."

Struggling to a sitting position, Grant said angrily,

"What the hell is going on here? We input the destination codes, so we shouldn't be feeling sick. We didn't the last time we gated to here. Maybe it's the wrong place."

Kane tottered unsteadily to his feet, putting a hand on the wall. "It's the same place."

The gateway chamber didn't conform to the standard specs that Grant, Brigid and Kane had seen elsewhere. It was very small, the walls not made of tinted armaglass shielding, but rather plates of sheet metal lined with lead foil. The door of the chamber was different, too, with a transparent panel set in its top half and a central wheel to open and seal it.

Philboyd, Grant and Brigid rose to their feet, collected their gear and waited while Kane turned the wheel lock until the solenoids popped open with a loud clack. They trudged out single-file. The jump chamber wasn't placed on an elevated platform, and it opened directly into a small control center, barely ten feet across. There was no adjacent recovery anteroom beyond.

They saw a single, simplified master control console running the length of one wall. There were a few of the basic command panels from the Cerberus installation. Many of the indicator lights were dark. Beneath the concrete floor they heard the rhythmic throb of generators, beating with a nerve-scratching loudness. Within a few moments, the sound hummed down to silence.

They weren't in a redoubt, but a Quonset hut, little more than a hutch standing between two bastions of rock. It was also brutally cold. It struck their faces, seeming to coat their exposed skin with frost almost instantly. The concrete floor was buckled in places, broken chunks thrusting up. Muted light glowed from beneath it, buried and distorted by inches of ice.

"There's the most likely reason for the rough transit," Brigid observed. "A ground slippage probably damaged the gateway's automatic settings, the target focus conformals."

"Probably," Philboyd said between chattering teeth.

Kane cast him a glance of mocking surprised. "Cold, Brewster?"

Philboyd dropped his rucksack and started pawing through it. "Yes!" he half shouted in defiance. "Don't you know that about seventy percent of your body heat escapes through your head, even if the rest of you is toasty warm?"

Kane did know that, but he said nothing. He, Brigid, Philboyd and Grant were all wearing the same kind of clothing. From throat to fingertip to heel they were clad in one-piece black leathery garments that fit as tightly as doeskin gloves.

Although the formfitting garments didn't appear as if they could offer protection from a mosquito bite, they were climate controlled for environments up to highs of 150 degrees and as cold as minus ten degrees Fahrenheit. Microfilaments controlled the internal temperature.

The manufacturing technique known in predark days as electrospin lacing electrically charged the polymer particles to form a dense web of formfitting fibers. Composed of a compiled weave of spider silk, Monocrys and Spectra fabrics, the garments were essentially a single-crystal metallic microfiber with a very dense molecular structure. The outer Monocrys sheathing went opaque when exposed to radiation, and the Kevlar and Spectra layers provided protection against blunt trauma. The fibers were embedded with enzymes and other catalysts that broke down all toxic and infectious agents on contact. The spider silk allowed flexibility, but it traded protection from firearms for freedom of movement.

Kane felt the shadow suits were superior to the Magistrate armor, if for nothing else than their internal subsystems. Built around nanotechnologies, the microelectromechanical systems combined computers with tiny semiconductor chips. The nanotechnology reduced the size of the electronic components to one-millionth of a meter, roughly ten times the size of an atom. The inner layer was lined by carbon nanotubes only a nanometer wide, rolled-up sheets of graphite with a tensile strength greater than steel. The suits were almost impossible to tear, but a large-caliber bullet could penetrate them and, unlike the Mag body armor, they wouldn't redistribute the kinetic shock.

Despite their internal thermal controls, the suits didn't keep out all the cold. Although it was midway through Antarctic summer, the average temperatures hovered in the minus forty- to minus fifty-degree range. Wind speeds of thirty to fifty miles per hour weren't unusual, and the resulting windchills averaged around minus one hundred degrees. They had brought additional cold-weather gear with them.

In the rucksacks were specially insulated clothing, food, water and even portable shelters. Reba DeFore had briefed them on the conditions and suggested they bring high-caloric foodstuffs, since most of the food people ate in the Antarctic went directly to generating heat. She had pointed out that even when a person felt comfortably warm, he or she was using over half the total caloric intake just to maintain body temperature, so the colder it became outside the body, the higher the required food intake.

Kane and Grant knew from their Magistrate missions in the Outlands that most people were so ill equipped for intense cold that they soon reached a state where they couldn't stay warm no matter how much they ate. Stripped naked at thirty-two degrees, human beings perished of lowered core temperature in as little as twenty minutes.

To provide shelter from the elements, they had brought along tents called Himalayan hotels. The Himalayan hotels were specifically designed for sub-zero climates. The tents incorporated a triple system of waterproof, breathable liners and thickly insulated outer shells.

The clothing they had brought with them to wear over the shadow suits was made from synthetic fabrics that trapped body heat, but let perspiration evaporate.

Philboyd tugged a knit cap over his balding head and began passing out the cold-weather gear to his companions. The clothing was donned layer by layer—thermal underwear, jackets and pants, hooded, fur-lined parkas and yet more pants. The hip-length parkas carried battery-powered heat filaments in the lining.

They put specially designed ski boots on their feet and chemically warmed protective gloves on their hands. Grant and Kane strapped their Sin Eaters to their right forearms and experimented with the actuators to make sure the spring and cable release hadn't been affected by the penetrating cold and that there was enough leeway between their right sleeves and heavy gloves to allow the weapons to jump into their hands if necessary.

Brigid inserted an Iver Johnson autoblaster into a zippered pocket of her parka. Philboyd carried a Copperhead, a close-assault weapon that had the potential to cycle 700 rounds per minute through the short barrel. However, the magazines of 4.85 mm ammunition held only fifteen rounds. Before giving it to the man, Grant had made sure the selector switch was set on 3-round bursts. In the hands of a trigger-happy amateur, the small weapon would be emptied within seconds.

Kane handed out full-face balaclavas and goggles all around. "Are we primed?"

"Set," Brigid and Grant responded automatically and in unison.

Philboyd shrugged, hefted the Copperhead and looked longingly toward the mat-trans unit. "You sure that thing will work well enough to get us back to Cerberus?''

''It should,'' Brigid said reassuringly. ''It's always a risk using an unindexed gateway. This is one of the prototype models anyway.''

Brigid earlier explained to Philboyd that not all installations containing a gateway were connected to the Totality Concept. Project Cerberus had mass-produced the gateways as modular units, and they were sent all over the world. Not even Lakesh knew how many were manufactured, or to where they were shipped. Even as overseer of the project, he wasn't privy to every detail.

Peeling back his glove, Kane consulted his chron, then moved to the door handle. ''Let's see what's out there.''

He turned the knob and pushed. Nothing happened. He threw his entire weight against the door, but it still didn't budge. Grant stepped up beside him and put his right shoulder against the door. They heard a prolonged, splitting crack somewhere off in the distance, outside the hut, and they stopped pushing. It sounded like a long roll of thunder, but it was interspersed with crashes.

Then the Quonset hut shook and shivered, as if a bomb had been detonated nearby. Seams of the tin roof popped loose, and little showers of snow sifted down.

''What the hell was that?'' Philboyd demanded, eyes bright with fear.

"Earthquake?" Kane glanced over his shoulder at Brigid for her opinion.

She shook her head. "I don't think so."

"It didn't feel like the kind of earthquakes New Edo was getting," Grant rumbled.

Kane returned his attention and strength to the door. Grant did the same. Under the steady pressure of the two men, the door sprang open with a groaning, tearing sound, breaking loose of the layer of ice that had sealed it.

As Kane kicked the door open fully, a shaft of milky sunlight slanted in over the threshold. The midmorning sunlight was veiled by cirrocumulus clouds, and it sparkled only dully on the sweep of snow. All they saw through the veils of wind-drifted snow was a range of low mountains, rugged and bleak in the far distance.

Grant grunted, and his breath stood out in a long plume from his nostrils. Ice crystals formed in his mustache, and he grunted in annoyance, fingering them away.

"Careful how you breathe," Brigid warned him, pulling the balaclava over her head. "If you get a buildup of moisture in your lungs, you could contract pneumonia."

"If I wanted medical advice," Grant muttered peevishly, "I would've asked Reba to come along with us."

Despite all the insulated clothes they wore, the sub-zero cold still penetrated. It bit at their nostrils, their lips, their eyes, anywhere it could find moisture.

Putting on his own balaclava, Grant stepped out of the hut, the hoarfrost crunching and squeaking beneath the thick treads of his boots. He consulted the readouts on the electronic sextant-compass held in his left hand. He glanced all around at the barren terrain, as if expecting to see something other than an icy wasteland stretching away in all directions.

The instrument suddenly slipped from his hand, but he managed to catch it with his other before it fell to the ground. He acted as if nothing happened, and none of his companions acknowledged by word or even expression that his fingers had momentarily lost strength.

Grant pointed northwest. "That way."

Chapter 20

Sunlight, even as diffuse as it was peeping through the cloud cover, still painted the white crest of the titanic glacier with warm hues of gold and orange. The glacier thrust up from an opening between mountain peaks, then flowed down in a sweeping curve in front of the pass.

Grant, Kane, Brigid and Philboyd had to travel cautiously past the foot of the glacier, watching out for hidden crevasses. As they neared the base of the vast, frozen flow, Brigid began a lecture. Kane didn't know if it was to educate them, to assuage Philboyd's nervousness or her own, but after half an hour, he found his irritation growing.

"In Antarctica," Brigid said, "there are both alpine and continental glaciers. Alpine glaciers are found in the high basins of mountain ranges and flow down into valleys. By contrast, a continental glacier forms on a continental landmass and flows outward from its source region."

"What would happen," Philboyd asked, "to Antarctica if the ice sheet did slip into the ocean?"

"If the ice were removed and the underlying rocks rebounded to their normal position," Brigid answered, "its bed would still be below sea level. Gravity pulls all glaciers and ice sheets downhill, and the Antarctic ice sheets are no exception. The ice in Antarctica is flowing to the sea at a rate of about one to ten yards per year. When glaciers flow over changing slopes or uneven land, the brittle top layers crack and form deep fractures called crevasses.

"Blowing snow can cover these crevasses with snow bridges. Some of these bridges are strong enough to support sleds, dogs and people—others are not. Thus, careful testing is required before passing over each crevasse on the snow bridges. Near the coastal and mountainous areas of Antarctica, the crevasses are the most dangerous."

"By the wildest of coincidences," Kane said sourly, "isn't that where we are, the mountainous area?"

Grant took it upon himself to answer. "That's pretty much it. So watch yourselves."

The four people had been trudging through the limitless ice fields, high snowdrifts without a break since leaving the Quonset hut. The wind wasn't dangerously cold at first, but it kept rising. Kane noticed Grant shivering violently as a gust of subzero wind buffeted them.

Within a minute, the wind moaning over the ice field turned into a shrieking wail that seemed to fill the entire world, tearing at the four people with a clawing fury. They were blinded by a white, stinging curtain. Breathing in the gale was difficult, since snowflakes and ice particles clung to the fabric of the balaclava covering their mouths and they inhaled the icy, semisolid mixture. It seared the moist, soft tissues of their mouths and sinus passages.

Grant, Kane, Brigid and Philboyd put their heads down and marched onward. The cold pummeled them, slapping at their bodies as they staggered and reeled, encrusting their goggles with a coating of frost. The billowing clouds of snow reduced their range of vision to only a few yards, and it froze the moisture in their nasal passages. Their faces, hands and legs grew numb, and ears and teeth ached fiercely. Blind, freezing and aching, they fought their way onward.

Neither Kane nor Grant feared becoming lost, so much as succumbing to the soul-killing cold and falling and freezing solid within minutes. They slogged onward and it was all they could do to maintain half-erect postures. Finally their bodies lost all feeling, numb to every sensation except the need to put one foot in front of the other.

Breasting the wind, Grant shambled and shuffled until he struck something hard and unyielding. He stumbled and nearly fell. Pawing at the frost on the lens of his goggles, he was just able to make out, through a part in the whirling streamers of snow, a dark mass. He called to his companions, and they huddled on the leeward side of a massive upthrust of ice-coated rock that shielded them from the direct bite of the wind. They stayed low to the terrain, trying not to breathe so deeply that the moisture of their respiration would cake up as frost in the balaclavas and soak through to their nostrils and lips.

After an hour of sitting, crouched together, the keening of the wind slowly softened, then died altogether. Wind-drifted snow had piled up high on the far side of the rock, and they were forced to struggle and slog through it to continue on the route. Clouds covered the face of the sun, and gusts of wind sporadically scoured them with tiny splinters of ice.

"Tell me again why I volunteered for this," Philboyd panted.

Her voice strained and raw, Brigid nevertheless managed to force out a chuckle. "Because you were getting claustrophobic."

"That's right," Philboyd replied. "Thanks for reminding me."

If hell were ice and snow, Kane reflected, it would be something like what they fought through. Everything was covered in ice and sleet that cut into them like animal fangs. Bright, shafting blades of cold sunlight occasionally pierced the cloud cover, casting sprawling shadows that confused the eye across the frozen surface of the glacier.

Crusted snow was a problem, too. They had to breast heaps of it, making it necessary to test the reliability of the footing before pushing through it. Only Kane's honed reflexes saved him from plummeting through a fissure.

As he backed away from it, recovering his balance and emotional equilibrium, he noticed the snow rippling. It rose in inch-high waves and advanced toward the fissure.

Kane stepped farther back. His three companions

did the same, none of them saying anything as they felt the ground rising beneath their feet amid the snap and crack of hoarfrost.

"What the hell is going on?" Grant half snarled out the question.

The words were barely out of his mouth when one of the glacier walls cracked with the sound of an artillery round. They watched as a huge sliver of the glacier slid down, grinding up plumes of pulverized ice as it dropped onto the snowfield with a mushrooming puff of snow.

With a grinding rumble, the fissure suddenly broadened and deepened. The sides collapsed in on themselves. The ground trembled violently under their feet, the frost-coated snow riven with ugly, spreading cracks.

With an earsplitting roar, an entire section of ground collapsed, plunging downward and carrying Philboyd with it. Instantly Grant snatched him by the sleeve, but he did so with his left hand. That, combined with the man's unsupported weight, caused him to fall flat on his stomach.

Philboyd dangled at the end of Grant's arm over frigid air, a void of impenetrable blackness. Kane secured a tight grip on Grant's ankles while Brigid worked forward on all fours to the edge of the fissure.

Between clenched teeth, Grant said, "Hold him long enough for me to—"

There was a crack of splitting rock, and Philboyd's weight abruptly increased. Grant slipped forward, and he fought to dig the toes of his boots into the frozen ground. Kane dug in his heels to keep him stable.

On her stomach beside Grant, Brigid reached down, groping for Philboyd. "Grab me with your other hand," she directed him.

Philboyd's free hand reached up, grasped her forearm just below the elbow, and Brigid was dragged forward a few frightening inches.

Kane stretched out with his left hand and grasped Brigid's ankle, stopping her slide. Straining every muscle in his shoulders, arms and back, he crawled backward, chunks of ice pressing cruelly into his thighs, buttocks and knees. Sweat slid down into eyes, and his limbs quivered with the strain.

Finally Grant and Brigid lifted Philboyd to a level where he was able to swing a leg over the edge of the crevasse. For a long moment, all of them lay on the ground, panting and gasping.

"Earth tremors," Philboyd husked out.

Brigid spit some ice particles from her mouth then said, "Not exactly. The glacier is calving."

Kane scraped the lenses of his goggles clean of slushy residue. "What the hell is that?"

"When glaciers and icebergs fracture and smaller pieces split off."

Grunting, Grant pushed himself to his feet. "Like they're giving birth to baby bergs?"

"Something like that. The tremors are due to the fact that when glaciers calf, the biggest breakaway portions are on the bottom—which, of course, are connected to the ice sheet itself."

Kane rose, brushing himself off. He extended a hand to Brigid, who affected not to notice it and stood without any help. She did give Philboyd an assist, since he was still shaken by his brush with death.

"How much farther until we reach the lake?" Philboyd asked Grant.

The big man didn't answer. He seemed fascinated by an outcropping of dark stone. At its base lay shards of ice, broken loose by the quake. Kane followed Grant's gaze, started to turn away, then did an abrupt double take. From the top of the rock twisted a lazy curl of steam.

Quickly the four people floundered through the snow to the rock. It wasn't huge, only about five feet tall. Nor was it a rock.

"Concrete!" exclaimed Philboyd, touching it. "Painted to look like stone."

"Yeah," Grant said dourly. "But why?"

Reaching inside his parka, he withdrew his combat knife, a weapon with a fourteen-inch-long tungsten-jacketed steel blade. He probed and prodded the top of the rock from where the steam issued. "Warm air escaping from below," Brigid observed.

Suddenly half the length of Grant's blade disappeared. It slid into a seam. Leaning forward, Kane examined it. "It's like a rubber seal."

"What the hell is it?" Philboyd demanded.

"A vent," Brigid explained. "Allowing warm air to escape from an underground source."

Philboyd didn't say anything in response. He watched as Brigid, Kane and Grant circled the rock.

They marked off a three-foot-wide circle around the base of the outcropping by digging their heels into the snow. "We can go through here," Grant announced, kicking the base of it.

Kane nodded. "Yeah, that concrete is probably pretty damn rotten at this point. It won't give us much trouble."

"Trouble?" Philboyd echoed. "What do you mean?"

"Watch and learn from the professionals, Brewster."

Kane dipped into the rucksack and brought out a coil of wire. As he unrolled it, walking backward, Grant selected a block of C-4. Brigid pulled on Philboyd's sleeve. "Come on, don't distract him."

It took Grant about five minutes to prepare the charge, lodging it at the base of the concrete outcropping where he had seen a network of cracks and flaking. He attached the detonation wire to the explosive, then walked calmly to join his companions, who were about fifty yards away. "Set?" Kane asked him, holding the detonator and the end of the wire in both hands.

"Set," Grant confirmed.

Swiftly Kane attached the wire to the detonator. "Everybody duck," he said, then flipped the switch.

The explosion wasn't as loud as Kane thought it would be. Most of the force was directed downward, where Grant had shaped the charge. Only a bit of the debris pattered down around them.

When the shifting planes of dust and smoke settled,

the four people cautiously approached the smoldering crater. Carefully they peered over the edge. They saw nothing but darkness.

"What the hell is down there?" Philboyd demanded waspishly, fanning the smoke away from his face.

Grant lifted the broad yoke of his shoulders in a negligent shrug. "We'll find out when we get down there."

Philboyd reached into the bag and produced a flare. "Why don't we try to light our way first?"

Kane nodded approvingly. "Good idea."

Philboyd ignited the flare and dropped the dazzling tube of paper-wrapped phosphorus. Despite the steam and smoke, all of them could see the walls of a glistening metal cylinder about ten feet in diameter. The flare apparently fell to the very bottom of the shaft. It became a tiny pinpoint of light, then disappeared altogether.

"What the hell happened to it?" Philboyd asked. "It shouldn't have gone out."

"It must've fallen out of our line of sight." Brigid picked up the rucksack and looked from Kane to Grant. "We're going down there, right?"

Kane nodded. "That's the general idea."

From the rucksack, Brigid began removing steel pitons, coils of nylon rope and climbing harnesses. Kane set the two pitons in the ice, driving them deep and hard with the hammer. He had no problem at all getting them to seat securely. Four sharp blows with the hammer wedged them in solidly. Although Philboyd eyed the pitons apprehensively, he allowed Brigid to help him on with the harness, though he winced when she cinched it tight around his waist.

"You know," he said, striving to sound casual, "nobody has mentioned why we're going down there."

"That's because we thought the why was obvious," Grant countered, threading the nylon rope through the carabiners of the pitons. "Unless you know of some other underground kingdom in the Antarctic, then this particular shaft must ventilate Ultima Thule."

Philboyd gestured to the metal wall of the cylinder. "That's refined steel," he said. "You can even see where sections are welded together if you look close. No way it was manufactured by a bunch of Vikings."

"You're forgetting that their dragon ship ran on diesel fuel," Brigid told him. "So they're a little more sophisticated than axes and bearskin shirts."

"I'm not forgetting. I just…" His words trailed off.

"You just didn't believe me," Grant finished genially. "That's fine, Brewster. If it makes you feel better, that's why we're going down there. So you can prove me a liar."

Kane smiled at the exchange, hearing an undertone of menace in Grant's tone that Philboyd was completely oblivious to. He strapped on the climbing harness and said, "I'll go first."

"Big surprise," Grant muttered.

It was almost traditional for Kane to assume the point man's position. It was a habit he had acquired during his years as a Magistrate, and he saw no reason to abandon it. Brigid and Grant had the utmost faith in Kane's instincts, what he referred to as his point man's sense.

During his Mag days, because of his uncanny ability to sniff danger in the offing, he was always chosen to act as the advance scout. When he walked point, Kane felt electrically alive, sharply tuned to every nuance of his surroundings and what he was doing.

Slowly, carefully, Kane edged out on the rim of the shaft and eased his weight onto the rope. The piton held. He slid farther out, slinging the rope through the loop on the harness until he sat within it. He pushed himself off into empty space, swinging for a moment pendulum fashion.

Although he wasn't afraid of heights, dangling over a pit of utter blackness sent a sudden jolt of superstitious terror jumping through him. He choked it down and began sliding down the rope, hand over hand, feeding it through the harness to control the speed of his descent.

The bulky parka made smooth motion difficult, and he had to be content with moving down a few feet at a time, then stopping to catch his breath and relieve the gnawing ache that settled in his hands, wrists, forearms and crept into his shoulder blades. He glanced up at the circle of light above him, at the comforting sight of Grant and Brigid peering down at him, rather than into the sea of darkness below.

He took his Nighthawk microlight from a parka

pocket and attached it to his left wrist by its adjustable Velcro strap, wearing it like a bracelet.

Kane descended another ten feet or so, casting the Nighthawk's 5,000 minicandlepower beam below him, noting how little the metal walls of the shaft were flecked with rust.

Sliding down the rope was harder work than he had envisioned. But it had been more than ten years since he had done any serious climbing and then it was part of a Mag training exercise, to upgrade his certification. Twice more he had to stop to relax some of the tension in his muscles. He was pretty certain he couldn't climb back up. With what seemed like maddening, infinite slowness, Kane continued to descend into the deep dark. When his toes finally touched a solid object, he almost laughed in giddy relief. He straightened, inhaling deep breaths and gingerly tested his footing. It was slippery and he figured he stood upon a patch of ice. He flexed his fingers, working and kneading the stiffness out of them.

Kane was suddenly aware of how terribly exposed he was in the darkness, pinpointing his position with his microlight. Just as he turned it off, he glanced down and saw he was standing on a dead man's face.

Chapter 21

Heart trip-hammering in his chest, Kane skipped backward, skidding on the ice covering the floor of the shaft and nearly falling down. He inhaled a calming breath, then switched the Nighthawk back on, cupping a hand around the beam.

The man was more a limb-twisted, discolored, life-size doll than a human being. He was completely coated in ice. Despite the distorting effect of what Kane guessed to be at least six inches of ice, he could discern the man's distorted but eerily well-preserved features—as well as the strange blue uniform he wore. It appeared to be made of heavy serge, with white piping around the V-necked collar. The clothing looked old, from another time period entirely, particularly the odd, flat black cap on his head that reminded Kane of a pancake. He could barely make out an insignia patch on the front of it, which appeared to be an anchor and a rope.

Casting the beam of the flashlight around, he saw four small square openings in the wall of the shaft where it met the icy floor. They were placed at equidistant points to one another. Ice nearly clogged all three of them. Only one was open, and Kane bent to peer into it. He saw the purplish-white glow of the flare and he guessed when it had struck the ice, it had bounced around before sliding on through.

Kneeling in front of the aperture, Kane shone his light around and saw only a cubicle with bare, featureless walls. Still, he felt the touch of warm—or warmer—air wafting in. It wasn't warm enough to melt any of the ice, but it still felt almost tropical compared to the frigidity settling in his bones.

"Kane!" Grant called down. "What's down there?"

"A man—but he's frozen solid, so I think it's safe enough for the rest of you to come on down."

"You think it's safe?" Philboyd asked in a harsh whisper.

"Yeah," Kane responded sarcastically. "Grant and Brigid trust my judgment. But since you apparently don't, maybe you should stay up there holding the rope until your mouth freezes shut."

There was no reply from the astrophysicist.

Kane detached the nylon rope from his climbing harness and Grant pulled it back up. As the heaviest of the three, he descended next. Brigid thought it best for her and Philboyd to remain topside, making certain the pitons remained anchored under his weight.

When Grant touched the bottom of the shaft, he gave the ice-sheathed corpse only a mildly interested glance and sent the rope back up. Brigid came down next, followed by Philboyd. To Kane's surprise, the man managed to descend without mishap.

Playing the amber beam of her microlight over the frozen corpse, Brigid announced, "He's wearing the uniform of the Kriegmarine, the German navy. World War II vintage.''

Philboyd shuddered and looked away. "A very long goodbye," he murmured. "And a big sleep."

Kane felt a sudden and surprising pang of sympathy for the man. He'd spent nearly two hundred years in cryostasis on the Moon, so the sight of a corpse, locked forever in the embrace of ice, evoked memories he preferred not to have floating through his mind.

Then again, Kane reflected, Brewster Philboyd and his fellow scientists were indirect but contributing factors to the events that led up to the nukecaust. Philboyd was of a type, the civilized man, the organization man.

Perhaps if civilized man, organization man hadn't allowed transitory political systems to kill his sense of adventure, his sense of responsibility, to kill his awareness that all around him was a living, wonderful world, then Earth would not have been such a sitting duck for the baronial takeover.

"What the hell is a German sailor doing here?" Grant demanded.

Brigid shrugged. "What the hell was a German commando doing only a few miles from here?" She made an oblique reference to Otto Skorzeny, the crazed German officer they had found in the old Nazi installation that the mat-trans unit had been installed to serve.

"Good point," Kane commented, directing his microlight toward the opening in the wall. "That looks large enough to wiggle through."

"Barely," Grant said dubiously.

Bending, Brigid shone her Nighthawk beam into the cubicle beyond the aperture. The flare sputtered, about to go out. She announced, "I see a groove, same dimensions as the shaft. Looks to me like a hatch slides out of one wall into the other."

"So?" Grant grunted.

"So," Brigid replied a little testily, "it's half-open."

"I didn't see that," Kane objected.

"There are a lot of things you don't see," Brigid retorted, dropping flat and worming forward on her elbows.

She crawled through fairly easily. Kane and Grant exchanged a look, then turned toward Philboyd and made an elaborate but unmistakable "after you" gesture. The astrophysicist hesitated only a second before lowering himself and sliding through the square.

Grant went next, crawling up to the opening. The fit was tight and he struggled, wriggled and kicked his legs to work his shoulders, then his hips through the frame. Kane planted a foot on his backside and gave him a shove. He cried out in alarm. Then, aided by the icy surface beneath his body, the big man disappeared into the cubicle as if he had been shot from a cannon.

Gripping the edges of the opening, Kane pulled himself through, his elbows and boots finding little traction on the floor. The narrow metal frame caught at his bulky coat. For a second, he was caught fast and he squirmed and cursed.

Grant reached down, grasped him by the collar and heaved. Kane shot forward, all the way across the cubicle and would have collided headfirst with the far wall if he hadn't put out his hands to catch himself. As he rose, he muttered sourly to Grant, "Many thanks."

"Don't mention it," Grant growled.

Climbing to his feet, he saw the half-open door Brigid referred to. She was already peering around it. Kane joined her, looking over her shoulder. A low-ceiling, rough-walled stone passageway stretched out before them. The twin light beams glinted off frost-coated mineral deposits embedded in the rough walls—broken chunks of ice littered the path and would prove hazards to walking. A blue-sleeved arm protruded up from the frozen ground. Three of the fingers had been snapped off like twigs, leaving only the middle digit protruding, as if the corpse were flipping the finger to eternity.

A brooding, unbroken silence bore down on them, like the pressure of a vast, invisible hand. Kane stepped out. "Let's go," he said, unconsciously lowering his voice.

The four people walked only a few yards before the passage branched into a Y. Kane chose the one on the right, because it had the strongest current of air. The ceiling of the tunnel was low, and they all had to walk nearly bent double. Shadows writhed across their path and the microlights reflecting from the ice confused the eye.

Once the shadows concealed the opening of a fissure and they nearly toppled into it. The crevasse was a slanted cut, as though a great ax might have chopped down at a forty-five-degree angle. They stood silently for a moment, staring down into it.

"This is where the path leads," Brigid declared at length.

Philboyd turned on her, his eyes bright with fear. "It's dark down there!"

"Oh, for the love of—" Kane stepped down into the fissure.

Philboyd visibly gathered his courage and tentatively walked into the crevasse. Grant and Brigid strode on either side of him. They didn't seem to walk so much as sink. Darkness closed around them, but beneath their feet they felt stone steps, like a stairway chipped out of granite, filmed with ice. The microlight around Kane's wrist poked out a pale glowing rod of amber that barely penetrated the darkness more than ten feet. They moved very slowly, very cautiously, as if they were treading on eggshells.

Kane carefully extended his right foot, seeking the next stone riser. It wasn't there. His foot touched only a smooth, icy slope. He tried to back up and skidded on the patch of frost beneath his left foot. He fell, sliding rapidly into the darkness and out of sight.

"Kane!" Grant boomed. Then, turning to Brigid and Philboyd, he shouted, "Watch it, you two!"

Neither one bothered to reply. Philboyd and Brigid

were too busy trying to keep from sliding down the slippery grade. Clutching at each other, they tried to set their heels, but like Kane, they fell down and slid out of Grant's sight.

Biting back a profanity-seasoned sigh, Grant crouched and followed them. Fortunately he didn't slide far, or for very long. He landed on his backside between Kane and Philboyd and narrowly missed kicking Brigid in the head. The four people quickly got to their feet, brushing themselves off in embarrassment.

"Now where the hell are we?" grated Grant.

"Still on course," Brigid replied with a wry smile. "Going down."

"We're in some kind of tunnel," Kane observed, shining his light around. "As man-made as the ventilation shaft...but a lot older."

It was apparent that the upper part of the shaft had obviously been constructed over many centuries, extending up through layers of bedrock and permafrost as it formed. At the moment, Kane wasn't interested in geology, but it was impossible not to observe the variety of strata as they crept down through them.

Then the shaft widened and they knew they were in the original, ancient shaft. The long-ago builders had cut it deep. Not even Brigid cared to guess how old the tunnel might be. They didn't go far before they realized they could discern the walls of the shaft down which they were walking without the aid of the Nighthawks.

Light seemed to rise from beneath them. The pass

dropped lower and the cold light deepened to a kind of sickly twilight. They still saw nothing but rock and ice, yet a sense of danger, of foreboding grew, so that Kane moved against it as a man breasted waves. He wasn't the only one who felt it—even Brigid's normally placid expression showed apprehension.

Suddenly the rock walls dropped away and the pallid dusk seemed to lift. Like the flicking of a switch, the murk was swept away and white daylight enveloped them, almost dazzling their eyes. They were no longer in a shaft. They saw a great dome of a ceiling above and a slanting wall of stone behind them. Below and beyond them they saw a strangely illuminated vastness.

Once their eyes grew accustomed to the brightness, they took a long visual survey of their surroundings. Beyond them was a stony slope widening out and down into a valley, a huge hollow of stone. Stalactites projected down from the domed ceiling, lending it the resemblance to a huge cathedral.

They saw a number of structures, buildings constructed of heavy, dark stone, but all around them were ruins, sheathed in ice. They were the strangest ruins Kane, Grant and Brigid had ever seen, in lives that were rich in ruins and high strangeness. The architecture seemed based on sword points and spear tips. They were just able to discern a collection of stone houses and tilled fields, all laid out as precisely as an estate garden.

Between chattering teeth, Philboyd demanded, in a

strangulated whisper, ''What in God's name is this place?''

Their eyes followed the concentric-ring pattern of the streets, picking out areas that might have been market places and temple squares. All along these streets towered the hollow carapaces of buildings, like the abandoned shells of sea creatures. The luminous coatings of ice blurred their outlines, adding a rich luster to the simplistic architecture. Ice climbed more than halfway up the sides of the buildings and hung down in fanglike icicles from empty doorways.

A cloudy shimmering seemed to hover right beneath the bowl-shaped ceiling, but it appeared to be more of an atmospheric distortion than actual cloud cover. Underneath the shimmer was a portion of the city that didn't appear to be coated in frost, although the buildings looked as abandoned as the other sections. In all the long streets and lanes, nothing stirred. They also heard no sound except their own respiration.

At the far edge of the stone structures, they saw the shore of a huge body of water, almost an inland sea. The black, heaving surface stretched for such an extent that its farther shore was only dimly visible. From the middle of it rose a towering pinnacle of stone, its summit wreathed in vapor. The island seemed to be the source of the cloudy umbrella that clung to the domed ceiling.

Quietly Brigid quoted, '''There shall come a time when the bands of the ocean shall be loosened and the vast Earth shall be laid open and new lands shall be seen beyond Thule.' "

No one asked her the source of the quote. Kane tugged down his balaclava and began walking down the slope, past upthrust boulders carved with runic characters.

They reached the edge of the settlement quickly and noticed several of the outermost buildings were undamaged and free of ice. Although the roofs had fallen in, they saw heavy timbers among the stones.

"These resemble Viking longhouses," Brigid murmured. "And the rune markings are definitely Norse."

The deeper they walked among the buildings, the warmer it began to feel, almost too warm after the bitter, marrow-freezing cold.

"Where is the light coming from?" Grant asked, tilting his head back.

Shafts of white sunlight speared down from dozens of round holes cut in the rock ceiling of the cavern. Each one appeared to be at least six feet in diameter. Inset within them were concave, transparent disks.

"Some sort of polarized sheets of plastic," Philboyd said, shading his eyes as he gazed up at them. "Light and heat can only pass in. We had something similar up on the Moon base."

"You wouldn't figure Viking barbarians would have something like that," Grant rumbled.

"No," Kane agreed. "But Nazi Germany would."

He started to say more, when his point man's sixth sense howled an alarm. The skin between his shoulder blades seemed to tighten, and the short hairs at the back of his neck tingled. What he called his point man's sense was really a combined manifestation of the five he had trained to the epitome of keenness. Something—some small, almost inaudible sound— had reached his ears and triggered the mental alarm.

He jerked to a halt, gesturing sharply for his companions to do the same. He flexed his wrist tendons and with the faint whir of its tiny electric motor, the forearm holster slapped his Sin Eater into his hand.

Grant's own handblaster jumped into his palm, and he looked around, eyes narrowed. "What is it?"

Then the Valkyries seemed to rise up out of the ground.

Chapter 22

Kane caught only disorganized, fragmented glimpses of gigantic horned figures bounding all around, shrieking like demons just loosed from Hell.

The figures were all female and of huge stature, several a good half head taller than Kane. Their bare legs were like marble columns, their long hair like gold, which matched the massive armlets binding their wrists and biceps. Glittering tunics of silver scale mail and the high-horned helmets added to their supernatural aspect. The bright, clear light glittered from the razored edges of axes, swords and spear points.

Grant and Kane reacted as quickly as their bulky garments allowed, instinctively shifting to back-to-back positions, their index fingers touching the trigger studs of their Sin Eaters. Philboyd uttered a squalling cry of shock and struggled to bring up his Copperhead. The wooden shaft of a spear struck the side of his head with an ugly thud. The man toppled to the ground, slamming against the legs of Kane and Grant, knocking them off balance.

Brigid Baptiste leaped in front of the two men, putting herself between the gun barrels and the Valkyries. At the top of her voice she shouted, *"Gefrieren! Gefrieren!"*

The Valkyries suddenly lurched to a halt. The bladed weapons weren't withdrawn, but they were lowered. Still, Brigid, Kane and Grant stood within a circle of menacing steel.

"I guess my pronunciation of ancient Germanic isn't as bad as I thought," Brigid side-mouthed to her friends. "I told them to stop."

Kane, his stomach muscles fluttering with adrenaline and tension, said tightly, "I think the fact you can speak their language at all combined with your coloring had more to do with it than your pronunciation."

Now that the women were no longer circling them, Kane realized they were less demonic than splendid savages—clean limbed and shapely despite their stature. Their skin was snowy white, their eyes varying in color from deep gray to bright blue. The loose, unbound hair that flowed down from the edges of metal helmets was blond or red or a shade in between, much like Brigid's sunset-colored mane.

There were only five of the warrior women, not the howling horde of Kane's first impression. But still their eyes blazed with ferocity and suspicion. The tallest of the women, whose helmet sported a pair of polished, curving bull's horns, addressed Brigid with a string of harsh consonants, her tone provocative and angry.

Brigid listened intently, frowning a little in concentration. When the woman finished speaking, Brigid said, "Her name is Gundrun, daughter of Thorfin's son, Ranir. She is chieftain of the Valkyries of Ultima Thule, the choosers of the slain.''

"Judging by her attitude," Grant muttered, "she's more like the choosers of *who* will be slain."

Not responding to his observation, Brigid continued, "She wants to know why two of my men have their faces covered. She asks if you are hiding something, or are you ashamed of something?"

Grant snorted and tugged down his balaclava, revealing his face. At his feet, Philboyd hiked himself up on an elbow and did the same. He started to put his eyeglasses back on, but a spear point darted toward him, lightly pressing against the side of his neck.

Gundrun's appraising gaze flicked over all of them and she spoke again, this time her tone rich with contempt. Brigid translated. "The outside world has changed greatly else the wolf, the black bear and the weasel would not hunt with one of our own orphans."

"You must be the black bear," Kane whispered to Grant. "And I'm the wolf."

"How do you know you're not one of the other two?" he shot back.

"Because I obviously don't look anything like an orphaned weasel."

"She didn't say orphaned weasel," Grant countered in exasperation. "She said—"

Gundrun half shouted a few words and shook her spear in their direction. The two men subsided and Brigid cast them an annoyed, over-the-shoulder glance. "Do I need to translate any of that?"

Both men shook their heads.

Gundrun snarled out a stream of invective, and Brigid replied, speaking hastily and stammering. When the woman fell silent, she and her Valkyries stepped back, gesturing with their weapons.

"Gundrun was ready to have you two chopped to seal meat," Brigid told Grant and Kane severely. "I convinced her that we have urgent news for her people. She agreed to take us to their ruler."

"If this was a movie, I'd say we should try to wow their ruler with feats of legerdemain," Philboyd muttered.

"Something tells me the Thulians will be a tough crowd," Grant commented.

Gundrun spoke again and Brigid said, "She wants our weapons."

Eyeing all the steel pointed in their direction and the implacable expressions on the faces of the Thulian warriors, Kane muttered, "I don't think that's a sound tactic. They seem awfully moody to me."

"Yeah, me, too," put in Grant.

"I agree," Philboyd said, putting his glasses on. Wincing, the man slowly got to his feet. "But if we don't do what they say, they'll try to kill us and we'll have to kill them."

"We're the interlopers here," Brigid reminded them.

Grant growled deep in his throat. "Their people came out to the Cific. They're the invaders. I'm here to put a stop to their raids."

"We're not that sure of our facts," Brigid replied

tersely. "That's why we need to talk to someone in authority."

Grant and Kane didn't move for a long moment. Then Philboyd unslung his Copperhead and handed it over to a Valkyrie. The woman examined the subgun briefly and smiled at him, almost in gratitude.

"They're just as nervous about us as we are about them," the man observed almost cheerfully.

"I can't imagine why," Kane commented. He leathered his Sin Eater, undid the buckles and tabs of the power holster and handed it over to Gundrun.

Glowering, Grant did the same. "Take care of that," he instructed, knowing she couldn't understand him. "I'll be really pissed if it picks up any rust."

With two of the Valkyries behind them and the other two flanking them, Brigid, Philboyd, Grant and Kane were marched through the settlement, bare rock giving way to frost-slippery pavement. As they approached the body of water, the air temperature rose appreciably and they saw less and less ice.

Kane leaned down close to Brigid and said lowly, "I noticed you didn't give up your gun."

A faint smile ghosted over her lips. "As long as the Valkyries didn't."

Kane repressed his own smile and felt his confidence rise.

Feet crunching on gravel, they followed a twisting lane that brought them out almost on the shore of the lake, near a small inlet.

The cove was of some size and it was literally crammed with the wrecks and hulks of old ships, some intact but most of them dismantled, either by tools or the merciless hand of time. They saw the stern of a coracle and the bowsprit of a longboat. They were marched past warped deck planking, broken masts, portions of keels, frames and even part of a wheelhouse with the glass in the portholes still within the brass frames.

The cove was less a graveyard of old ships than a maritime junkyard, where seagoing vessels had been brought to be dismantled and cannibalized. There didn't seem to be an order of placement, either by ship type or era; they were all heaped together in a clutter. They tramped over old wooden belaying pins, blocks, tackle, hatches, oars, sails that had rotted to little more than scraps of canvas. Rearing up out of the clutter they saw the carved dragon figurehead of a Viking longship. The bow was a wreck, the hull planking caved in and splintered.

On the far side of the wreckage yard, a sleek dark vessel loomed large on the rocky shore, half submerged so it resembled a beached killer whale. Its hull was made of rust-streaked steel plates. A conning tower arose from its sleek surface amidships. It was canted over on its port side, half-crushing a much smaller vessel that reminded Kane of a small schooner.

Although the paint was peeled, a serial number was still visible on the conning tower—as was a simple swastika.

"An *unterseeboot*," Philboyd murmured in awe.

"A what?" demanded Grant.

"A U-boat," Brigid explained. "A submarine. That's obviously what brought the Kriegmarine sailors here."

She turned to Philboyd. "I didn't know you spoke German, Brewster."

He shrugged. "When you work in anything to do with space travel, you're bound to run into a few German scientists. I picked up a smattering here and there."

"But why were there dead German sailors in the ventilation shaft?" Kane inquired.

"Two possibilities," said Brigid. "The crew of the sub either volunteered to help out around here as part of the community, or they were enslaved."

The Valkyries herded them toward a twelve-foot-long boat made of planks, tethered to a boulder by a length of leather. With its upcurving bow, it resembled a gondola. With prods of the spears, Philboyd, Grant, Brigid and Kane climbed aboard. Gundrun and another Valkyrie climbed into it while the other two remained on the shore.

One of them snatched the tether free and pushed the boat easily into the water. To the surprise of the four outlanders, they saw an outboard motor clamped to the squared-off stern of the vessel. Gundrun started it with a single yank of the pull-cord. She gunned the throttle, turning it toward the open water. The prow cut through it on a rush of foam.

"Really an odd mixture of technology," Philboyd whispered. "Late bronze age melded with middle twentieth century."

Brigid nodded contemplatively. "They managed to adapt and borrow without changing the basic underpinnings of their culture."

Grant knuckled his chin. "Somebody taught them how to repair motors like these...perform maintenance on them."

"Not to mention provide them with fuel," Kane interjected.

"The Germans, maybe," Brigid ventured.

"Maybe," Kane said doubtfully.

The farther the boat pushed out into the lake, the warmer the air became. On impulse, Grant removed a glove and put a hand into the water. It felt like tepid bathwater. He withdrew his hand, his voice registering surprise. "The water is warm!"

Brigid nodded. "I figured as much. This lake must be fed by some sort of volcanic geothermals."

Kane experimentally plunged his hand in, as well, eliciting a glare from Gundrun. He said flatly, "A lake warm enough not to freeze is one thing. This has to be at least seventy degrees. That can't be natural."

Brigid nodded again. "My thoughts exactly."

By the time they were able to see details in the island of rock thrusting up out of the middle of the lake, the air was so humid sweat formed on their bodies. They opened their jackets, then as they went on, they shed the parkas altogether. Fortunately the shadow suits adjusted to the new temperature and quickly made them comfortable again.

As dark crags rising from the lake began towering above them, Kane felt the prickling of apprehension at the base of his spine. It wasn't an island at all, but more of a rocky spire, projecting out of the water like a sheer-walled cone at least one hundred feet tall. The sides rose up to the rim, which was wreathed in fog and steam. No shoreline was visible, only a deep, V-cut cleft. Within it a great flight of stone steps climbed from the lake surface to the pinnacle.

Gundrun piloted the boat expertly over the waves, to the foot of the stone stairs. She steered the craft slowly between dark ramparts of rock. When the hull grated on stone, she cut the engine. She tossed a mooring line to her companion, who climbed out and looped it securely around a rock.

Gundrun spoke to the other Valkyrie, only a few words, but the four outlanders heard and understood one word among all the others. It was "Asgard."

"Asgard," Philboyd echoed, his eyes widening. "As in home of the Norse gods?"

Kane shook his head and murmured grimly. "No— Asgard as in a volcanic peak that's heating up the Antarctic ice sheet to the melting point."

"The conflict of ice and fire," Brigid said in a hushed tone. "Ragnarok indeed."

THE CLIMB TO THE TOP of the peak wouldn't have been so strenuous if the air hadn't seemed to become more stiflingly hot and humid with every step. Even with the shadow suits' internal thermal controls, the four outlanders perspired freely. Kane reflected that the temperature didn't feel much different than that on Thunder Isle.

When they reached the pinnacle, sidling between two bastions of rune-covered rock onto a flat plateau, they were almost too tired and hot to be impressed by the sight that met their eyes.

A broad avenue paved with white pebbles stretched away in front of them. White buildings chased with golden porticoes shouldered each other. A row of fluted, slender towers rose at the end of the avenue, giving the illusion of being tall, but in actuality they weren't more than three stories high. They stretched up in twisting spirals, colored in fantastic hues of gold and red and blue. Above them hung the umbrella of steam, which shifted and rolled.

"This doesn't even look real," Philboyd murmured in a voice hushed by an awe so deep it was almost shock. "It's like something out of an amusement park."

The Valkyries growled gutturally and gestured to the tallest of the towers at the end of the white-pebbled avenue. It was centered between a pair of smaller structures. The four people fell into step behind the two warriors. Water dripped down from above—not quite a drizzle or mist, but every surface gleamed with moisture.

They didn't march for very far. Long before Brigid, Kane, Philboyd and Grant thought to have reached the tower, they were entering an arched doorway.

"What the hell?" Grant grunted, mystified.

Kane looked around with baffled eyes and guessed the tower was situated in the exact center of the plateau.

Philboyd said, "Optical foreshortening...every-
thing is built up here on a forced perspective to give
this place the feeling of being much larger than it is."

Kane didn't say anything, but he was impressed by
how quickly the man figured it out. Escorted by the
Valkyries, they were marched into an open hall, the
walls of which were of marble with golden scrollwork
crawling across them.

A concourse of Valkyries stood stiffly along the
walls, each one gripping a long spear. Tall winged
helmets were on their heads, and armlets of gold and
silver, all gem encrusted, gleamed on their bare arms.
Each one carried a round shield with the Thulian
swastika embossed on the surface. The honor guard
paid no heed to the people as they entered the hall.

On the floor a series of gold-inlaid tiles stretched
forth, and in the center of the chamber, they formed
a collar around a disk of a translucent substance. A
blaze of yellow-and-orange light shimmered from below the tile-collared disk. Kane estimated it was
twenty feet in diameter if not more.

On the far side of the collar, the tiles resumed their
straight line. They led up to a broad, elevated platform upon which towered an elaborate, high-backed
throne. Sitting on the throne was a figure that caused
Kane's throat to tighten and what little moisture remained in his mouth to dry to a dusty film.

A huge man sat slumped there, silent and brooding,
one gauntleted hand idly fondling the jeweled hilt of
a gleaming broadsword lying across his knees. His

massive limbs were clothed in blue-tinged mail. His entire torso was covered in a fantastic armor that appeared, at first glance, to be wrought of pure ice that sparkled in the light dancing from a disk in the floor.

A cloak of sky-blue hung from his wide shoulders, fastened by a huge brooch pin. The man was very old—a snow-white beard fell halfway to his waist. Hair of the same bleached-out hue tumbled around his shoulders. His right eye was covered by a blue leather patch with a swastika design worked into it with gold thread. His left eye was deeply sunk under his grizzled brow, but it blazed as if from a fire within. An ornate helmet sat on his head, which made him seem even more of a giant. It too appeared fashioned of gold, with curving horns of a burnished alloy that arched backward over the jeweled crest of the headpiece.

The man exuded a palpable aura of age, mystery and power. His single eye was like a window into a forgotten past, which was full of only dark memories and glories long past. Although it was hard to tell in the wavering light, the man appeared to be at least six feet tall—sitting down.

The four outlanders gaped up in astonished silence at the enthroned giant and didn't hear Gundrun's hissed commands. Only when she struck the back of Kane's knee with the shaft of her spear and made his leg buckle did they realize she was ordering them to kneel.

Even Grant was too stunned to do more than scowl at the Valkyries when he lowered himself to one knee.

Gundrun stood before them and spoke in a loud, stentorian voice, the echoes booming and chasing each other under the arched roof.

"What's she saying?" Kane asked Brigid.

She listened for a moment, then in a strained, hoarse tone said, "Kneel in the presence of Wothenjaz, the high one. Kneel before the father of the golden realm."

"Wothenjaz?" repeated Grant under his breath.

Brigid nodded. "Otherwise known as Wotan, Woden and…Odin."

Kane squinted up at the figure on the throne. "That can't possibly be the same guy…can it?"

She shook her head in rueful resignation. "I'm not sure of anything at this point."

Chapter 23

Her head bowed, Gundrun spoke reverentially to Wothenjaz. The inscrutable mask of the bearded man's face did not so much as twitch, but Kane received the distinct impression their arrival had caught him off guard.

Wothenjaz stared down at them, then made an imperious gesture with his right hand, lifting it from the naked blade of the broadsword and spreading his fingers wide.

The gesture had meaning to Gundrun, because she tapped Brigid lightly on the shoulder with her spear and jerked her head suggestively toward the man on the throne.

"I guess it's time for me to convey the important news," she murmured as she rose. "And explain ourselves."

"I hope she makes the explanations quick," Grant whispered to Kane. "My knees are killing me."

Grant's hope was in vain. Brigid stepped close to the platform and spoke to Wothenjaz at great length—first haltingly and uneasily, then with greater confidence. When the one-eyed man responded, it was in a deep, husky voice that sent ghostly echoes chasing each other under the arched roof.

Kane used the opportunity to look around the hall. The lack of any male warriors struck him as distinctly odd, but he figured the honor guard of Valkyries was more than sufficient to handle any threat. He counted two dozen of them, all of them topping six feet in height.

He eyed the gold-collared disk in the center of the floor and figured it was a capped fire pit, a vent of some kind extending down to a volcanic core. Tilting his head back, he studied the ceiling. Projecting from a socket in the roof directly over the fire pit was a thick-walled, heavy-gauge pipe. It reminded him of the barrel of a huge artillery piece. By visually measuring it, he realized it was just the right diameter to fit within the fire pit.

Philboyd's whisper commanded his attention. "Are you thinking what I'm thinking?"

Kane cut his eyes over to him. The man gazed upward, too. "Probably not," Kane replied. "What are you thinking?"

"I'm thinking that big-ass pipe is a vent that can be lowered into the volcanic well. I'm thinking the heat is pumped up through it, and through the top of the tower to the roof of the cavern. And on top of the roof, on the surface, is the ice sheet. I'm thinking that if enough heat is tapped and vented up to it, the whole shebang loosens up and melts, day by day, hour by hour."

"I stand corrected," murmured Kane. "That's exactly what I was thinking."

Brigid turned toward them, her expression very

troubled and grave. Although Gundrun towered over her, she appeared somewhat sad, not threatened. "You can get up now."

The three men did so, although Grant had difficulty, cursing under his breath. Without looking at him, Kane put a hand under his arm and heaved upward. The big man lurched unsteadily to his feet, grimacing in pain.

"What's going on?" Philboyd asked, casting his eyes nervously from the foreboding figure of Wothenjaz to Gundrun.

"We're guests of the golden realm," Brigid replied. "At least until Grigori Zakat and his crew return."

Both Kane and Grant jerked their shoulders in reaction to the name. "So the son of bitch is part of this place," Grant growled.

Brigid ran her gloved fingers through her tumbles of hair. "Yes and no. I'll explain later when we're alone."

A FORM OF NIGHT FELL swiftly over Ultima Thule. Grant, Brigid, Kane and Philboyd sat unguarded in an inner room not far from the audience chamber. Grant half reclined on a couch, while the others sat in wooden chairs. Nobody objected that he took the couch. Despite his efforts to conceal it, his limp had become more pronounced over the past couple of hours.

All of them sampled the ale and viands a Valkyrie served from golden platters and cups. Heavy, blue velvet hangings decorated the walls, and bits of bric-a-brac, some of it exquisitely made, were scattered carelessly all about.

Rubbing one of the hangings between thumb and forefinger, Brigid said, "Blue. The royal color of Odin."

"Does that one-eyed old guy really think he's king of the Norse gods," Philboyd asked with a smile, "or is he really the king of the Norse gods?"

Brigid chuckled. "Neither. Wothenjaz is more a title than a proper name, at least here. He inherited it from his predecessor—fifty years ago."

Kane took a sip of the bitter ale and made a face. "Did he tell you about this place?"

Brigid nodded. "He tried, but beyond a couple of hundred years ago his knowledge is very vague and mixed up with myths and legends, some of it very improbable. But one thing I'm certain of—at this point in history, Ultima Thule is the oldest extant nation in the world."

Philboyd's eyebrows drew down toward the bridge of his nose. "How do you figure that?"

"Easy," Brigid answered. "They've existed unchanged and basically unchanging for at least two thousand years, maybe even longer than that. They've survived everything since before the birth of Christ, including the nukecaust and skydark."

Philboyd frowned, and Kane couldn't help but smile at the man's discomfort. As a scientist who expected everything in the universe to be classified and pigeonholed, he was knocked on his analytic ass when confronted by something outside his field of study.

"Essentially," Brigid continued, "the Thulians are the descendants of a Nordic colony that settled in and around Antarctica. Because of the heat provided by the volcanic cone here, they made it their primary city."

"Which came first?" Grant asked. "The legends of Hyperborea, Asgard and Thule, or these people?"

Brigid shrugged. "A little of both, I would judge. They patterned their civilization on aspects of the old Norse religion while adding to it, which then filtered out and became part of the entire myth cycle."

"Why weren't they discovered before now?" asked Philboyd suspiciously.

"Extensive exploration of the Antarctic continent didn't begin until the twentieth century," Brigid answered. "Besides, they were discovered—or rather the Thulians discovered the outside world. They weren't exactly hiding, although their existence was cast into doubt for many hundreds of years. Apparently they preyed on shipping lanes at will, but the ships that went missing were assumed to have succumbed to the treacherous polar seas."

She smiled wryly. "And witnesses who reported seeing Viking raiders in dragon ships weren't believed."

"Except," interjected Kane, "by the Nazis."

Brigid nodded. "I'm afraid so. They made contact with the Thulians before the end of World War II, and after it, some high-ranking Nazi officials fled here, hoping to base a new reich from Thule.''

"Why didn't it work?" Philboyd asked. "World conquest sounds right up the Thulians' alley.''

"From what I gathered from Wothenjaz, the Nazis tried to rebuild Thule. They gave them technology—like the engines, the polarized plastics and the ventilation ducts…but they tried to enslave them. So the Thulians killed them.''

Philboyd wagged his head in denial. "This is too incredible. It's absurd. An intelligent culture living in isolation here for over two thousand years, barely advancing beyond their ancestors?''

"You're ascribing our own culture's domination by technology to them," Brigid told him. "They picked and chose from technology, bits and pieces that would help them, not take them over. That was the main point of contention between the Thulians and Nazis. And the entire technology debate has been revived again—due to the arrival of Zakat.''

Grant lifted his head from the couch. "How so?''

"Zakat was found out on the ice pack by a hunting party. Obviously he came through the gateway and rather than try to jump to a more hospitable environment, he decided to explore…or walk until he died of exposure.

"A Valkyrie named Sif found him lying senseless not too far from the ventilation shaft. He was the first outsider she had ever seen. She brought him into Thule, more or less as a curiosity. Zakat was terribly injured, but he recovered in due time. Soon he learned their language and all of the inner mysteries of Thule."

"Inner mysteries?" echoed Kane.

"Wothenjaz wasn't really clear on that," Brigid admitted, "but I have a feeling he was referring to the technology left here by the Germans and other bits they had collected over the years. Most of it wasn't used or in disrepair. Zakat set about making it operational again.

"According to Wothenjaz, the desire for power stirred in the man and he coveted his throne. He scourged him, hoping to prove Zakat a coward, but he did not break. Instead, he gained the admiration of many of the warriors. He began filling their heads with dreams of glory, of sallying forth into the outside world as their Norse ancestors had done, to plunder and conquer.

"Zakat began plotting with other warriors to unseat Wothenjaz. For months there was a series of plots and counterplots and finally an attempted coup. Warriors and Valkyries alike died, but in the end neither faction triumphed."

"Why not?" Grant asked.

"The Valkyries had sworn allegiance to Wothenjaz—to the title, at any rate. If they betray him, they are doomed to an afterlife where they wander for eternity through a gray purgatory of ice and snow, never knowing redemption or rest. Besides, all the Thulians fear Wothenjaz, even those who chose Zakat. They believe him to be more god than ruler. The only way Zakat can usurp Wothenjaz is to prove himself a god…and the only way to do that is bring about Ragnarok.''

Kane rolled his eyes. ''That sounds just like something out of that religion of his. What did he call it?''

''The tenets of causitry,'' Brigid replied automatically. ''Zakat studied the volcanic extrusion here and realized only a portion of the cone is above water level. The reservoir of hot magma that provides all the heat is also cooled by the water.''

''How come the water doesn't just boil away?'' Grant wanted to know.

''From what I can tell, this is what's known as a shield volcano. The column of lava doesn't rise out of the central conduit to the summit, but expands and forms domes on the sides. The cone increases in diameter, so an eruption isn't likely under normal circumstances. Zakat apparently intends to bring one about by tampering with it.''

Philboyd sighed in frustration. ''Why didn't Wothenjaz just have Zakat killed instead of trying to discredit or humiliate him?''

''Tradition,'' Brigid said bleakly. ''It has been a tradition since the beginning of Thulian time that a warrior who covets kingship must fight for his crown—or have a champion do it for him. Zakat's champion is someone dear to Wothenjaz, so he won't engage in single combat.''

''Let me guess,'' grunted Grant in disgust. ''Sif, the Valkyrie who found Zakat, is Wothenjaz's daughter and she fell in love with him.''

''Worse,'' Brigid said. ''Sif is Wothenjaz's wife,

once his queen, once leader of the Valkyries. Now she has gone out voyaging with Zakat to bring back the means to jump-start Ragnarok.''

The corners of Kane's lips twitched in a humorless smile. "Is it just me, or does this sound *really* crazy?"

"It's not just you," Brigid confirmed dolefully.

Grant gusted out a sigh and lay his head on the couch. "And you can't understand," he intoned, "why I want to retire."

Chapter 24

Kane awoke instantly, upper body snapping erect and dislodging Brigid's head from his shoulder. For a split second he wasn't certain what had awakened him. Then he heard trumpets blaring a fanfare of triumph. Drums thundered and voices shouted and bellowed in a noisy, victorious clamor.

Consulting his wrist chron, Kane saw by the glowing digits they had been in the room for over eight hours. His companions stirred, sitting up and blinking. Philboyd lifted his glasses and rubbed his eyes. "What's going on?" he asked, stifling a yawn.

Kane didn't answer, a cold knot of tension forming in the pit of his stomach. Footsteps tramped heavily outside the door. He stood, Grant and Brigid following suit. After a moment, Philboyd did, too. The door handle turned.

Grant, Brigid and Kane instantly recognized the tall, lean man who stood in the doorway, despite the mailed armor he wore—and the scar cutting down across his forehead. Grigori Zakat stared at them expressionlessly, then he hugged himself as if he were cold. His body trembled and he bit his lips. Tears swam in his eyes.

Pulling a great sob of air into his lungs, Zakat managed to regain control of himself. His shoulders and legs continued to quiver, but it was due to unrepressed joy. "At last," he breathed, touching the phallic amulet hanging from his neck. "Privately I feared the events I set into motion wouldn't cycle through in the proper sequence to bring all of you to me. But my devotion and faith has been justified."

Forcing a note of studied indifference into his voice, Kane said, "I think it has more to do with a ledge I didn't see in the dark than that little holy peenee around your neck." He paused to arch an eyebrow. "Or is that really your peenee?"

Zakat roared with genuine laughter, and the unshed tears in his eyes spilled down his cheeks. He turned his head and in between gales of laughter, spoke several guttural words.

A giant blond armored woman suddenly pushed past him into the room. "I just told Sif what you said," Zakat stated. "For some reason, she didn't find it as amusing as I did."

"Yeah," Kane replied, eyeing her apprehensively. "I notice she's not laughing."

Sif beckoned to Kane with a crooked forefinger. Zakat, his guffaws now more like snuffling chuckles, said, "She wants to show what happens when a Thulian warlord is disrespected."

"When she brings me a Thulian warlord instead of a fused-out Russian," Kane declared, "I'll be very interested."

"I'm afraid I must insist you cooperate. Otherwise,

Sif will demonstrate on one of your companions. The delectable Miss Baptiste, for example.''

Kane took a deep breath and stepped forward. Brigid plucked at his arm, whispering urgently, ''Don't do it.''

He didn't respond. He crossed the room and halted before Sif, gazing up at her with a neutral expression. Sif's knee flashed up, thudding solidly into Kane's midsection. Air left his lungs in a loud whoof, and he stumbled, off balance, but the shadow suit redistributed the worst of the impact. Still, the impact caused little pinwheels to ignite behind his eyes. Before they stopped whirling, Sif secured a stranglehold.

Fingers like flexible iron bands locked around Kane's throat, the thumbs pressing against his larynx. Kane brought his forearms up and knocked the Valkyrie's hands away—or tried to. Her hold didn't break. She drove a knee into his groin and, as he doubled over, folding in the direction of the pain, Sif released him. He fell to his knees, and she kicked him in the side.

Zakat spoke quietly to her and she backed away, a cold, cruel smile playing over her face. ''I think that will suffice,'' he announced.

Kane staggered to his feet, dizzy, panting and nauseated. Grant steadied him as he drew in great gulps of air. Brigid strode aggressively up to Zakat, her eyes seething with jade flames of fury. ''You're still a crazy bastard, Zakat.''

The Russian struck her across the face with the back of his gloved right hand. Then as if alarmed by his lack of self-control, he caught his hand and held it to his breast.

"I apologize," he said in a sibilant whisper. "The strain these last few months has been almost intolerable. If you knew of the planning…"

Between clenched teeth, Grant bit out, "Planning for what? More piracy?"

In a soft, soothing voice, Zakat replied, "Planning for a venture to build a new world, a new empire of discipline and order. An empire none of you will ever see. In a sense, I regret killing you, Mr. Grant and Miss Baptiste. However, Kane has deeply wronged me and must be punished. Part of his punishment is death, of course, but the other part is watching all of you die before him."

Kane lurched toward him. "How did I wrong you, Zakat? You were my enemy and when an enemy tries to kill you, you try to kill him in return. That's the first law of nature."

"There are other laws, Kane. By the right of *lex non scripto*, the unwritten law, you believed you could kill me and suffer no consequences. But it was not so much you trying to take my life as the potential for power you wrested from me."

A hungry light suddenly flickered in Grigori Zakat's eyes and he thrust his head forward eagerly. "The facets of the Shining Trapezohedron, Kane— where are they, what did you do with them?"

"The same thing I tried to do to you—chucked them off a cliff."

The Russian glared at him, first in suspicion then in righteous wrath. "I believe you did that."

"Would I lie to you?" Kane inquired sarcastically.

Zakat shook his head, his hair flying around his face in a flurry of witchlocks. "You don't obey the law of power, and that's why you will suffer. All power has its price, whether in blood or dignity. Depending on the market value of the power sought, the price goes up."

"I heard that before." A taunting smile creased Kane's lips. "Right before you went over the cliff."

"I know you thought I'd perished in Agartha, and you assumed that because I wished you to." Zakat met the taunting smile with one of his own. "As it was, I was injured." He fingered the scar on his forehead. "Contusion, abrasions, lacerations, even a few broken bones. Painful, but I can control pain."

Zakat's eyes wandered as he fell into his narrative. Kane knew it was to their advantage to keep him talking. "So you climbed back up and left Agartha?"

The Russian nodded. "You make it sound so simple, Kane. I wandered the length and breadth of those subterranean labyrinths for days, often in complete darkness. By the time I found my way, I was half-dead from want.

"I began the long return trek up the mountain pass to the monastery on foot. I encountered a pack of bandits, and I sought to gain their aid. I identified myself as Tsyansis Khan-po, the King of Fear. Do you know what they did next?"

Before Kane could respond, Zakat snarled, "They

laughed at me. They called me a liar. They claimed they had already met the true King of Fear. They knew he was the true monarch because he kept death up his sleeve. I knew it was you to whom they referred, Kane. You stole my title!''

Kane recalled the incident with vivid clarity. ''I killed the bandit chief, and the rest of them called me the King of Fear. I earned the title—I didn't steal it.''

Zakat waved away Kane's objection. ''Nevertheless, they kept me with them for a day and a night—torturing me, buggering me, beating me. On a whim, they decided to let me live and to free me. But first they held my right hand—my gun hand, my sword hand—in the fire until it was black and the all nerves were dead. Then they cast me out on the trail naked.''

Zakat clamped his lips together. The light in his eyes was wild as he glanced down at his right hand. ''You will never know my suffering on the mountain pass. No man could ever know the full horror of it. But I lived and made it back to the monastery.

''I forced the sole monk who remained there to treat my wounds, but I feared to recuperate there, since he seemed immune to my influence. So I took food and clothing and used the mat-trans unit to escape. But only one of the destination codes showed an active receiving unit.''

He cast his eyes upward toward the ice fields above. ''And there my beloved Sif found me and nursed me back to full health.''

''Yeah,'' muttered Philboyd, ''we can see she's a real Clara Barton.''

Zakat shifted his gaze toward him. "I don't know who you are, but I have a feeling you deserve everything that's about to happen to you."

"Which is what?" Grant challenged.

Grigori Zakat grinned fiercely. "And I thought you might be afraid to ask."

THE THRONE ROOM WAS thronged with a glittering, armored host. The blare of golden trumpets rang across the hall as Zakat entered with Sif, Kane, Grant, Brigid and Philboyd in tow. Wothenjaz gazed down from his throne, as motionless and expressionless as a statue.

As they drew closer to the fire pit, Kane saw a wooden pallet resting on the floor. It was loaded with a number of metal drums marked with the letters HDX and several canisters and tanks.

"Is that what I think it is?" Grant whispered to Kane.

"It is," he answered grimly. "Enough incendiary and combustible chemicals to turn a dormant volcano into a nuclear bomb."

The Thulian warriors jeered and jostled the four outlanders as they walked a gauntlet of armored men toward the dais. Wothenjaz gestured toward Sif, and she marched toward the platform, climbing a short flight of steps to take a place beside the throne.

Standing near the fire pit, Zakat threw a smirk toward the outsiders. "Here is the culmination of the long months of planning. I struck a deal with the Pit boss of your quaint baronies who was engaged in smuggling. He in turn introduced me to a contact, who provided me with the proper weapons and materials I needed...not just to trigger Ragnarok, but to establish a new Thule.''

Brigid said coldly, ''By causing a new ice age? By being responsible for the deaths of hundreds of thousands of people and ravaging a world that is just now beginning to crawl back up out of barbarism?''

''Yes,'' said Zakat. ''That will give me what I need.''

''Do you need a world destroyed by floods and ice?'' Grant demanded.

''At this time, yes, I do. For many reasons, most of which you wouldn't understand, because you don't understand the principles by which I live.''

Kane stared at him. He had no idea if Zakat's idea of increasing the volcano's heat output would actually send the Antarctic ice sheet sliding into the sea, but he knew even if he and his friends escaped, he couldn't leave the man in a position of power. Grigori Zakat was insane, unable to conceive of the horror of a world crusted in ice.

To Grant, he whispered, ''I'm going to try something.''

''What?''

Kane didn't answer. Instead he put his head down and loped across the intervening yards between him and Zakat. The Russian saw him coming and fear glinted in his eyes. A few armored Thulian warriors made grabs for him, but Kane was too fast. He left the floor in a flying dive and collided with Zakat.

Both men went down in a tangle of arms and legs. Kane was atop him instantly, his Magistrate-trained reflexes and fury driving him forward, knees slamming solidly into the man's flat stomach.

He pistoned both fists into Zakat's face beneath him in a flurry of jabs and left and right hooks. The Russian's head rocked back and forth under the steady tattoo, blood springing from his nostrils, flying from split lips.

Then strong arms grabbed Kane and hauled him backward. Kane shouted, "I challenge you, Zakat! You and me! I issue the challenge!"

A spear stabbed into his midsection but failed to penetrate. While the warrior gaped in astonishment, Kane snatched the shaft in his two hands and struck him in the belly with the butt of it.

Then men piled all over Kane, pinning his arms behind his back, punching him in the stomach. All through it, Kane roared, "I challenge you, Zakat!"

The Russian spit blood and stalked toward the restrained Kane, his lips peeled back over his red-filmed teeth. "You have no rights here!"

"We'll have the rights ceded to us," Brigid shouted.

With no one around her, she rushed to the foot of the throne platform. When a Valkyrie reached out to stop her, Wothenjaz straightened in his throne, gesturing for her to stand aside. Zakat growled like an animal and caught Sif's eye, who shook her head. Brigid Baptiste had been granted an audience with the ruler, and no one could now interfere.

In the Thulian dialect, Brigid said, ''The man who has come among you, Grigori Zakat, is a liar. He represents a greater threat to your people's freedom than did the Nazis of long ago. He wishes to be king, to be a monarch, the master of the Ragnarok he will use you to engineer.''

Sif stepped to the edge of the dais and gestured contemptuously toward Brigid, then the others. Stridently she shouted, ''Grigori Zakat has mighty plans for a mighty people! If the outer world is overrun by barbarians, he will aid us in bringing the lesser breeds to such a pass that their only hope for survival lies in surrender to Thulian domination!''

Brigid started to speak again, but Wothenjaz cut her off with a raised hand. His attitude was one of weariness, of having heard it all before. ''Enough,'' he proclaimed. ''Debate is not our way. Thule has existed for countless centuries bound by our customs and traditions. One of those traditions is that anyone who wishes to wear the helmet of kingship must fight for it, or have his champion do so. Zakat's champion is Sif, and I cannot fight her. I have no champion to fight in my stead.''

Brigid inhaled a deep breath. ''I think you do.''

She glanced questioningly toward Kane, still caught fast in the grip of the Thulians. He nodded curtly.

Chapter 25

Gundrun snapped the manacle around Kane's left wrist and gave the slender chain an experimental tug. She said something and Brigid translated. "'Don't be fooled—this chain is as strong as the one that bound Fenris.'"

"Whatever the hell that means," Kane muttered.

Gundrun fed the other end of the chain through an eyelet in the pipe. A Valkyrie on the far side connected the end link to an identical manacle and snapped it around Sif's wrist. She stared at Kane expressionlessly across the fire pit. The venting pipe had been lowered from the ceiling and it was positioned four feet above the cover disk.

Zakat spoke earnestly to Sif, who listened intently, a look of serene detachment on her face. Her long flaxen hair was tied in a single thick braid that hung down her back. She was stripped of her armor, her Valkyrie's finery and wore a dark, close-fitting leather tunic, cinched at the waist by a length of knotted rawhide.

Kane was dressed similarly. The Thulians had insisted on it. He wasn't sure if the mode of garb was traditional for single combat, or because the warriors became suspicious when they couldn't gut him during the melee.

Grant muttered, "Even if you win, it may not change anything. Zakat has a lot of support here."

Kane shrugged. "At the very least we'll delay Zakat dumping all those chemicals down the gullet of the volcano."

"I've been thinking about that," Philboyd announced. "I doubt he'll get the result he's hoping for. More than likely, he'll set off underground explosions that will blow vents in the sides of the cone below the water level. They'll get one hell of a steam bath and probably parboil all of Ultima Thule in the process."

"That's nice to know," Kane drawled. "But we'll still be here and get boiled right along with them."

Philboyd swallowed. "I guess you're right," he replied inanely.

Brigid glanced into Kane's face. Her eyes were worried, her expression pinched. "I wish I could be sure what the outcome of this contest will be. If you kill Sif, Wothenjaz is liable to kill you right along with Zakat."

Kane smiled thinly. "That possibility occurred to me, but I think he's a man of honor."

Grant pursed his lips, as if he tasted something exceptionally sour. "Wouldn't that be a nice change?"

Wothenjaz lifted his voice above the murmuring throng, shouting, *"Kampfen!"*

A male warrior and a Valkyrie removed the two sections of the fire-pit cover. Kane felt the intense heat rising out of the well in an almost solid column, like a physical assault.

A man handed Sif a short-handled ax. A Valkyrie pressed a twin to it into Kane's hand. He hefted it, checking its balance. Then Sif gave the chain a terrific yank and Kane catapulted off the floor. He managed to keep his footing, but he staggered on the lip of the pit. He teetered, arms windmilling, squinting away from the orange-and-red glow from below. It was like looking down the throat of Hell.

Sif sprang in, chopping at Kane's head, but it was a feint. The Valkyrie meant to make a swift and shifty fight of it. Kane returned the blow with a cut at Sif's legs. The woman bounded high, clearing the blade easily and in midair hacked down at Kane's head, meaning to separate it from his shoulders.

He hurled himself to one side and the ax blade chopped into the collar of tiles, slicing one in two. Kane didn't hesitate—he shot out his left leg in a sweeping kick that caught the backs of Sif's ankles and dumped her over on her back amid a heavy thud and a bellow of outraged surprise.

They struggled to their knees on the rim of the fire pit. The wavering heat waves drew sweat out of both of them. Kane almost felt as if his skin were shriveling under its blast.

Sif swung her ax again in a whistling curve, and Kane's flashed up to meet it. Steel rang together with a painful clash and both blades shattered, flying fragments nicking their flesh and drawing blood.

The Valkyrie gaped at the wooden haft in her hand,

then dropped it and reached for Kane's throat. But her arm was numbed by the force of the blow and Kane easily slapped it aside. A fierce jab opened a gash above Sif's eyebrow. Scarlet oozed into her eye, blinding her.

With a screech of fury, Sif tried to exchange punches with Kane, but her flailing fists missed their weaving target or rebounded from his forearms. She hurled herself forward, fingers bent into claws.

Kane caught her wrists, noting fearfully it was like grabbing two bars of tempered steel. They tumbled over the floor, locked in each other's arms. Sif's fingers slipped on Kane's sweat-slick arms, and her grasp was so powerful his skin peeled away in strips as if it were scalded.

Sif drove a fist against his chin, jarring his teeth together. He clutched the braid in her hair and jerked. She shrieked and struck at him again. Unwilling to release his hold on her hair, Kane slid to one side, feeling Sif's fist skim along the side of his face, tearing at his ear. Kane raised his knee, driving it into Sif's belly.

Sif swung again, howling with rage. The malletlike blow caught Kane on top of the shoulder, briefly numbing his arm. Sif looped the slack of the chain and dropped it over Kane's head, tightening it around his neck. She struggled to rise behind him. Kane knew she intended to garrote him to death, so he heaved back and forth, twisting within the noose of the chain and scraping his flesh raw. He struggled to get to his feet, and for an instant he was nose to nose with the Valkyrie. Only cold, naked fury showed in Sif's eyes. Kane thrust the crown of his head at the woman's face, but she turned her head and caught the blow on the side of her jaw.

Still, Sif bent over backward, over the lip of the pit. Kane was forced to throw himself in the opposite direction to pull her away so she wouldn't drag him down, as well. She fell inside Kane's reach. He threw his left arm out, locking it around and behind Sif's right arm, trapping it.

Sif struggled to get free of the hammerlock, and Kane slid his right arm around her neck. He forced her down on the tiled collar encircling the rim of the fire pit. They had already absorbed the terrific volcanic heat and when her cheek touched a tile, he heard a faint sizzle as of meat tossed on a griddle and she howled in pained agony.

Kane lifted her clear of the tiles. Sif gagged, clutching at the Kane's arm. She inserted her fingers into the crook of his elbow and to his astonishment she actually began prying it away. Kane increased the pressure, bearing down. Zakat shrieked something, and Kane glanced up to see him nearly dancing in mad frustration, crimson-flecked spittle flying from his lips.

Brigid's sharp voice cut through the murmur of the onlookers like a knife. "Zakat is telling her not to yield! He wants you to kill her!"

Kane could only guess at the reason, but he figured the death of Sif at the hands of an outlander might sway both the Valkyries and Wothenjaz to his side.

Sif hissed a stream of words in Thulian, and although he couldn't understand them, he gleaned their meaning. She told him she would never yield, never surrender.

Despite her tone of defiance, Sif's respiration was strained and panicked. Kane reached a swift conclusion, with only the vaguest concept of how his decision might turn out.

He released Sif, pushing away from her and standing. As he backed out of range of her arms and legs, he shouted over his shoulder, "Baptiste! What are the Thulian words for 'I give you back your life'?"

Sif slowly climbed to her feet, regarding Kane with a glare of pure venom. She touched the reddened welt on her cheek where the tile had burned it.

"Baptiste!" Kane yelled again, not daring to take his eyes off the Valkyrie as she advanced on him, gathering the slack of the chain in a loop in one hand and slapping it against the other.

Suddenly Brigid shouted out a string of confusing consonants. At the top of his voice, he repeated the words as best he could. He bellowed it twice, still trying to back away from Sif.

Wothenjaz suddenly rose from his chair, assuming his full, formidable height. He spoke, and his roar of a voice was like thunder. He lifted his great broadsword over his head. Sif instantly jolted to a halt. Her blond head swiveled toward her husband, her eyes wide with shock.

Brigid came quickly to Kane's side. In a voice quivering with relief, she said, "It worked, Kane. You worked it out when I couldn't. Wothenjaz was hoping you'd do what you did.''

Grant and Philboyd bracketed them. "Just what did you do?'' Grant demanded. "What's going on?''

"By sparing Sif's life,'' Brigid explained, "when Kane could have taken it, she can no longer champion the cause of Zakat.''

Kane gulped in oxygen and rubbed his neck, glad to be away from the scorching air around the fire pit. As he unlocked the manacle around his wrist, he said, "That's what I figured he was up to when he agreed to a trial by combat, even though I wasn't a Thulian. Zakat outsmarted himself by having Sif as his champion, whom Wothenjaz wouldn't fight.''

Grigori Zakat stared in openmouthed terror as Wothenjaz majestically descended from the platform, the broadsword in his hand gleaming like quicksilver. The milling throng parted for him. The man was at least seven feet tall, and he looked almost as broad. He was a living juggernaut, a figure not just of legend but vengeance, justice and death.

Zakat screamed at Sif, rushing to her, clutching frantically at her arms. She shook him off, not looking at him, as if his touch tainted her. Zakat turned his gaze toward Kane, his lips working, mouthing words no one could hear. He glanced into the implacable faces of Valkyrie and warrior alike, but none of them acknowledged his presence. Even if any one of them were inclined to interfere, they were forbidden by ancient ritual, custom and law.

Zakat spun toward Wothenjaz, who strode toward

him with the confident swagger of a tiger approaching its prey, his blue cloak belling out behind him. If he so coveted the rulership of Ultima Thule, Zakat knew he would have to duel Wothenjaz for the crown—and even Sif knew he couldn't possibly emerge victorious.

Nostrils flaring, Zakat stared wide and wild-eyed toward Kane. His face contorted. He began to tremble violently, his eyelids flickering, spittle collecting at the corners of his mouth.

Kane met his gaze and snarled out a mocking laugh. "Why don't you tell him about the time you were the King of Fear, Grigori? That might make him change his mind about chopping you into about a hundred pieces and feeding you your peenee."

Zakat's left hand clutched at his amulet. His body quaked, a thousand changing sparks of light dancing in his eyes. Then he threw back his head and screamed, a howl of terror, of fury torn from the roots of his soul.

He bounded toward Kane, hands raised, fingers curved like talons. Grant made a motion to intercept him, but Kane elbowed him back. He whiplashed the chain across the floor separating him from the on-rushing Russian. The manacle struck Zakat's temple with a loud crack of bone, spinning him and sending him staggering to the edge of the fire pit.

His feet scrabbled for purchase on the gilded tiles, then he slipped over the rim. The fingers of his left hand hooked onto the edge and he hung there, over the terrible heat. Kane sauntered over to the pit and gazed down at Zakat, his face twisted in exertion.

"We've been in this situation before, Kane," the Russian gasped.

Kane nodded. "I remember." He bent over, extending a hand. "This time I won't let you fall."

Zakat's eyes widened in surprise—then the looming figure of Wothenjaz cast a shadow over his face as he stood shoulder to shoulder with Kane.

"I understand why," he said hoarsely, great globes of perspiration forming on his forehead. "You prefer to see me humiliated before you see me dead."

"Actually," Kane replied smoothly, "I don't care what order they're in." He reached down. "Make up your mind."

Grigori Zakat's lips writhed over his teeth in either a grin or a grimace when he released his grip. Kane caught only a glimpse of him as he plummeted down the volcano's conduit and into the inferno of its belly. He didn't see or hear his body plunge into the magma, but the unmistakable stench of seared human flesh and scorched hair wafted up in a noxious cloud.

Wothenjaz nodded brusquely as if deeply satisfied with the way everything turned out, as though it had all gone according to an intricate plan. He regarded Kane solemnly for a long, silent moment, then his lips quirked in a smile beneath his beard.

With a flourish of his cloak, Wothenjaz pivoted on his heel and marched over to Sif. She dropped to her knees before him, head bowed, eyes downcast.

Grant whispered to Kane, "Think he'll kill her?"

Kane shook his head. "Not after all of this."

Philboyd stepped up close and asked, "Will he take her back?"

Kane pondered the query for a moment, but before he could answer it, Brigid said quietly, "There's an old Latin saying, *Victoria et pro victoria vita*—victory, and for victory, life. Wothenjaz won a great victory for himself and for us. No one could wish for anything better. He'll take her back."

Then the assembled Thulians shook spears and swords and axes over their head and began singing about the glorious days to come.

Stony Man is deployed against an armed
invasion on American soil...

FREEDOM WATCH

An unidentified stealth craft takes out two U.S. satellites before
making a forced landing in the dangerous border region of
Afghanistan and China. White House advisers claim the mystery
machine originated in Siberia and urge the President to retaliate
with a nuclear strike. Stony Man deploys Phoenix Force and
Able Team to find the enemy who's using technology linked
to Area 51 and who are prepared to unleash its devastating
power to attack the free world....

STONY MAN

*Available in
February 2003
at your favorite
retail outlet.*